T0152532

CROSS PURPOSES

Visit us at www.boldstrokesbooks.com

By the Author

Unexpected Sparks

Unexpected Ties

Cross Purposes

CROSS PURPOSES

by
Gina L. Dartt

2016

CROSS PURPOSES

© 2016 BY GINA L. DARTT. ALL RIGHTS RESERVED.

ISBN 13: 978-1-62639-713-2

THIS TRADE PAPERBACK ORIGINAL IS PUBLISHED BY
BOLD STROKES BOOKS, INC.
P.O. BOX 249
VALLEY FALLS, NY 12185

FIRST EDITION: OCTOBER 2016

THIS IS A WORK OF FICTION. NAMES, CHARACTERS, PLACES, AND INCIDENTS ARE THE PRODUCT OF THE AUTHOR'S IMAGINATION OR ARE USED FICTITIOUSLY. ANY RESEMBLANCE TO ACTUAL PERSONS, LIVING OR DEAD, BUSINESS ESTABLISHMENTS, EVENTS, OR LOCALES IS ENTIRELY COINCIDENTAL.

THIS BOOK, OR PARTS THEREOF, MAY NOT BE REPRODUCED IN ANY FORM WITHOUT PERMISSION.

CREDITS
EDITOR: SHELLEY THRASHER
PRODUCTION DESIGN: SUSAN RAMUNDO
COVER DESIGN BY MELODY POND

Acknowledgments

I have to acknowledge my betas, Pam and Jay, who read everything I throw out there, not just the stories about the characters they like, and do their best to give quality feedback on all my ideas. Also, my friends on the tennis courts, Norma, Cindy, and Sherrill, who always listen to my plots, even when they make no sense. And to my sister, Cathy, who patiently watched me walk around Grand-Pré as I figured out the logistics of trespassing on a national park. For the reader, please know that all the locations in this book actually exist, even if the geography is slightly altered here and there for dramatic purpose.

Dedication

To my sister and brother-in-law, Cathy and Doug,
who are always there for me.

CHAPTER ONE

The wipers struggled to keep up with the rain pounding the windshield. Beneath her wheels, Lana could feel the powerful rush of water tugging insistently at her Jeep Wrangler, pushing it to the left. Exhaling in relief as she finally reached the other side of the small bridge, she carefully navigated the corner leading up the Kent Hill Road. A glance in the rearview mirror showed even more chunks of ice choking this side of the bridge, forcing the water across the pavement. In another twenty minutes, she suspected even a four-wheel drive wouldn't be able to traverse the flooded section safely.

This is going to be such a pain in the ass, she decided glumly as she followed the road rising along the riverbank. Every year, there was a warm spell in February, a sort of annual joke played on Nova Scotia by Mother Nature for a couple of weeks before she imposed winter once more. In good years, people would go outside to bask in the warm sunshine and fool themselves into thinking that perhaps, this year, spring would come early. In bad years, when there had been a lot of snow and ice over the previous two months, and the warm spell came in the form of constant rain rather than sunshine, people didn't bother fooling themselves. Instead, they started hoping for cold temperatures again before the ice broke up, clogging narrow passages, while snow melt from the surrounding forests and fields filled the many brooks, streams, and rivers, overflowing the banks and causing widespread flooding.

Obviously, this was going to be a bad year. Forecasts were calling for a lot more rain over the next few days as the ice continued to shift in the swollen tributary. The bridge at the bottom of the hill was the quickest way into the small village of Kennetcook from the north. A small co-op, garage, diner, and post office made up the four corners of the tiny crossroads, providing the people in this part of the county with most, if not all their necessities. People on that side of the river would be fine if the bridge was submerged beyond safe passage, but those on Lana's side were looking at an hour's drive in the other direction to the nearest town that, though a lot larger than Kennetcook, was terribly out of the way. And that was assuming there were no more flooded areas between here and there. If that happened, then it could take two or more hours of navigating the various back roads to reach a town of any size.

Lana remembered a February ten years earlier when the bridge had not just flooded over, but had been utterly destroyed. It had taken a month for the Department of Highways to replace it, and she had discovered just how much she relied on Kennetcook for the little things that made life bearable.

Well, with any luck, she thought philosophically, the bridge will hold. In the meantime, her quick trip to the store meant she was well stocked up on groceries if she was cut off for a few days. After that, if she had to travel all the way to Windsor to pick up her milk, bread, and Xtra Brownie ice cream, then she supposed she could survive it. She always had the option of moving closer to a larger town, but then she'd have to give up the log cabin. Long summer evenings relaxing on the porch as she watched the placid waters flow by easily made up for those few winter days when the river became an engorged, soaked beast frantically trying to escape the confines of its willow-lined banks.

Glancing out her side window toward the rampant torrent of ice and water rushing several meters below the hill, she abruptly put on her brakes, the Jeep skidding to a stop.

At first she wasn't quite sure what had caused such a reflex. With the sound of the wipers squeaking loudly in her ears, she squinted through the darkness and pouring rain. It took a moment before a stray glint on metal let her know something was down on the riverbank. Something that hadn't been there when she'd driven past earlier on her way into the village. Only long familiarity with the road and river had prompted her to notice it. Otherwise, the current conditions would have concealed it completely.

After shifting her vehicle into park, she leaned over and fumbled in the glove compartment for a flashlight. It would probably turn out to be nothing, she decided grumpily, but if someone had actually gone off the road, then they were most likely in trouble. The bank was steep, rising to the road for about ten meters, with only a few small spruce trees and some alder bushes preventing a slide into the raging water below.

Cursing a bit under her breath, Lana climbed out of her Jeep and turned on the flashlight. After she reached the edge of the road, she shone it down the slope, the shrunken and drenched snowbanks reflecting white among the dark slashes of winter-ravaged vegetation and mud. She started as her thin beam of light flashed over a shape in the darkness. Quickly she brought it back to reveal a crumpled bumper emblazoned by a green-and-white Enterprise sticker.

What the hell is a rental car doing way out here? she wondered in amazement. Even during tourist season, this road wasn't exactly on the way to anywhere. Eventually it led to Windsor, of course, but there were easier, more picturesque routes through the Rawdon Hills. And frankly, in February, it was all rather bleak at best and downright desolate at worst.

"Hello, is anyone there?" she shouted.

She could feel the icy trickle of water go down the back of her neck beneath the collar of her winter jacket as she waited for an answer, the wind driving pellets of freezing rain into her face. She bent her head, lowering the brim of her baseball cap against the onslaught, and called out again.

"Hey there, is anyone in the car?"

Was she going to have to go down there? She stared uneasily at the steep gradient falling away beneath her. Suddenly, she heard a squishy sound, a tearing away of mud and turf as the car slid forward a little, held back only by the fragile and uncertain strength of some alder bushes. That was when she heard the scream, rising thin and faint above the roaring rush of wind and water.

"Shit!"

Dashing back to the Jeep, she flipped open the rear hatch and shoved aside bags of groceries to get at the nylon rope she kept there in her emergency kit. A headlamp she exchanged for the small flashlight gleamed weakly when she switched it on, indicating she should have been more conscientious about changing the batteries. Hastily, she tied one end of the rope to the bumper and yanked on it sharply to make sure it was secure before she started down the bank.

"Hang on!" she yelled as she scrambled through the wet mire of snow and mud. "I'm coming!"

Wondering why she didn't feel more scared, she decided it was just the heat of the moment. Afterward, she'd be terrified, assuming she didn't go arse over teakettle into the river, eventually ending up as a decomposing Popsicle in the Bay of Fundy.

As she descended, she could see the snow churned up around the driver's door. Obviously, someone had tried to get out earlier but made little headway up the slippery slope. Just then, the car slid forward again and the interior light flashed on as the door opened. Whoever was inside was bailing, deciding to take their chances on the bank and rain rather than end up in the river. A shapeless form landed in a heap on the ground.

"I'm almost to you!" she shouted again, and this time she could see the pale circle of a face turned upward in her direction. She found precarious purchase among icy rocks as she moved as rapidly as she could toward the kneeling form. Tree branches snapped and metal creaked as the car abruptly resumed its interrupted course to the river. A large splash erupted just as Lana reached the woman, grabbing her around the waist as she began to slide after the car.

"Hey, I got you."

Sea-green eyes swam up into Lana's startled gaze, framed by long reddish hair and offering a look that combined entreaty and annoyance. "Damn it, I don't think they'll be giving me my deposit back."

Pure honeysuckle laced the tone, straight from the American South and completely out of place in the Maritimes. Startled, Lana laughed. "Probably not," she said. "Are you okay?"

"Wet and cold, but at least I'm not in the water."

They both looked down to see the dark form of the car list to the right and start to float down the river, the torrent powerful enough to move even its bulk.

"Come on, let's get back up to the road."

The woman clung tightly to Lana as they began the difficult ascent. Lana noted that she was wearing stylish high-heeled shoes, completely inappropriate for stumping about anywhere other than on the flattest surfaces. Her clothing wasn't particularly suitable for the weather either, a sheer blouse and trousers beneath a thin trench coat, soaked through and covered with mud. Lana could feel her shiver convulsively against her side as she continued to cling to a large briefcase. It made their movements up the slope even more awkward, but she showed no inclination of letting it go, and Lana didn't complain. After all, it was undoubtedly everything the poor woman had managed to recover from the car. The rest of her luggage was probably in the trunk.

"I'm Lana," she panted as they climbed. "Lana Mills."

"Michelle Devereaux. So nice to meet you. Too bad it's not under different circumstances." The woman's tone was deeply ironic and Lana laughed again, impressed by her spirit in such difficult conditions.

Finally, they reached the summit and clambered onto the side of the road, slipping a bit on the ice that had formed as the temperature continued to drop. Lana was glad she'd left the engine running and turned the heat up to full once they were inside. Shifting into drive, she glanced over at the woman huddled in the passenger seat. Michelle was small and slender and, now that she was safe, starting to shake like a willow in the wind.

"It's an hour to the nearest town," Lana explained as she pulled onto the road again. "We'll never make it back down to Kennetcook, and there's no place to stay there anyway. My house is just up the road a bit. We'll get you some dry clothes and some tea."

"Sounds perfect," Michelle managed between chattering teeth. She hugged her briefcase close to her body, as if afraid to set it down, and Lana wondered if shock was setting in.

"Not long now," she promised in an attempt to reassure her. "I'm just at the top of the hill."

She pulled into her driveway and navigated the short slope that was becoming icier by the minute. She had a small, detached garage at the top used for storage, leaving no room for her Jeep. She regretted that fact as she stepped out into the driving rain now mixed with ice pellets. The motion light at the corner of her cabin barely illuminated the yard, and she was surprised to see her hand shake as she unlocked the back door. Probably a reaction to her little adventure, she thought. It was good to know she wasn't completely dead inside after all.

Flipping on the lights, she drew Michelle into the kitchen where it was warm and dry. She dropped her keys on the island counter, then continued past it, down the hall to the bathroom, where she turned on the faucet in the tub. After finding some towels, she left them on the back of the toilet before returning to the kitchen where Michelle waited, an uncertain expression on her face as she clutched her briefcase to her chest.

"I've started the tub," Lana told her. "While you get warmed up, I'll find you something to wear."

Michelle looked relieved. "Thank you."

Once Michelle disappeared into the bathroom and shut the door behind her, Lana trotted back out to the Jeep to retrieve her groceries. She quickly put away the frozen items, then left the rest and ran upstairs to her bedroom. Changing out of her damp clothes, she pulled on a pair of sweatpants and a T-shirt before gathering up the same, along with some hiking socks. Michelle was smaller than she was, so she didn't have much chance of finding anything that would fit well, but warmth was more important than style anyway. She hesitated over her underwear drawer, wondering if Michelle was more inclined to the naughtier silk-and-lace garments or the simple matronly cotton panties.

Suddenly, as if in response to the provocative thought, the lights went out, leaving Lana in total darkness.

CHAPTER TWO

Michelle eased into the water with a sigh of mingled relief and pleasure. She still felt like a block of ice from her fruitless attempts to scale the slope on her own, and the soothing heat was just what her aching muscles needed. Though the cabin looked quite rustic on the outside, made of real logs no less, the interior was a charming mixture of modern and country. Thankfully, Lana apparently enjoyed her creature comforts, even out here in the middle of nowhere, with high-end, top-of-the-line appliances, electronics, décor, and furnishings that were clearly expensive to Michelle's discerning eye.

And while it was the middle of nowhere as far as Michelle was concerned, her plan of sticking to the back roads hadn't protected her. She was just surprised Lana hadn't asked her how her accident had happened. Michelle supposed that was a topic for later conversation and she'd worry about it then. For now, she was content to lean back and let the steamy heat chase away the last of her chill. She was surprised when everything shut down a few minutes later, leaving her blinking blindly in the blackness.

"Don't worry," she heard from beyond the doorway a minute later. "It's just a power failure. Should have expected it, really, considering the weather. Are you all right?"

Michelle was tickled with Lana's Maritime accent, the elongated "o" in the "worry" and the way "all right" came out as "aahl right." She really was here, finally, in the land of her forebearers. Would she be speaking in a similar way by the time she left?

"I'm great," Michelle called back. "Still in the tub."

"I have some clothes and a candle. May I come in?"

"Please."

The candle threw wild shadows as Lana entered, a bundle of clothing tucked under her arm. She placed the candle on the sink counter and the clothes on the closed lid of the toilet, eyeing the briefcase resting on the closed bowl. "I don't have much to offer, I'm afraid."

"I'm sure they'll be fine. Thank you."

Michelle studied the attractive features closely, detecting a great deal of character in the set of her jaw, the high cheekbones framed by thick, dark hair boasting random strands that feathered over Lana's forehead. But the eyes were the real attention-grabber, a deep, soulful brown, displaying depths and indications of a whole lot more going on just beneath the surface. A swift glance at Lana's left hand revealed no ring, but that didn't necessarily mean anything. She might have been divorced or never married. Or she could have simply taken off her jewelry after changing out of her damp clothes. She had initially been dressed in a blue silk shirt and designer jeans, beneath a navy ski jacket and leather gloves. Now she wore dark-gray Nike sweats and matching T-shirt, similar to the garments she'd provided for Michelle's use.

Michelle hadn't bothered to cover up her nakedness, and she saw Lana do a quick scan of her body beneath the placid water and then look away, a slight flush darkening her cheeks. That didn't mean anything either. She could just be shy around other people or a bit prudish when it came to the human body. Yet Michelle's gaydar continued to ping like a sub about to be hit by a torpedo, and she believed she might have detected sincere appreciation rather than simple evaluation in that quick glance.

"Are you hungry?"

The question caught Michelle by surprise, and she had to bite back her first answer that was completely inappropriate, though fully in tune with where her thoughts had been leading. "Starved," she admitted. "I had something to eat in—uh, Truro, I think it was called, but that was at lunch."

"I should have something in the fridge. It should be ready by the time you're done in here."

"Thanks."

Lana disappeared out the door, leaving Michelle to finish her bath. She didn't rush it, basking in the water as long as it remained hot. After toweling off, she tried on the clothes. The athletic pants were long in the legs, but they stayed up thanks to the drawstring, while the black T-shirt was faded and soft to the touch.

After tying her hair back in a loose ponytail, Michelle carried her wet clothing out into the kitchen, where a battery-operated hurricane lantern cast a soft glow over the granite countertops and tiled floor. She looked around the cabin's open-concept design, from the kitchen and dining nook at the rear of the house to the living room at the front, both featuring large, arched windows looking east. A big woodstove resting on a raised hearth, with a slate rock wall behind it, served as the partition point between the two. It had a glass door, and behind it, flames crackled and snapped, making everything appear warm and cozy. A covered pot, along with a cast-iron teakettle, sat heating on the soapstone surface.

"I'll take those and put them in the laundry for now," Lana said, retrieving the sodden mass. "Once the power's on again, I'll do them up for you."

"Do you think it'll take long for it to come back?"

"I'm not sure. There's a lot of flooding and this isn't exactly a high-priority area for the power company." Lana walked into the laundry room just off the kitchen. Michelle could see her through the door, placing the clothes in a basket. "I do have a generator, but that's looking after the water heater and the freezer right now. I don't want to waste it on anything else."

"Candles are fine." Michelle smiled and then added, "Romantic."

Lana shot her a sharp look as she returned to the kitchen but didn't say anything. Instead, she started rummaging around in the various drawers and cabinets, bringing out plates and utensils, napkins, and other accouterments. Michelle took a seat and watched, trying not to feel useless as Lana efficiently set the table before bringing over the pot. When Lana lifted the lid, a thick chili offered a savory aroma that made Michelle's mouth water. Crusty bread with accompanying knife was placed on a wooden cutting board, and Michelle wasted no time in reaching out for it.

Lana smiled faintly as Michelle didn't speak. She merely offered the ultimate compliment to the chef by cleaning up her bowl in record time and reaching out for seconds.

Lana goggled when she went for thirds. "How do you stay so tiny?"

"Fast metabolism," Michelle mumbled around a mouthful of bread, red kidney beans, and beef. "Like a hummingbird."

"Lucky you."

Finally, replete after a bowl of some kind of brownie-laced ice cream for dessert, Michelle leaned back in her chair, sipping a cup of coffee. It was instant since the water came from the teakettle, but it still warmed her insides. She watched as Lana went over to a door that must have led to the basement, where she retrieved a tin dishpan. Filling it with water from a bucket, she placed it on the stove to heat for the dishes. It was clear that Lana was quite self-sufficient, regardless of the circumstances, though Michelle supposed she had to be, considering how uninhabited the area seemed. With the weather the way it was and the rental car at the bottom of the river, it was unlikely anyone knew where she was.

For the first time today, Michelle allowed herself to relax. She was safe, at least for the time being.

"So what happened?"

Startled, Michelle looked up to meet those sharp eyes regarding her as if they could strip away every artifice and lie. Resisting the urge to squirm, she managed a smile. "I guess I didn't take that curve at the bottom of the hill very well," she said carefully. "I couldn't keep it on the road, and then, the hill was so slippery when I tried to climb back up, I couldn't get anywhere." She offered a small shudder that wasn't entirely feigned. "I'm really lucky you came along when you did."

Lana hesitated, her features softening. "You must have been frightened."

"It wasn't the most pleasant experience." Michelle offered a half shrug. "But it was an adventure. I'll be talking about this one for years."

"You probably will."

"The time a beautiful woman saved my life," Michelle added silkily, just to see what the response would be. It came in the form of a blush dusting those high cheekbones and those wonderful wide eyes sliding away from hers.

"I need to get the dishes done." Lana turned her back, retrieved some oven mitts, and picked up the tin dishpan, carrying it over to the sink.

Michelle watched her for a few moments, smiling faintly to herself, then rose from her seat to retrieve a dishcloth from the counter.

"You don't have to do that," Lana protested quickly as Michelle took a plate from the rack and began to dry it.

"I want to." Michelle glanced at her. "You saved me, you fed me, and you took me into your home without hesitation. Very kind of you considering I'm a complete stranger. The very least I can do is help with the dishes." She was impressed at how well she'd been treated so far from home and hadn't been aware people were so hospitable outside the South.

Lana didn't seem to know how to respond to that either, so the next few moments were filled with the slosh of water, the clink of dishware, and the steady tick of freezing rain pelting the window above the sink. Michelle didn't try to fill the silence with conversation, content to enjoy the peaceful quiet between them.

"So what do you do?" Lana ventured finally.

"I'm an associate professor of American history at Tulane in New Orleans."

"I see. That explains the accent."

"What accent?" Michelle stared blankly at her.

Lana laughed a little and pulled out the last dish from the soapy water. "So what are you doing up here?"

"What do you know of the Acadians?"

Surprise ghosted across her face, and Lana turned her head to look at her directly. "Just what I learned in school," she said in a doubtful tone. "They were French settlers originally living here in the Maritimes. Nova Scotia was actually known as Acadia back then and was owned by France. There were various wars between them and England. The province got handed back and forth until England finally claimed it one last time and gave it to a Scottish knight who renamed it New Scotland in Latin. The French settlers were rounded up and expelled by the British. Many ended up in—oh, yes, now I see—a lot of them ended up in Louisiana. The Canadian connection is where the word 'Cajun' came from. There are still quite a few communities here in the province."

Impressed with the rather comprehensive, if brief, history lesson from an apparent novice, Michelle nodded. "I'm of Acadian heritage myself, which is why I specialize in the Great Expulsion," she explained. "I'm here researching a—uh, a paper."

"Not exactly the best weather for it," Lana said.

"So I discovered." Michelle smiled broadly and was rewarded by a slight curve of full lips, though Lana looked away from her again. "So what about you?"

"What about me?"

"What do you do?"

"Oh, I'm a writer."

"Really?" Michelle was delighted.

"Yes, fantasy novels."

"Would I have read any of them?"

Lana shook her head and dumped the dishwater into the sink, turning the pan over to let it drain. "Probably not. They're aimed at a specific audience."

Michelle folded the dishtowel she'd been using and draped it over the handle to the nearby oven door. "Try me. Give me some titles."

"Well, there's *Dark Ice, Dark Fire, Dark Wind*...There were actually eight in that series. The titles are fairly standard. Pick an adjective and stick various nouns behind it."

Lana ducked her head shyly as she picked up the hurricane lamp and carried it to the living room, placing it on the coffee table. Intrigued, Michelle followed, curling up in an armchair situated close to the woodstove while Lana sat down on the wine-shaded plush sofa across from her.

"Uh, let's see, I also wrote *Shadow Rider* and *Sky Rider*... Well, you get the drift." She grinned somewhat sheepishly. "That's where I took a noun and threw various adjectives in front of it."

Michelle just stared at her. "Oh, my God," she said, unable to keep the wonder out of her voice. "You're L. S. Mills. I just loved *Dark Storm*, even though I was sorry the series had to come to an end."

Lana looked briefly confused and then, just as quickly, completely astonished. "You've read my books?"

She sounded as if she couldn't believe anyone ever had, but once she actually grasped the concept, her expression immediately became even more guarded. Michelle had a good idea why. All L. S. Mills's books had lesbian protagonists and were considered as much romance as they were fantasy. Published by a smaller house that specifically catered to that market, they weren't the sort of books a reader picked up casually at an airport newsstand. Michelle's gaydar had proved accurate after all.

It was too bad the real reason she'd come to Nova Scotia left so little room for pursuing such a lovely distraction.

CHAPTER THREE

Lana felt a ripple of something she couldn't fully identify surge through her when she realized Michelle was most likely gay. She'd just assumed, as she always did, that Michelle was straight, and now she was forced to readjust her thinking. It wasn't an unpleasant adjustment, but it was a bit disconcerting. She wasn't quite sure what to say next.

"So what are you working on now?" Michelle sounded eager and cheerful, apparently her normal operating state, even after being half drowned and nearly frozen to death.

"I'm not," Lana said shortly. "Working on anything, I mean. I'm still—it's just not where I'm at right now." She really didn't want to get into the reason she hadn't been writing for the past two years, but she had a sinking feeling Michelle was going to ask.

"Why? You used to put out two books a year, sometimes three. Writer's block?"

"Something like that."

Lana was happy to go with the misconception. And it *was* writer's block in a way, just not in the traditional sense of the word. The fact that actually trying to imagine worlds where happily-ever-after worked out and love conquered all was still far too painful to contemplate, but she wasn't about to share that with Michelle.

"What's the S stand for?"

"Um, Sarah."

"That's your middle name?"

"No, it's…" Lana faltered, feeling the familiar dull ache in her chest. "It was my wife's name. Sarah helped me out a lot on plot and characterization."

Michelle immediately sobered. "Was?"

"She passed away a year and a half ago." Lana managed to keep her tone even, but it was an effort. "Breast cancer. She was diagnosed three years ago."

"Oh, God, I'm so sorry." Michelle abruptly appeared stricken, eyes going wide. "I'm just—I'm sorry, I didn't know."

Lana lifted a hand, not in dismissal, but as a sort of wave of acknowledgment. She still didn't know how to react to the sympathy and condolences. That was probably why she spent most of her time to herself, cooped up here in her cabin, rarely drawn out by friends and family. Eventually she was going to have to move on, maybe even start writing again. She just wasn't there yet.

She attempted a smile, hoping it didn't look as awkward as it felt. "So, you're researching a paper on the Acadians? Where were you headed? The Valley? Grand-Pré?"

"Yes, as a matter of fact, that's exactly where I'm headed." Michelle seized on the change of subject with enthusiasm. "I want to check out a church there."

"Well, it's beautiful country, though perhaps not this time of year." Lana suddenly remembered how the woman had ended up in her living room. "Tomorrow, we'll contact the Mounties and tell them about your accident. I suppose I can drive you to Windsor after that. That's probably the closest place with a car-rental agency."

"Mounties?" The tone sounded uncertain.

"The Royal Canadian Mounted Police," Lana elaborated, reminded she was dealing with someone from far away. It seemed the farther south one went in the States, the less they knew about Canada. Still, she thought an expert on a part of Canadian history would be a little more aware of the rest of the culture. "They have jurisdiction. I'd call them tonight, but without electricity, the phones don't work and my cell doesn't really have good service out here. Too many hills."

"Good. I mean, there's no hurry. I'm safe, after all, and they probably have more things to worry about tonight than a stranded tourist, anyway."

"That may be true, but I'm a little concerned that someone might find the car and think the driver drowned."

Michelle peered toward the front windows where nothing could be seen but the reflection of the hurricane lamp on the glass. "In this?"

Lana followed her gaze and laughed a little. "It *is* dark as pitch out there," she said. "Chances are, no one's going to spot a car in the river tonight." She glanced at the clock hanging on the wall, surprised to see it was almost ten. "Time to turn in."

Michelle fixed her with a direct gaze, one that made Lana feel uncomfortable, but then she looked away and the feeling was gone. "I like reading before I go to bed. I don't suppose you have a book you can lend me?"

"Of course. Follow me."

Picking up the hurricane lamp, Lana led Michelle back toward the bathroom. To either side of the short hallway, doors led to bedrooms, one of which Lana used as her office. Inside, the walls were lined with shelving that sagged beneath the immense collection of hardcover and paperback books.

"Help yourself," she offered dryly.

Michelle laughed and wandered in, looking around at the books and the desk in the corner where a large, high-definition monitor resided on the neat surface. Although Lana hadn't been writing, she was usually on her computer once a day, catching up on her e-mail and the few things that still intrigued her. After Sarah's death, it had taken months before she even turned it on. That time was a big black hole to her, without memories of any significance at all, outside of enduring pain and heartbreak.

Lost in thought, she started a bit when Michelle pulled a book from the shelf and smiled at her in a way that made her look young and mischievous. The expression was infectious, and despite the path her mind had wandered, Lana found herself returning the smile.

"Found one?"

"Yep, one of yours." Michelle flashed the book cover at her and Lana felt her cheeks heat. "It's been a while since I read it."

Still feeling awkward, Lana didn't respond, instead easing out the door and across the hall to the guest bedroom. She'd made up the bed with fresh linen while Michelle was in the bath.

"You'll probably want to leave the door open," Lana suggested as she put the hurricane lamp on the nightstand. "The heat from the woodstove should be enough to keep you warm. There are some old T-shirts in the dresser that you can use for pajamas if you'd like, and some toothpaste and new toothbrushes in the top drawer of the vanity in the bathroom. I'll be upstairs if you need anything else."

"I'll be fine. Thank you." Michelle put her hand on Lana's forearm, making her pause. Looking down at it, Lana was surprised at how much that simple physical contact made her body respond with an unusual intensity. When had she become so starved for human contact?

"I mean it, Lana," Michelle told her warmly. "Thank you for everything you've done."

"I'm glad I could help." Lana turned to leave.

"Wait! Won't you need the lamp?"

A veteran of many late nights spent pacing the empty rooms of her cabin or just sitting huddled by the fire, staring emptily into the flames, too devastated to sleep alone in their empty bed, Lana shook her head. "I know my way around in the dark." She glanced back over her shoulder. "Good night, Michelle."

Despite her words, she retrieved a flashlight from one of the kitchen drawers and filled the woodstove again before heading upstairs to the master bedroom and the adjoining ensuite. As she brushed her teeth and undressed, she could hear the wind whistling about the eaves and lightly shaking the house, while ice pellets peppered the glass.

"Not a night fit for man nor dog," she muttered as she looked out the bedroom window and saw nothing but darkness. The lights normally dotting the hills across the river were conspicuously absent, indicating the power outage was extensive. Those houses weren't even on the same grid as hers.

Sighing softly, she looked down at the nightstand where she'd placed her wedding ring after changing out of her wet clothes earlier in the evening. Gently touching the simple gold band with her forefinger, tracing the perfect circle, she felt loneliness well up so strong and sharp in her throat it nearly choked her. She'd thought it had dulled over time, the jagged edge of loss blunted a little more as each day had gone by. She didn't know why it had returned so fresh and powerful tonight, except that perhaps having another person underneath her roof made her customary solitude feel even emptier than usual.

Tossing and turning restlessly on the cool sheets, she tried to think of other things, of what she needed to do in the morning if the power was on and what she would do if it wasn't, whether the road to Windsor would be clear and how many alternative routes she would need to take if there was more flooding. Her thoughts were so disjointed and jumbled she didn't hear the footsteps ascending the stairs until they hit the squeaky step third from the top.

Startled, Lana froze, then rolled over, blinking as the soft illumination of the hurricane lamp appeared in the doorway. Rising onto her elbow, she peered at the slender form standing there, dressed only in a pale-blue T-shirt that hardly maintained decorum, the hem brushing the top of her smooth, bare legs.

Lana felt her mouth go dry. "Michelle? Is there something you need?"

Michelle lifted the lantern a bit higher, revealing emerald eyes that regarded Lana in a molten gaze. "Yes, there is." Her voice was low and smoky with an implication of something that couldn't possibly mean what Lana thought it did.

"What?" It wasn't the most brilliant response, but it was the best she could come up with on such short notice.

Michelle smiled faintly and padded across the polished wood floor on bare feet, setting the lamp gently on the nightstand. Astonished, Lana watched as she eased onto the side of the bed, Sarah's side of the bed, and turned toward her.

"You," Michelle said simply. "I need you." Then she leaned over and kissed Lana before she could utter a word of dissent or otherwise protest. Michelle's lips were soft and warm, and her mouth tasted minty fresh.

I guess she found the toothpaste, Lana thought dazedly. It took a few seconds before she realized she was returning the kiss, responding instinctively rather than with any clear thought. With an effort, she broke it off, pulling back as she struggled to draw air into lungs that felt too constricted to fill properly.

"Wait!" she said, disturbed when the word came out more as a squeak than an actual objection. With an effort, she cleared her throat and tried again. "I don't do this."

"Do what?" Michelle asked softly, her attention intent.

Cheat on my wife was Lana's initial response in her head, harsh and terrible as it crossed her mind even as she knew that it was no longer applicable in this situation. "Kiss people I don't know," she managed instead, though that wasn't quite true either.

"You know me," Michelle responded, sounding vaguely amused. "We met earlier today, remember?"

"That's not—it's just—I haven't," Lana said, her heart pounding in her chest. "Not since Sarah." Longer than that, because for a considerable time before her death, while Sarah was ill, any brief physical intimacy between them had been palliative rather than passionate.

Michelle's gaze became compassionate, eyes warming perceptibly. "I think I'd already figured that out. Look, I'm just passing through," she added gently. "And I'm not expecting or asking for anything beyond a nice warm body to help pass a cold, windy night. If you don't find me attractive, just say the word and I'll go back downstairs. No harm, no foul."

"No, I do," Lana said, embarrassed to hear her voice crack. "Find you attractive, I mean, but I can't…"

She wondered when this surreal situation became something that no longer shocked but rather felt like a really good idea, stirring things in her she'd thought long dead and buried. Michelle didn't move, patiently watching as Lana struggled with the realization that for the first time in a very long time, her mind and body wanted something other than not just to hurt.

To do more than merely exist.

CHAPTER FOUR

Michelle could see the uncertainty in Lana's eyes, and the fear, but she could also see the growing acceptance of her offer, the sudden need and yearning that came with it. Perhaps she was making a mistake by coming upstairs, but she wasn't the sort to deny her baser impulses. She'd been drawn to Lana from the first moment she'd looked at her. The tragic story of her lost love only enhanced that irresistible aura of brooding allure.

Once she was certain Lana wasn't going to refuse her, she reached out and laid her fingertips lightly on her cheek. There was a swift intake of breath, but nothing further, and carefully, Michelle leaned forward to cover those full lips again, sinking into the sweet warmth of her mouth. A whimper at the back of Lana's throat sent a thrill of desire through her, and Michelle deepened the kiss, slipping her arms around her and pulling her closer. She could taste the hunger in Lana's kiss, felt the desire in the hands roaming over her back and sides. Now that she'd surrendered to what was about to happen, Lana was no longer holding back.

Neither made a move to turn off the hurricane lamp. Perhaps Lana needed to see her, Michelle thought briefly as she pulled the T-shirt off over her head. If only so she wouldn't be confused for someone else in the dark and bring back memories better left untouched in this moment. Michelle was willing to accept that. Besides, she wanted to be able to see Lana as well.

Easing down onto the mattress, Michelle moaned quietly as she felt the full length of Lana's lush curves beneath her. She felt so good, so warm and soft, so utterly welcoming. Running her hand along her side and then up to cup Lana's breast, Michelle brushed her thumb lightly over the velvet-soft skin of a nipple that hardened immediately. Lana groaned softly, pressing into the caress, and her fingers raked through Michelle's hair as they kissed until they were breathless.

There was something so delicious, so incredibly right about lying together in the dim glow of the lamp, the sound of the freezing rain a delicate counterpoint to the soft whisper of skin on skin, of tiny murmurs of passion. Michelle had never been averse to finding her pleasure wherever she could, but now she was taken aback to find that this felt different. Maybe it was because Michelle had been in such peril earlier and Lana had been her knight in shining armor, coming to her rescue. Or perhaps it was simply because Lana was so responsive, and Michelle understood it had been so long for her. The situation made each touch more exquisite, every kiss a little sweeter.

It made her want to go slow, to make everything right for Lana. If she was to be her first after losing Sarah, then pride demanded Michelle do it right. She lingered over the soft swells of Lana's breasts, using her lips and tongue to tease each nipple into attentive points of sensation. Lana whimpered and squirmed under the relentless attention.

"Breast woman?" she managed with a breathless laugh.

Michelle smiled. "I'm an all-woman type of woman." She paused to look down at her, peering deeply into the depths of those limpid eyes. "Don't worry, darlin'. I'm just getting started."

"Oh my."

Amused, Michelle resumed her loving assault on Lana's breasts before leisurely trailing down over the lean plane of her stomach. She paused briefly to tease her navel with the tip of her tongue, sparking a soft giggle, then down to the waiting treasure. She caught her breath as she parted Lana's legs, immersing herself in her full range of senses as she covered the tender flesh with her mouth, basking in the musky scent and flavor of her. Lana jerked reflexively, tangling her fingers in Michelle's hair, tugging helplessly, encouraging her to continue.

Michelle was more than glad to comply. She loved this. She loved pleasuring women, loved hearing their soft moans and cries of delight, loved knowing she was the one to offer them such intimate joy. Lana was even a more special joy. To know what she had lost gave a piquant twist to the encounter that most didn't for Michelle.

It was almost too much because when she thought about it in those terms, when she thought of Lana's heartbreak, tears stung Michelle's eyes and her heart skipped a beat. It took a second for her to regain her composure, surprised that Lana's loss affected her so deeply. Forcing her attention back to the matter at hand, she once more fluttered her tongue over Lana's ridge, slick with desire. Silken thighs closed about her head, tightening as pleasure grew. Lana's hips arched, bucked once, then twice, and a sound of such sweet surrender issued from her lips that Michelle felt a strong throb in her own groin.

She lightened her touch and kissed her way back up her body, trailing languidly along each line and curve until she reached her face. Lana had her eyes closed, a lazy grin curving the corners of her mouth, revealing a hint of a dimple. Lana kissed each eyelid lightly, then brushed her lips down the elegant nose before covering her mouth, inviting a welcoming kiss that came instantly, deep and delightful.

"That was amazing," Lana whispered once they'd parted.

"You're amazing," Michelle murmured.

She felt the restless urge of need sizzling along her nerve endings but forced herself to be patient, wanting Lana to enjoy her first physical intimacy in a long time to the absolute fullest. Besides, if she'd judged correctly from the tenor of the love scenes in her books, Lana should prove to be a considerate lover.

She didn't disappoint. Her hands soon began to trace over her, and Michelle sank fully and willingly into the pleasure of her touch.

Lana flipped them over so that she was on top, her thick, dark hair falling about their faces as they kissed, hard and passionate now, as she made Michelle her own. Michelle was thrilled, surprised by the depth of Lana's desire, but eagerly matched it. Then Lana's skilled fingers were on her, and deep within her, and Michelle lost all connection with coherent thought.

Afterward, she lay in boneless satisfaction, stunned at how easily Lana had overwhelmed her. Beneath her cheek, she could feel the steady throb of Lana's heart, a soothing counterpoint to the thin howl of wind whistling past the nearby window. Tenderly, Lana's fingers traced through Michelle's hair, stroking with passive energy.

"Thank you." It was an almost inaudible whisper in the night.

Michelle smiled. "Oh, anytime," she said playfully.

"No, I mean…" Lana hesitated, and Michelle heard her swallow. "Just thank you."

Sobering, Michelle rubbed her cheek against the smooth skin of Lana's breastbone. "You're entirely welcome."

Running her fingers lightly over the slope of Lana's belly, teasingly, tracing each line of surprisingly defined muscle, she felt desire stir once again. "Of all the people who could have been passing by, I sure am glad you were the one who fished me out of the river."

Lana chuckled. "I am, too." Her breath caught as Michelle's fingers trailed down to scratch luxuriously through the dark triangle, exhaling into a soft moan. "Exceedingly glad."

Michelle rolled on to her, delighting in the warm length of her body beneath her own. Lana was significantly taller, five eight to her five four, and the difference in size made her feel almost giddy at the thought of all that wonderful flesh to explore. Lana made a sound as she proceeded to do so, a bit surprised, it seemed, but mostly appreciative.

They made love again, slow and languid, almost drowsy as they caressed and stroked, bringing each other to a mutual peak. Sleep came quickly after, a natural sinking into the balmy black of oblivion. When Michelle awoke, the window was still a black square, reflecting the light from the lamp, and carefully, she eased away from the warm body next to her, slipping from between the sheets. Pressure building in her bladder, she took a chance on a nearby door, pleased to discover it led to an ensuite. Carrying the lamp, she felt her eyebrows lift as she entered, discovering a positively luxurious layout that included a twelve-jet whirlpool tub along with a glass-and-chrome shower big enough for three people. It boasted an overhead rain nozzle along with a massaging head and dual body faucets, and she made a mental note to take her shower there in the morning, assuming the power had returned. It appeared writing was a much better gig than she thought. Or perhaps Sarah had been the one with the money. Either way, Michelle could have found herself in worse situations.

After using the facilities, she descended the stairs on catlike feet, avoiding the squeaky one three down from the top automatically. In the guest room, she retrieved her briefcase from beneath the bed. Opening the lid, she checked the contents, reassuring herself that everything was still there and unharmed: the tattered diary written in tiny script, old maps and drawings, and most importantly, the letters she'd discovered during her research in the university archives. She felt the same shiver she always did when she saw them, the slightly sick mix of guilt, terror, and excitement. If anyone discovered she had taken them…

Who was she kidding? He *had* found out. Otherwise, that dark sedan containing two men wouldn't have been following her all the way from Truro. Hell, those guys must have been following her since she'd left New Orleans. She found it highly unlikely anyone in Nova Scotia knew about what she'd discovered or what she had planned. It had to be Hector. He was the only one who understood what this meant to her, because it meant much the same to him.

She should never have told him about the letters. Rich and powerful, he was also dangerous, regardless of their personal relationship. His guys probably thought they'd taken her out of the game earlier that day, and if it hadn't been for a lucky alder bush and a lovely woman, they most certainly would have succeeded.

Involuntarily, she glanced upward, thinking about Lana and wondering how much she dared tell her. How much she *could* tell her without involving her in something she had no right to lay at her door. Sighing quietly, she shut the briefcase and locked it, sliding it beneath the bed once more. Somehow, she would have to convince Lana not to contact the authorities while she arranged to rent another car. How she would do the latter and not let on to any rental company that she'd already lost her previous vehicle was a complication better left for the morning. In the meantime, she was cold, and it made no sense to stay down here while such a warm and welcoming woman waited for her.

Creeping back upstairs, she eased back into bed, carefully snuggling up behind Lana and wrapping her arms around her. Lana stirred briefly, turning her head.

"Y'kay?" she muttered.

"I'm fine," Michelle whispered soothingly. "I just went to the bathroom. Go back to sleep."

Lana sighed, a soft exhalation, and settled back onto the mattress. It took significantly longer before Michelle was able to mimic her.

CHAPTER FIVE

It took more than a few seconds after Lana woke up for her to realize the cozy, loving place she found herself in was neither a dream nor a journey back in time. It wasn't Sarah wrapped so warmly around her from behind, but a stranger, someone just passing through, and any sense of comfort and intimacy offered was merely temporary. Yet, her presence made Lana feel so good and sheltered that she couldn't deny her need to linger in the slender arms, to want this time to go on forever.

Suspecting any such indulgence would only leave her lonelier in the aftermath made Lana ease away from Michelle's enticing embrace. Maybe it wasn't worth remembering how good a connection could be, when she now knew how bad it could be without it. Slipping from between the sheets, Lana stood there briefly, wood floor cold under her bare feet as she took a moment to look down at the beautiful woman sleeping in her bed, the blankets tangled gloriously about her slight body, long, rich auburn hair the color of fall maple leaves spread over the pillows. Inside, Lana's heart gave a painful thud, and quickly, she pulled on her robe and shoved her feet into her slippers. Moving as quietly as possible, she gathered up some clothes before heading out the door. Taking her shower in the downstairs bathroom rather than the ensuite seemed like a prudent idea.

She was relieved to find that the power had returned, repaired sometime during the night, and as she glanced out the window, she noted that the rain and wind had eased, though it remained gray and foreboding. Taking a brief detour down into the basement, she turned off the propane generator maintaining the freezer and fridge, switching back over to the main power before heading back upstairs to put Michelle's damp clothes in the washer.

In the safe haven of the shower in the downstairs bathroom, she let the hot water wash over her and wondered why she'd given in to her desires the night before. She supposed it was the first time in a long while she'd felt *interested* in something. And she couldn't deny that Michelle was the most interesting thing to come along in years.

As she dried herself off, she could hear movement above her and knew her guest had awakened. The soft sound of water in pipes indicated Michelle had found the ensuite, and with images of that lithe body writhing beneath gushing water to plague her thoughts, Lana quickly dressed and went out to the kitchen, where she started preparations for some western omelets. A knock on the back door interrupted her as she was about to pour her mixture in the pan, and she frowned as she put down the ceramic bowl. She hadn't heard a car, but when she glanced out the window above the sink, she saw the official vehicle parked behind her Jeep.

Emily Stone, tall and solid, dirty blond hair harshly subdued into a neat bun, light-blue eyes piercing beneath the brim of her cap, dipped her head briefly when Lana opened the door. "Good morning, Mrs. Mills, I just stopped by to make sure everything was all right."

Lana smiled. Being addressed so formally relayed the fact Stone was officially on duty, as if the uniform wasn't enough of a clue. "I'm surprised to see you, Emily. How are the roads?"

"They're a bit challenging," Emily admitted as she stepped inside. "I wouldn't attempt any travel unless it's an emergency. We've had to block off the bridge down below."

There was more than a slight flavor of the Rock in her voice, the lively lilt of Newfoundland lacing her otherwise officious tones. Mounties weren't generally posted in their hometowns, but they could choose their home province. Instead, Stone, after graduating Depot in Regina, had spent a few years out west in Saskatchewan, then in Southern Manitoba, before finally settling in Nova Scotia. Lana had ferreted out that much during the many meals they'd shared down at the diner whenever she'd been picking up takeout at the same time the constable was stopping by for a break from her patrol of the surrounding area. Somehow, Emily always managed to convince Lana to eat her fish and chips there with her rather than take them home to eat in solitude.

Lana supposed she couldn't exactly call her a close friend, since the meals at the diner were the only interaction they shared—outside of the time Emily had stopped her for speeding and let her off with a gravely delivered warning rather than a ticket and fine, for which Lana had been suitably grateful—but they were more than mere acquaintances. It warmed her to know the visit was as much personal as it was official, since she doubted Emily was stopping by every house on this side of the river between here and Windsor just to see how people were doing.

"Does it look like the bridge is going?"

"We hope not, but it's too early to tell." Emily absently shifted the heavy Sam Brown belt that contained her cuffs, radio, and Smith & Wesson 4956. "I hope you're well supplied because it takes about three hours to get from here to Windsor now."

"I am. I went down to the store last night," Lana told her. "I think I just made it over the bridge before it became too deep to try. It was a little scary. Fortunately, I don't plan to be going anywhere for a while."

She paused, about to tell her the rest when she saw Emily's eyes widen in what could only be consternation. Uncertainly, Lana turned to follow her gaze, feeling her jaw slacken when she saw Michelle descending the stairs, dressed only in another of Lana's T-shirts and very little else. A white towel was wrapped around her recently washed hair, her green eyes big and bright. She looked positively decadent and somehow younger than she'd seemed last night.

A range of emotion flooded through Lana—astonishment, desire, chagrin, and a little guilt—when she saw Emily's raised eyebrows. For someone who was supposed to still be in mourning, this was a little difficult to explain.

"Oh, my, the police. Is the flooding that serious?" Honeysuckle didn't just flavor the words now: it positively dripped from the golden drawl, as if Michelle had just stepped out of a Civil War-era novel.

Lana swallowed hard, managing to break the silence that followed. "This is Constable Emily Stone," she said politely. "Emily, this is Michelle Devereaux. She's—"

"An old and dear friend of Lana's," Michelle said smoothly and completely untruthfully as she came to stand beside Lana, wrapping her arm tightly and rather possessively around her waist. "I'm staying with her for a while."

Lana blinked, too bemused to contradict the tale of old friends reconnecting years later that Michelle was spinning to the constable, who appeared to be so taken aback by the lack of clothes involved, that she wasn't saying anything in reply. The next thing Lana knew, Michelle had smoothly and confidently eased Emily out the door, shutting it firmly behind her before turning to regard Lana with an ambiguous expression.

Lana shook her head, confusion reigning. "What the hell was that? Why did you lie to Emily?"

"Oh, Emily, is it?" Michelle eyed her archly. "Not Officer Stone?"

"*Constable* Stone." Lana corrected her automatically. "Why did you lie to her? Why tell her we'd been friends for years and that you were here on a visit? I don't understand."

"I didn't want her to know what really happened," Michelle offered in an unexpectedly reasonable tone.

"Why not?" Lana struggled to make sense of what was happening. It didn't help that how Michelle was dressed, or rather, undressed, was serving as a distraction. She stared at her and then at the door. "Look, we need to call her back and tell her about your car. If they find it and think someone drowned, they'll be searching for a body."

"It works for me that people think that."

That got Lana's full attention. "For God's sakes, why?"

Michelle hesitated. "Because I didn't exactly go off the road on my own. Someone forced me off."

Lana stared at her blankly for a moment as the words percolated through her mind. "You'd better tell me exactly what's going on." She was aware of the frost edging her tone and the rising sense that she'd been played for a bit of a fool.

"I'd rather not," Michelle told her cheerfully. "In fact, the less you know, the better. So what's for breakfast?"

She made a move toward the kitchen and Lana reached out, not quite touching her, but with a strongly suggestive gesture nonetheless. "Stop." She hadn't sounded like that for some time, she knew, but Sarah had always said she had the most authoritative voice she'd ever heard. The sexiest, as well, according to her, but this wasn't the time or place to consider that point. Michelle turned, her eyes widening and pupils contracting. She even made a little sound of surprise, almost a squeak.

"Start from the beginning. Tell me everything. Are you even really a professor from Tulane?"

"Uh—" Michelle's eyes darted to the side. "I don't have tenure."

"Of course you don't." Lana could feel her shields going up, realizing only after the fact how far they'd fallen. "And your research?"

"That part is true. I am here, researching something." She hesitated. "I may have been a little vague about what that is, specifically." She squirmed beneath Lana's gaze, seeming unable to look her in the eyes but also unable to continue the dissembling.

"Not the Acadians?"

"Oh, yes, to do with the Acadians."

"What, exactly?"

"You know there was a church in the Annapolis Valley?"

"At Grand-Pré, yes. It's been rebuilt."

"But not quite in the same place."

"No, they don't know exactly how the original settlement was laid out," Lana said, trying to remember the vacation when she and Sarah had visited the museum located on the site.

"I do."

"What?" Lana crossed her arms over her chest. "How?"

Michelle cast a pleading glance in the direction of the kitchen. "Can we continue this over breakfast? I'm starving."

"Are you sure it's your metabolism?" Lana said icily. "Maybe you just have a tapeworm."

Flashing her a narrow look because of the waspish comment, Michelle sighed. "Look, I can explain better over a meal."

Lana sighed. "Fine. But it better be good or I'm calling Emily back here immediately."

"Well, don't let me stop you," Michelle threw over her shoulder as she headed for the table. "But let's be sure it's about me and not just because you want to see her again."

"What?" Again, Lana felt unbalanced as she turned the heat on under the frying pan and stirred her omelet mixture once more. "What the hell's that supposed to mean?"

"Oh, come on. That woman wants you."

"Wants me?! She's a friend. She's not even a lesbian!"

"Who told you that?" Michelle regarded her, openly skeptical. "Of course she is, and she makes a point of stopping by to see you whenever she has a legitimate excuse, but only then. Because you're widowed, you see, and it would be unseemly for her to make the first move. You have to do that."

Lana didn't want to hear this. Furthermore, she suspected it was Michelle's way of confusing the issue, which was that— Which was…

What exactly was the issue again?

CHAPTER SIX

Michelle forked into the omelet with a sense of relief that Lana had appeared to let the whole thing go for the moment. So when it turned out that Lana was merely waiting politely until she finished breakfast, then pinned her with a look that penetrated to the bone, Michelle was taken aback.

"Talk to me." Lana's dark eyes glinted and her jaw had set to something rock hard, chin lifted haughtily. "What's going on?"

Michelle considered her options, suspecting she didn't have many if she didn't want Lana to be on the phone immediately to that very attractive law-enforcement agent. That had been a hell of a jolt when she realized the voices downstairs had included someone in a uniform with a gun on her hip. She'd barely had time to scurry back into the bedroom and pull on a T-shirt she'd found at the foot of the bed, making herself look as provocative as possible before descending the stairs and distracting everyone quite nicely.

Still, the expression on the cop's face had been interesting indeed. A clear display of devastated disillusionment before firming up into a more official and impassive mask of impartiality. And it was undoubtedly that sense of deep disappointment that had enabled Michelle to ease Stone out of there without further investigation. Michelle didn't know how long that would last. She needed to get on the road as soon as possible.

Unfortunately, the only way to do that was in Lana's Jeep. Unless she was prepared to do something drastic like steal it, she needed Lana to drive her where she needed to go, if not to Grand-Pré itself, then to the nearest car-rental place. Come to think of it, could she even rent a car without being immediately identified as someone who'd lost her last vehicle under suspicious circumstances?

Realizing she had no other choice, she caved. "There's a gold cross," she admitted reluctantly. "King Louis XV gave it to the Father of St. Charles's church in Grand-Pré."

Lana looked skeptical. "The king of France gave a gold cross to a little village in Acadia? Why?"

"Something about a mistress and an illegitimate son no one knew about who ended up becoming a cleric. Consider it a sort of eighteenth-century child support. It was all very secretive and not recorded in the history most people know." Michelle was a little irritated at the corner she'd found herself maneuvered into. "It's the Acadians' greatest treasure."

"I wasn't aware they had a greatest treasure. So you're a treasure hunter," Lana said, a certain condemnation in her tone. "Rather than a historian."

"On the contrary, I want to find it so it'll go to the university or a museum, rather than fall into the hands of a private collector," Michelle said, offended.

"And is either the university or museum in Canada, or the United States?"

Michelle stopped, confounded by the question, realizing she hadn't really considered it before. "Uh," she said, somewhat stupidly.

"How did you find out about it?" Lana demanded, apparently bypassing the subject for the moment.

"A series of letters I discovered between the father and another priest in Port Royal. After the Great Expulsion, Father Beauséjour lived in Louisiana for twenty years before finally returning to Canada, where he died in 1803."

"And those documents indicated he possessed some kind of golden cross?"

"Yes, hidden when the British rounded up the families in Grand-Pré and left behind when the Acadians were expelled from Nova Scotia," Michelle said. "The British burned down the entire settlement, and the cross was never found."

"You were forced off the road because of this?"

Michelle dropped her eyes, feeling that grim stare penetrate to the bone. "I first came across the letters and Beauséjour's journal in the university archives, but to go further, I had to contact a private collector who had the rest of the documentation, the actual piece that tied everything together and revealed where the cross was hidden. In order to see his, however, I had to show him what I had."

"This collector?"

"Christ almighty, are you sure you aren't a cop yourself?"

Lana's jaw tightened perceptibly. "You're asking me to lie to the Mounties. Worse, you're asking me to deceive a friend. I'd better have a good reason for it."

Michelle smiled. "Does that mean you're willing to consider the idea?"

Now it was Lana's turn to look away, to drop her gaze. "Tell me everything," she insisted.

"His name is Hector Duperies," Michelle said. "Very wealthy. His family consisted of Acadians who remained in Louisiana. He's quite proud of his heritage and would do anything to add the cross to his collection."

"Including trying to kill you?"

Michelle looked away, unwilling to go into the complicated situation any deeper. "He has a bit of a reputation," she said instead.

"He's a criminal?"

"Not proven, but rumors are that his business practices are a little—" Michelle searched for the right word. "Shady."

"You knew this going in?"

Michelle hesitated, then lowered her head. "Yes."

"Wonderful."

Lana stood up and began to clear the table, her motion agitated, the plates and mugs clinking together. Michelle stayed where she was, not wanting to irritate her any more than she already had, if irritation was the right word. She recognized that she'd time to get used to the idea that she was on the verge of a great discovery. It was all new to Lana, and Michelle had to give her space to absorb and accept the reality of it.

If she could. Michelle was aware that her quest for the cross could end right here, that Lana could simply throw up her hands and be done with it—contact the police and tell them about the rental car and the accident. By the time Michelle had dealt with all that, found another car and made her way to Grand-Pré, Hector's men would probably have caught up to her again.

"What do you want me to do?" Lana asked finally as she stacked the dishes in the dishwasher.

"Duperies' men probably think I've been stopped," Michelle said. "But if you take me to Grand-Pré today, we'll get the jump on them."

"Oh, 'we' will, will we?" Lana's tone was heavy with sarcasm. "They probably already have it, if they know what you do."

"They don't. They're going on memory," Michelle said in her most persuasive tone.

"But didn't you say you only had part of the puzzle?" Lana pointed out, looking confused. "You said their boss had the key piece."

"He *had* it," Michelle said. She got up and went into the spare bedroom to retrieve her briefcase. "Now I have it."

She set the case on the island counter, dialed in the combination for the lock, and opened the lid. Inside lay a stack of yellowing and brittle documents, each individual piece protected with some kind of polyester sheathing, along with two battered journals. Lana stared at the pile and then at Michelle.

"You stole them?"

"I borrowed them," Michelle said.

"You couldn't photocopy everything?"

"I didn't want him to have them." Michelle shrugged. "Besides, there wasn't time."

"Oh, my God," Lana said, walking away. "What have I gotten myself into?"

"Look, all I need is a ride to the Annapolis Valley," Michelle said, shutting the briefcase. "I know exactly where the cross is supposed to be. I'll go in, retrieve it, and then we can take it to the authorities."

"Which we can't do right now because you possess stolen property," Lana said, beginning to pace about the kitchen like a caged tigress. "And now that I didn't say anything to Emily, I'm an accessory at the very least for failing to report an accident."

Michelle started to protest and then prudently shut her mouth, clamping her lips tight. Obviously Lana considered herself an upright, law-abiding citizen and didn't like any of this. Either she would help or she wouldn't, and Michelle suspected anything she could say wouldn't make an impact on the decision. She'd heard that Canadians tended to be more uptight when it came to certain things. It would be easier to convince her if she was from New Orleans, Michelle thought. We have a more laissez-faire view of legal boundaries.

"Why are you doing this?"

Michelle blinked at the question. Lana had stopped pacing and had now pinned her with another of those sharply piercing looks. She hesitated and decided she'd better be as forthright as possible. Sometimes the truth was more useful than a lie. "Because if I find this thing and give it back to the Acadians, back to my people, it means I've accomplished something extraordinary." She tilted her head sheepishly. "And it wouldn't exactly hurt my future career options."

Lana frowned darkly but didn't say anything sarcastic, for which Michelle was grateful. In the short time she'd known her, she had discovered Lana's tongue could be as sharp as her pen, and she really didn't like being the focus of it.

"If I help you, if we find this cross, then we'll take it to the authorities here," Lana said finally. "It's Canadian and it belongs in Nova Scotia. I don't really give a damn about the New Orleans end of it."

Michelle wanted to argue, but at the determined expression on Lana's face, she finally inclined her head for the sake of agreement. "All right," she said reluctantly. After all, she supposed, she'd still be credited with finding it and that was all she really wanted, wasn't it? Whether the cross ended up in an American museum or a Canadian one was irrelevant, or at least it should be. "We need to leave as soon as possible."

"I have to clear up a few things and leave a note."

Michelle stared at her. "A note? What about? To who?"

"A note detailing everything that's happened so that if something goes wrong, they'll know how and why and who was behind it."

"They?" Michelle eyed Lana skeptically. "You mean 'she,' don't you? You're talking about that good-lookin' lady cop."

Lana's face became wooden. "She's the only one who might care if something happens to me."

That struck to the bone and Michelle winced. Still, it was better than the alternative, where Lana called the constable immediately and the whole thing ended with Michelle achieving nothing more for her troubles than an outstanding bill for a rental car that had been swept out to sea.

"I understand," she said, moderating her tone to its most conciliatory inflection. "I know this is a major deal for you, and I'm really very grateful."

"Give me an hour to pack a bag," Lana said gravely. "We'll stop in Windsor and pick you up a few things, especially some winter clothes. You'll need them if you plan to be running around outside." She frowned briefly and headed for her study.

Michelle watched her go, struck by a sudden thought. She understood why she was doing this, why she felt she had to go on this adventure, on this pursuit of some mythical dream no matter what the danger. What it might cost her in the long run.

But why was Lana doing it when all common sense said she should simply call back her cop friend and end it all here and now?

CHAPTER SEVEN

Stunned, unhappy, Emily barely paid attention to the road as she drove from Lana's cabin, unable to believe what she'd seen. Not that she had any claim on Lana, of course, but still, she'd thought—she'd hoped—that when Lana was ready to move beyond her grief, she would see Emily and how she felt about her. Now it looked as if Emily had missed her chance, which made her chest roil with regret and disillusionment.

Noticing the needle creeping up on the speedometer, Emily deliberately lightened her foot, slowing the cruiser. There was no point in running off the road over this. Exhaling in a rush, she shook her head and turned off one of the side roads to avoid the flooding that lay ahead. Her patrol included most of the Rawdon Hills, which had a lot of back roads with isolated houses on them that required her attention. For the most part, it was a quiet and peaceful assignment, the only excitement being an occasional speeder or a domestic dispute that could usually be calmed with some practical suggestions and pointed warnings. It had been an unexpected though gratifying bonus to discover one of her favorite authors lived there.

Not that she'd ever let on to Lana. Besides, when she first met her, Sarah was still alive, though gravely ill, and after her death, Lana had been plunged into a dark morass of mourning. Emily could offer only a passing friendship and a shoulder if Lana ever required it, though, outside of their shared meals at the diner in Kennetcook, Lana never had. Now, just as it seemed Lana was surfacing from her pool of misery, appeared to be shaking off the worst of the lingering sorrow, some stranger had swooped in to offer more at just the right time, leaving Emily with nothing but a heavy heart and a myriad of *what ifs*.

It gnawed at her all the way back to Windsor and the RCMP detachment, where she parked the cruiser and slammed the door with unnecessary vigor. Inside the squat building that housed their offices, she ran into fellow regular member Paul MacDonald, who sat at the desk opposite hers, filling out paperwork. Tall and broad-shouldered, with his dark hair cut high and tight, his hazel eyes perpetually amused, he took one look at her face and lifted his bushy eyebrows.

"What's going on, Ems?"

Emily shot him a look and forced her agitation down deep into the pit of her stomach where it lay like lead. "Just tired of winter," she said.

"A couple more months of it, anyway," he replied philo-sophically. He eyed her narrowly over his computer monitor. "No, really, you came in here looking like you were loaded for bear. What's up?"

He was a good friend, and on the occasions when it called for it, he operated as her partner on patrol. She'd been to his house many times for dinner with his family: Hannah, his wife, and his two kids, boys, Seth and Cory. If Emily had to talk to anyone, it might as well be him, she decided. Besides, he knew all about Emily's pathetic little crush, told to him one night during a particularly tedious stakeout of an illegal marijuana grow field.

"Just got caught off guard this morning," she admitted as she sat down and powered up her computer.

"Lana?" His tone was silky, and a teasing light shone in his dark eyes.

She exhaled audibly. "I stopped by to see how she was doing with all the flooding." The next was a bit painful. "She had a guest."

"Huh," he said noncommittally. "So?"

"So, she was a personal-type guest," Emily went on as she filled out her paperwork, trying to distance herself a little from the situation. "Her name is Michelle and she's from New Orleans. She came downstairs dressed in nothing but a T-shirt, looking about eighteen, except for the eyes." Emily paused, thinking about it. "The eyes looked a hell of a lot older."

"Oh, wow, that's a surprise," he said, and his angular dark features softened a bit. "Sorry, Ems. Guess your favorite author's over her mourning period. Maybe this means she'll start writing again. But it doesn't necessarily mean there's no chance for you. In fact, this could all be good news. Obviously, Lana's ready to move on. And if this girl is from New Orleans, then she's probably not sticking around." He paused. "How do you suppose they know each other?"

Emily shrugged. "I got the impression they were old friends." Except it was Michelle who did the implying whereas Lana had seemed a lot less comfortable with the idea, Emily remembered belatedly, as she began to go over the encounter in more analytical detail. In fact, Lana had seemed surprised at some of what Michelle had been saying.

"Maybe she's a reader, some kind of fan of Lana's books. I need to run a background check on her, see who she really is."

Paul lifted his head, staring at her. "I doubt that's a good idea," he said mildly.

"No, I didn't—" Emily felt her face heat as she realized how her plan sounded. "I don't mean for personal reasons. It's just now that I'm thinking about it, there was something hinky there."

"Emily, you know how much I respect your instincts," he pointed out, his voice becoming serious. "But this could be going over a line you really don't want to cross." He shook his head. "Look, you're off for the next few days. Think about it, and if you really believe there's something there, you can always run a background check when you get back."

"You're probably right," she said, though a sense of dissatisfaction remained.

Swallowing it back, she began to finish her remaining paperwork. She didn't often have three days off in a row and had been planning to enjoy them. In fact, that was part of the reason she'd stopped by Lana's cabin that morning. She'd hoped to talk Lana into, if not a date exactly, then some sort of outing, a movie in Windsor perhaps, or maybe just another lunch at the diner in Kennetcook, only without her being in uniform and having to go back out on patrol immediately afterward. Now Emily wasn't anticipating her time off nearly as much, but she still needed to wrap up as much as possible before leaving.

She changed out of her uniform in the locker room at the end of her shift and stuffed it in a gym bag, which she carried out to the parking lot where her ruby-red Dodge Challenger, the R/T Scatback Shaker model, was parked. As she was pulling out of the lot, an incoming cruiser stopped and she braked in response, looking over to see Norma Stewart, another member from her detachment.

"You come in from Kennetcook?" Norma said, rolling down her window as Emily did the same. "Route 14?"

"I turn around in Kennetcook," Emily explained. "That's the edge of my patrol. Northeast Nova Division has it from the other side. Stewiacke detachment. Why?"

"They just fished a rental car out of Lattie's Brook near Maitland. Considering how strong the current was, it might have gone in on our side."

"I didn't hear anything from the locals," Emily said. "There was no sign of an accident during my pass through this morning, but there's a lot of flooding around there. The driver?"

"No sign."

"Do they think he's in the river?"

"No, the car was empty, the doors shut, and the windows were up. It looks more like it was dumped or abandoned. Women's luggage still in the trunk, though. The paperwork in the glove compartment was ruined, so they're checking with Enterprise now to see who rented it."

"Women's luggage? Well, if it went in on our side, then Paul will have to handle it," Emily said. "I'm off for the next three days."

"Lucky you," Norma said dryly. "See you on Tuesday."

But Emily didn't leave right away as the police cruiser pulled away. Instead, she sat in her car and thought furiously. If the rental car belonged to Michelle, why wouldn't she have said something when she was there? Why wouldn't Lana? And why did she even think it was Michelle who'd rented the car in the first place?

Nothing more than my gut, Emily thought uncomfortably, and that was hardly enough to warrant going back inside with her suspicions. But it was enough for her to turn right toward the highway instead of left into downtown Windsor, where her apartment was located. The V8 beneath the hood rumbled pleasantly as she accelerated onto the TransCanada, and she wished she could travel this fast the entire way, but only a couple of kilometers later she was easing down the ramp and back onto the twisty, broken pavement leading through the Rawdon Hills.

She chafed at the detours she had to take on the way to Lana's place, some little more than fire roads through the forest before coming out onto the main highway once more. It was well after dark when she arrived at the cabin, and her heart sank when she saw no lights in the window. She hoped that indicated another power outage, but when she pulled in, the motion light at the corner of the garage immediately activated. Now that she was here, doubts and self-consciousness rushed in. What the hell was she doing?

Hesitantly, she opened her door and got out of the Challenger. It was raining again, a cold, fretful rain that made her blink, a misty halo outlining the bulb of the outdoor light. Squaring her shoulders, she steeled herself and climbed the short flight of stairs leading to Lana's back door. She knocked firmly, a bit louder than she intended, and winced at the harsh sound.

No response. Frowning, she looked around and realized that Lana's Wrangler wasn't in the yard. She closed her eyes in consternation. All this way and she wasn't even home. Except— hadn't Lana said she wasn't going anywhere for a while, that she'd be staying away from the flooding? This was all very strange, mostly because it wasn't what Emily recognized as normal behavior for Lana. And Emily had paid attention to every aspect of her behavior from the second she'd laid eyes on her three years earlier. Though immediately attracted to the darkly beautiful features, what really had ensnared Emily was Lana's courage and grace in the most dreadful of circumstances, her quiet dignity and small flashes of humor that colored their conversations at the diner.

She wasn't proud of what she did next, but she couldn't help herself. She had to know. Sliding her hand behind the deck post by the door, she retrieved the spare key that Lana kept hanging there. She'd revealed the place of concealment during one of their lunches, presumably because being a police constable made Emily so trustworthy. Feeling a bit sick, but determined to get to the bottom of the situation, Emily slipped the key into the lock and turned it.

Inside, a fire still smoldered in the woodstove, but the place held a definite aura of emptiness. Emily took a step forward, hesitated, and decided she'd violated Lana's privacy quite enough. Ashamed and chastened, she turned to leave when she glimpsed a white envelope propped up on the toaster on the counter beside her.

Emily's name was on it, written in Lana's artistic scrawl. Stunned, she took it and opened it, pulling out a two-page, stapled letter printed from Lana's computer.

If you're reading this, Emily, I've either gone missing or something else, something unusual, has happened to me.

Emily blinked. It sounded like something out of one of Lana's novels. Shaking her head in disbelief, she quickly scanned the letter, then reread it. As she did, one part of her mind noticed that Lana wrote letters in the same style that she wrote her books: descriptive, flowing, and with a good eye for setting a scene, providing all the details of a daring rescue the night before and a treasure hunt that Lana needed to pursue for reasons she didn't really explain in the letter.

That Emily now needed to pursue, because she was damned if she was going to leave Lana alone in this situation, especially with that Devereaux woman, who Emily hadn't trusted from moment one.

Locking the door securely behind her, Emily stuffed the letter into her jacket pocket and descended the back stairs in a rush, heart pounding as she ran for her car.

CHAPTER EIGHT

Lana was aware of Michelle's gaze on her as she drove, the emerald eyes studying her as if she could somehow read her mind. She doubted Michelle would find much of use in there. Lana didn't really understand why she was going along with this scheme, or what she hoped to accomplish, but there she was, driving through the rain and gusty wind to Grand-Pré. In February. With half the roads impassible because of flooding.

She should be home, tucked up in her cozy cabin by the fire, reading or tying flies or any of the other pastimes she enjoyed. Of course, she hadn't really enjoyed those pastimes since Sarah's illness. And her cabin hadn't felt anything more than empty for some time now.

"How much farther?"

"Assuming we don't run into any more flooding, it shouldn't be long," Lana explained. "We'll turn off for Wolfville at the next exit. The museum is on the way." She paused. "It won't be open, you know. It's only open from spring to fall."

"I know, which is better for us." Michelle glanced out the window. "We should find a place to stay and wait until dark. That way, we'll be sure no one will see us."

"What makes you think we'll be able to find anything in the dark?"

Michelle flashed her an impish smile. "Oh, we'll find it." With her red hair covered by a new black toque and the scattering of freckles across her high cheeks no longer obscured by makeup, she looked a lot younger than Lana had initially assumed the night before.

They had stopped at the mall in Windsor where Lana replaced Michelle's lost clothes, phone, and toiletries, as well as provided her with some outerwear more suited for a Maritime winter. Now that she was dressing her, driving her around as if to a soccer game, and feeding her to boot, Lana was beginning to feel rather uncomfortable. It wasn't that she minded the expense. Between what Sarah had left her and her book royalties, she could easily afford to indulge this whim of hers, but it suddenly occurred to her that perhaps she shouldn't be sleeping with a woman who might be as much as a decade younger. Not first thing out of the gate.

"Any ideas on where we should stay?" Michelle asked, interrupting her train of thought.

"There's a motel right across the road leading to the historic site," Lana offered. She and Sarah had stayed at the Evangeline Inn one spring for the Apple Blossom Festival. She wasn't sure she wanted to deal with the onslaught of memories staying there would bring, but it was the most convenient venue for what they had in mind. "I don't know if it's open year round."

"I guess we'll find out."

As they pulled off onto Trunk 1 leading to Grand-Pré, Lana was struck by how bleak the scenery was in winter. She'd only been down to the Annapolis Valley in the spring and summer, when it was green and vibrant, where every view was a lush vista of fields and orchards. February was definitely not conducive to tourism, so she was surprised to discover the Evangeline Inn open for business rather than closed for the season.

As she parked the car, she glanced over at Michelle. "Should we stay in the inn or the motel part?"

"Motel," Michelle said shortly. "It's cheaper and more anonymous."

Lana felt her lips twist in a smirk. "Yeah, anonymous doesn't really work in places this small," she said. "Especially this time of year."

But she was unprepared for how many cars were in the parking lot, and as she and Michelle headed for the office, she took note of more than one rainbow triangle sticker displayed in the vehicles' back windows. Inside, behind the wooden counter straight out of the 1940s, a slender woman with bright eyes and dark curly hair was on duty. Her small, gold nametag read Cindy Sullivan.

"Afternoon, ladies," she said with a smile. "Are you here for the Rainbow Weekend?"

Since Lana had no idea what she was talking about, she just stared at her blankly. Michelle, however, was quick to jump on it.

"Yes," she said, and wrapped her arm around Lana's waist, yanking her close. "We spent our honeymoon down here so we couldn't resist coming back for the dance."

Left in the dust once more, Lana could only goggle as Michelle registered them for a room with a king-sized bed, though she was required to dig out her credit card again since it was quickly apparent that Michelle wasn't going to offer any of her own. Lana wondered if she had lost all her funds in the accident.

"If you wouldn't mind, could I ask you an odd question?" Michelle smiled charmingly at the innkeeper as her accent deepened. "You haven't seen a couple of men come through here, have you? One has dark hair, kind of swarthy, and a Spanish accent, while the other is bald with a scar over his right eye and a tattoo on his neck and face."

Cindy, who'd been filling in the receipt on the computer, paused and looked at her, her cheerful expression abruptly disappearing. "As a matter of fact, I have," she said, frowning. "They came in last night, and when I asked if they wanted a double room for the weekend, they said they didn't and looked so offended I decided it might be better if they found other accommodations. I told them we were already fully booked."

Lana blinked. "Why?"

"Most of our guests are here for the weekend events," Cindy said, as if it should be obvious. "I thought it would be awkward to have patrons staying here who were—less than okay with everything that was going on. Do you know them?"

"Not really. We just met them in our travels and heard they might stay here. You were right. They wouldn't much like what's going on this weekend." Michelle blithely accepted the room cards. "Thank you so much." She flashed a smile at Lana. "Get the bags, dear."

"What the hell was all that about?" Lana demanded after they'd moved the car down to the other end of the lot where their unit was located and were unpacking the trunk. "What weekend? And those men you were asking about. Are they the ones who forced you off the road?"

"Yeah, Pierre and Juan," Michelle responded. "I didn't see who was in the car that ran me off the road, but I figured it was them. They're Hector's muscle. We're lucky they aren't welcome at the inn this weekend. It means they had to find another place to stay, and that should delay them even though they're a day ahead of us."

"What is this weekend again?" Lana dropped her suitcase onto the bed and looked around the room. It was simply decorated, but clean and bright, even on a late-February afternoon. "And how do you know about it?"

"I read the poster when we were coming in," Michelle said, giving her an odd look. "Didn't you see it? It's Valentine's Day tomorrow. Today, there's a farmer's market in the Port Williams fire hall for artists and craftspeople, a brunch tomorrow morning at the inn's restaurant, feminist seminars going on at the university in the afternoon, and finally, a dinner/dance tomorrow night at someplace called the Warehouse in Wolfville."

"Valentine's Day." Lana was honestly astonished. She hadn't even thought about the date or its significance.

"It's a gay and lesbian event," Michelle said. "Which makes it a perfect cover for us. And also explains why Miss Cindy didn't want a couple of homophobes staying here."

"Is that why you only booked one room?" Lana demanded. "For cover?"

Michelle leaned over and patted her on the right hip. "Not just for that," she said, her voice dropping huskily. "We might as well enjoy each other while we're here."

As much as she still had doubts about this whole situation and about Michelle, now, as well, Lana couldn't deny the chill of desire that spiked through her, or the sense of anticipation that rose as Michelle threw an enticing glance over her shoulder as she headed for the bathroom. The sensations felt so new and unfamiliar after so long that she wanted to cherish them rather than reject the notion of being attracted to someone again.

"Shall we try out the restaurant?" Michelle's voice floated through the bathroom door.

"Sure," Lana said, swallowing against a mouth suddenly gone dry. Maybe this wasn't the best idea for her, but with her heart and body waking up again, it was impacting her like a tidal bore, powerful and impossible to resist.

The dining room attached to the motel wasn't exactly a restaurant, more in line with a café, but they did serve burgers and some chowders. Lana ordered the seafood while Michelle made do with a grilled chicken breast on a Kaiser roll and a Caesar salad instead of the French fries she initially wanted.

"What kind of place has burgers but no fries?" she complained after the waitress had left.

"A place that doesn't have a deep fryer," Lana pointed out dryly. "Just a grill."

"Fine." Michelle looked around, an expression of dissatisfaction on her face. The walls were a simple wood panel with white accents on the windows and doors, and a few photos on the wall. "This isn't what I expected."

"What did you expect?" Lana took a sip of her soda as she regarded the other woman thoughtfully.

"I don't know. Something more historic, more—well, more Acadian."

"Hey, the motel's only been around since 1948, and even the inn isn't that old," Lana pointed out. "The Acadians settled in the 1680s and were expelled in 1755. The inn was the boyhood home of Sir Robert Borden, who was prime minister of Canada from 1911 to 1920. The name, Evangeline, has to do with the Longfellow poem, not the war between the English and French."

Michelle fixed her with a stare. "How do you know that?"

"I just read it," Lana said, smiling. "There's a whole history lesson printed beside the breakfast menu."

Michelle looked even more disgruntled and Lana laughed out loud, surprising herself. How long had it been since she had laughed so easily? Too long, she suspected.

"After dinner, we should check out the site," Michelle said after their meal arrived.

"I think we should wait until much later in the evening," Lana said, injecting a note of caution into this madness. "Like midnight or something, when we're sure no one's going to be around. Maybe even around one or two. It's Friday night, date night. We don't want to come upon some teenagers out parking."

Michelle stared at her. "That's good thinking. Are you sure you haven't done this before?"

"I just don't want to get caught," Lana said darkly. "And if we're going to do this, we should be smart about it."

"I can't argue with that." Michelle suddenly paused, holding up a finger to indicate Lana should stay quiet. Bemused, Lana looked at her and belatedly realized Michelle was eavesdropping on the conversation at the next table between the waitress and two patrons about a break-in of some sort earlier that day.

Michelle turned around in her chair. "Hello there, I'm sorry to interrupt, but did you say the museum was broken into?" She offered up one of her smiles, and of course, all three women immediately became completely cooperative. Lana wondered how Michelle managed it. And how susceptible she was to that oddly provocative Southern charm.

"Not the museum, the Memorial Church," the waitress said, pinking up at Michelle's attention. "A few items were taken, some historical stuff, and the door latch was broken. The police think it was kids."

"It's always kids, isn't it?" Michelle said, her drawl deepening.

She turned back to Lana. "They don't even know the church isn't where the original one was," she said in a low, excited voice. "Pierre and Juan must have just taken the items to make it look like a random burglary. And to add to Hector's collection."

Lana's heart sank. "But now the police will be looking out for criminal activity in the area."

"I doubt they think the site will be hit again." Michelle brushed off her concern with a casual wave of her hand. "No, we should be able to get in somewhere. Besides, we shouldn't have to break into anything. What I'm looking for isn't in a building. It's outside."

Michelle grinned. "What could go wrong?"

CHAPTER NINE

B ack in their room, Michelle slipped out of her winter coat, tossing it onto an armchair. The briefcase was sitting on the dresser and she checked it automatically, making sure it was still locked and that no one had disturbed it while they were in the café. Assured the precious contents were safe, she looked back at Lana, who lay on the bed, stretched out as she glanced through the pamphlets she'd retrieved at the counter after paying for their dinner.

"Learning anything?" Michelle asked playfully as she kicked off her boots and crawled onto the bed next to her.

She really was beautiful, she thought wistfully as she looked over at her. Lana was a bit older than most of the women Michelle dated, but her body was still fit, breasts high and firm, waist and hips trim, legs long and shapely, her musculature surprisingly well defined. Clearly, she maintained a regular workout régime. That, or she had some incredible genes.

Desire flared, but Michelle was hesitant. Flirting was one thing, but would Lana really want her after all the revelations and the knowledge that Michelle found truth to be an esoteric concept, one that should be utilized only as a last resort?

"I'm learning that the British gathered up all the men in the Church of Saint-Charles to tell them all their personal goods were forfeit to the crown and they were being deported," Lana said as her dark eyes scanned the pages. "I try to imagine what it was like for them to go home and tell their wives that they had to leave behind everything they knew, everything they'd built. Go someplace that, honestly, is as different from Nova Scotia in climate and environment as you can get."

Trust Lana to zero in on the human aspect of it, Michelle thought fondly. Gingerly, she put her hand on Lana's stomach, the soft knit of her royal-blue sweater warm from her body, rising and falling with every breath. Lana either didn't mind the touch or didn't notice. Michelle hoped it was the former.

"It wasn't easy for anyone," Michelle said. "Many died on the ships transporting them to the British colonies, and those that survived had to start all over again in strange surroundings. Maybe it's not surprising that a lot of them came back as soon as they could." She began to move her hand in slow circles, caressingly, careful not to be too quick. "And it was all from an inability to commit."

"Isn't that simplifying it a bit?" Lana said, tossing the pamphlet onto the nightstand and linking her hands behind her head. If she noticed Michelle's stealthy caress, she was pretending not to. More importantly, she wasn't pulling away. Michelle took the opportunity to tug the sweater from where it was tucked into Lana's jeans, allowing her to slip her hand beneath it and touch Lana's stomach directly, her skin soft and silky smooth beneath her fingertips.

Easy, Michelle reminded herself. Slow.

"The French wanted the Acadians to fight with them or at least fight against the Mi'kmaq tribes allied with the British, which they didn't want to do," she said, forcing herself to continue the conversation even when she really wanted to just jump all over Lana like a lion on a gazelle. "When their part of Acadia became Nova Scotia in 1713, they agreed to live under British rule but refused to sign an oath of allegiance to the British crown. That was a bone of contention for forty years. I guess they thought they could remain in the middle forever, but you know what happens when someone tries to stay neutral between two superpowers."

"Yeah, eventually, one or the other or both run them over," Lana said. "They were probably lucky they were just deported. They could have just as easily been exterminated."

"Which is what happened to a great many Indian tribes in the States." Michelle pressed closer, and her fingers drifted upward to Lana's bra with its front clasp. Deftly, she undid it and then paused. "Do you want me to stop?" she asked directly.

"The discussion or what you're doing?" There was a definite purr in Lana's tone, her dark eyes sultry. A ripple of longing spiked from the juncture of Michelle's legs all the way up to her throat.

"Either," Michelle said huskily. "Both. Neither." She ran her fingertip over Lana's freed breast, rubbing across the soft nipple that stiffened immediately. "What was I saying?"

"About the inability to commit to something," Lana said, and her breath caught, just a little.

Accepting that as a green light, Michelle took the tender protrusion between her forefinger and thumb, rolling it back and forth as she leaned over, capturing Lana's full lips in a searing kiss.

"Commitment can be hard," Michelle breathed, when they finally parted. "Uh, so it'll be a few hours before we can check out the site. I have an idea or two about how we can pass the time."

Lana unlinked her hands and reached up, slipping her arms around Michelle's neck and pulling her down for another kiss, her tongue dancing over Michele's lips. "I think I really like your ideas," she said throatily.

Michelle smiled and left the soft swell of Lana's breast, slipping down over her stomach to the waist of her jeans. Unfastening them took only a second, and with determination, she slid beneath the silk of Lana's panties, through the wiry tangle to the warm folds, moist and waiting, her forefinger rubbing over the ribbon of sensation with lavish intent.

Lana made a soft sound of pleasure, a sort of pleased murmur, which made Michelle smile again. Suddenly, the need was unbearable and she sat up, using both hands to tug at Lana's jeans, pulling them down her legs.

Lana took the opportunity to divest herself of her sweater and bra, then reached out for Michelle, helping her out of her long-sleeved shirt and jeans. Then the full luscious length of Lana was on top of Michelle, pressing her down onto the mattress as she kissed Michelle with unrestrained passion. Michelle pulled her closer, her hands roaming over Lana's warm back, down to the full swells of her buttocks, squeezing them with a sort of delirious joy.

She's just so wonderful, Michelle thought dazedly. So compassionate and generous without seeming to expect anything in return, unlike practically everyone else she knew. For a brief second, she tasted real regret and grief at the thought that Lana could never really be hers, could never really be part of her life in any way. But she could be hers for right now, and that was enough.

Lana rose a little, enough that she could touch Michelle, fondling her with firm precision. As she looked down at her, she smiled, her teeth a bright white that contrasted with the rich wine of her full lips. Her expression was almost haughty, possessive, and it made Michelle quiver from her toes to the top of her head. Maneuvering without words, Michelle urged Lana's thighs apart so she could reciprocate, and for a few moments, it was sheer heaven, Lana incredibly wet against her fingers as she fondled the warm, willing folds, sliding in and out firmly before concentrating her caress on the sensitive center.

Meanwhile, Lana plied her with lavish attention, her fingers so skilled and dedicated as they drew out the most exquisite sensation. She kept kissing her as well, wonderful, shattering kisses, left off only when they both needed to breathe, a requirement that became progressively urgent as their desire grew ever more intense.

"Oh, I'm almost there," Lana whispered, her breath hot in Michelle's ear.

Michelle wanted to indicate some kind of agreement, but the most she could manage was a helpless whimper, the sensation building in powerful waves. It was increasingly difficult to separate her pleasure from Lana's, wanting them to reach the peak together, but Lana was too quick, shuddering above her as her touch grew erratic, briefly interrupted as she groaned in release. Michelle waited, hovering on the precipice, aching and open, jerking involuntarily as Lana resumed her caresses with renewed concentration. Michelle lightened her touch, easing Lana down from her peak as she surrendered to her own, focusing all her attention now on Lana's touch, the heady taste of her mouth covering hers, the perfect union of lips and tongue and fingertips granting her benediction both spiritual and physical.

For long moments afterward, she basked in the sensation of Lana's body on hers, tremors still rippling through her as both of them relaxed into the golden warmth of afterglow.

"Wow," Lana muttered finally, her dark hair draped across Michelle's face. Michelle blew several strands away so she could breathe.

"Very nice," Michelle agreed, feeling the sweat dry on her skin, cooling her to the point of being uncomfortable, even with Lana's warmth on top of her. Shifting with unspoken accord, they managed to pull the comforter over them and settle against the stiff linens of the motel mattress.

Lana nestled her head on Michelle's shoulder, right arm and leg draped companionably across her chest and pelvis. Michelle thought Lana's presence should feel confining, but it didn't. She just felt nice and somehow safe, protected in the security of Lana's embrace.

"You know, I'm really sort of glad you came into my life," Lana said quietly.

"You mean despite the circumstances?" Michelle exhaled slowly. "And that I lied to you?"

"Well, it would have been nice if you'd told me everything from the beginning, but maybe I wasn't in a place to listen before we—well, you know." Lana spread her fingers over the upper part of Michelle's chest, brushing over the freckles there. "I might not be here, now."

"You're okay with being here?"

Lana laughed, low and dirty. "Oh, yes. This part is fantastic. It's making me feel alive again. As for the rest, well, maybe I can't deny that's part of the appeal, too."

"So you like bad girls," Michelle murmured with a smile.

"I am a bad girl," Lana admitted, surprising Michelle. "Or at least I was before Sarah. She was so steady and calm and infinitely patient with all my stupidity." Lana sobered. "Then she got sick, and I had to take care of her. I couldn't be the wild artist anymore. I had to be the responsible one. The grown-up."

"Define 'wild,'" Michelle demanded, curious.

"Well, in college, I liked to drink quite a bit and partied like there was no tomorrow," Lana admitted. "Out all hours, cutting class, working my way through all the lesbians and any straight chick willing to give it a go, just generally having more fun than was good for me. Honestly, if I hadn't met Sarah, I probably wouldn't have graduated Dal."

"Dal?"

"Dalhousie University," Lana explained. "I was an English major, of course, and she was getting her RN."

"Sarah was a nurse?"

"Yes," Lana said. She paused and swallowed hard. "She was the most caring and compassionate person I'd ever met."

"She sounds wonderful," Michelle said honestly. "I'm really sorry you lost her, Lana."

Lana made a pained sound, not necessarily one of negation, but an indication she was ready to change the subject, possibly because it was becoming too prickly. "It was a good life while we had it," she said, her voice a bit thick. "Her parents left her the land and that's why we built the cabin there, even though it wasn't a great commute to Truro where she worked at the hospital. The place might not look like much this time of year, but in the summer, it's wonderful. We'd go hiking and mountain-biking in the woods behind our house, and we have friends down the road who own horses. We rode a lot, and went canoeing and fishing in the river."

"It sounds very outdoorsy," Michelle noted.

"It was." Lana sounded more wistful than sorrowful now.

"Not anymore?"

"Well, I haven't felt like doing anything for a long time."

"But you're so fit," Michelle blurted without thinking.

"What?" Lana sounded puzzled.

"I just meant that you look really good," Michelle said. "That usually takes dedication." She almost added "at your age" and managed to swallow it back in time.

"Well, the thing with exercise," Lana pointed out, her voice deadening a little, "you don't have to think about it. In fact, it's really good for not thinking about anything at all while you're doing it."

"Oh, yeah, I got you," Michelle said, kicking herself internally for poking the sensitive spot again. When would she learn? "Sorry."

"No, it is what it is." Lana lifted her head and nuzzled closer to Michelle, kissing her gently. "Then you came along and turned it all upside-down. And that's a good thing. I needed it. I didn't know how much until it happened. So thank you."

"Glad to be of service," Michelle said, dryly. She glanced at the digital clock on the nightstand. "Still got a few hours before we conduct our mission. Want to go again?"

Lana purred and stretched, pressing her curves against Michelle. "As many times as possible."

"Oh, boy," Michelle mumbled, wondering if perhaps she hadn't bitten off more than she could handle.

CHAPTER TEN

Emily shut the door of her apartment more firmly than she intended, but she was in a hurry. Tossing the duffle bag containing her uniform onto the kitchen counter, she went into the bedroom to pack an overnight bag. She didn't know how long it would take for her to catch up to Lana and the Devereaux woman, so she packed for the whole weekend, including an extra uniform in case she had to come into work on Tuesday directly from wherever she ended up.

As she packed her toiletries, a photo of herself and her father hanging on the wall caught her eye, and she stopped, once again assailed by doubts. Should she really be doing this, chase a woman she knew only from an occasional meal at the Kennetcook diner?

She looked at the picture again, her first tour as an RCMP constable, dressed in her red serge uniform, her father in his, his ruddy features beneath the brown, felt, wide-brimmed campaign hat beaming with pride. She had grown up wanting to be a police officer like him, rather than a lawyer like her mother. Her parents were still in St. John's, both retired now, though he was still the first person she called whenever she had a difficult case.

Not that she had difficult cases anymore, not since her tour just outside Winnipeg in southern Manitoba. The Weaver murder had been a tough one, and once it was closed and she had the opportunity to transfer to the more serene and quiet posting in

Nova Scotia, she'd taken it. The choice wasn't great for her career, but it had done wonders for a psyche scarred from encountering too many brutalized children and too many battered women, unable to help any of them as much as she wanted. Not that there weren't the same problems here in the Maritimes, but with a much smaller population density, she encountered correspondingly less crime of the type that had wounded her so deeply.

Her father had been a little disappointed in her choice, how the transfer had interrupted what had been a steady rise through the ranks, but her mother had been greatly relieved to know Emily was in a far more peaceful posting and that she was closer to home. She really should take the time to visit them more often, Emily thought unhappily. This weekend would have been perfect for that. It would have been so easy to book a quick flight to Newfoundland and spend the whole three days with them.

Instead, Emily was preparing to pursue a woman who might or might not be in trouble, just because she had a crush on her. A woman who probably didn't even see her as anything more than an occasional meal companion.

Except, she reminded herself as she touched the envelope in her jacket, this letter had been addressed to her. Not to any of Lana's neighbors, nor to any of Lana's immediate family, her mother in New Glasgow, her sister in Brookfield, or her brother in Moncton, and not to any of her other friends. No, it was as if Lana had known Emily would be the first to notice she was gone, the first to miss her, and the only one who would keep checking in on her even after she'd done her best to push her away.

Her cell phone erupted suddenly, the brief 70s rock tune indicating the call was from her friend Joanna.

"Hey," she said, bringing the phone to her ear as she stuffed the letter back into her jacket and resumed packing. "What's up?"

"That's what I was about to ask you." Joanna was incredibly cheerful, relentlessly optimistic, and apparently thought Emily's life was a lot more exciting than hers because she always claimed to be living vicariously through her. Emily couldn't see how, considering Joanna had a great partner, Collette, two kids, and frankly, one too many dogs. "If you're not working, come by for dinner tomorrow night. We're having turkey."

"Sounds great, but I'm going out of town this weekend," Emily said, zipping up her bag.

Joanna immediately perked up. "Oooh, with anyone I know?"

"Nope, just on my own." Emily did a quick run-through, making sure her apartment would be all right for the next few days. Pausing by the large cat condo, she reached in and stroked Maxine, her calico, who purred a little but otherwise displayed little interest. Considering how much Emily was gone because of work, that was normal. Maxine was used to being on her own and liked it that way so long as her food dish was full and her pet fountain kept running.

Emily tended to both now as Joanna continued to chatter in her ear.

"Where are you heading?"

"Grand-Pré," Emily told her. "Down the valley."

"Why?" Joanna sounded astonished. "It's the middle of winter. Nothing's open—Oh, wait, are you going to the Rainbow Festival?"

"The what?" Emily frowned as she resealed the cat-food bag.

"You know, the whole Valentine's Day weekend thing down there in Wolfville," Joanna explained. "Dinner, dance, seminars at Acadia, displays at the farmer's market, all kinds of things. Collette and I were planning to go, but we couldn't find a sitter for the whole weekend. We thought about asking you but figured you'd be working. Damn it, I wish I'd known you were available."

"Huh," Emily said, pausing to think. She didn't like to lie, but the event provided an easier explanation than why she was really headed there. "Yeah, sure, that's why I'm going."

"Well, it's about time you meet someone. It's been awhile since Amanda. You could always use a little pussy play in your life."

Emily lifted her brows. "Really? That's what you're calling it now?"

"Hey, just because Amanda turned out to be a bitch doesn't mean we all are. Besides, you have to get back on that horse sometime." She paused. "You are a mounted police officer, after all."

"You're funny," Emily said, in a tone that indicated the opposite. "C'mon, Amanda wasn't a bitch. She just couldn't deal with my being on the job. She was always worried I'd get hurt."

"She was a bitch," Joanna said firmly. "Trust me on that. I've known her longer than you. So when you're down there, meet up with someone hot and get it on. You need that."

Emily smiled. Joanna was relentless when she got a thought in her head. "We'll see what happens," she said noncommittally. "Listen, I have to go. I'm on my way out the door."

"Well, have a great time," Joanna ordered her. "And be sure to call me when you get home so I can hear all about it." She sighed. "Oh, to be single and on the hunt once again."

Emily laughed. "Sure, that's what you'd be doing if you were single."

"I would! I'd be screwing everything that wasn't nailed down. So if I can't, you have to. Take full advantage of being hot and young and gainfully employed."

"You think I'm hot?"

"Oh, you know you're hot," Joanna said. "So go find yourself another hottie and see if you can spontaneously combust."

"You'll stop by and check on Maxine?"

"The cat hates me, you know. She knows I'm a dog person."

"Just make sure her dishes are full and the litter box is scooped. You don't have to pet her. She doesn't like it anyway."

"Don't worry, I got it. Go get yourself laid, lady."

Emily shook her head as she hung up. That was the one thing about Joanna. Five minutes on the phone with her and she was ready to tackle the world. A tiny part of her even regretted that she wasn't headed to Grand-Pré for this celebration, whatever it was.

However, with a festival going on, it would be considerably busier in the area than she'd initially anticipated, which would make it that much harder to find Lana and the Devereaux woman.

Locking the door behind her, Emily descended the back stairs in a rush and went out to the yard where her Challenger was parked by the dumpster used by the China Rose. She'd rented the apartment over the restaurant when she was first posted to Windsor, but ended up staying because she liked being in the downtown area and the couple owning the restaurant liked having a cop living upstairs. She provided a certain sense of security, and they provided great food, available at the most convenient times, especially after a long shift when Emily didn't feel like cooking.

As she pulled out of the alley running beside the building, she turned on the stereo, her playlist starting off with a Bob Seger tune perfect for driving. She continued to rehash the letter in her mind, trying to figure out if Lana had been under any kind of duress when she wrote it, any type of coercion.

Instead, all she could think was that a definite excitement had been threaded through it, a sense of adventure she hadn't expected of Lana or sensed in her personality before outside of her books. Was it possible she didn't really know Lana at all?

She was both relieved and worried when she finally pulled into the Evangeline Motel & Inn. Relieved to find it was open this time of year, but worried there'd be no more room. It was nine o'clock in the evening and pitch dark, rain falling steadily, making everything look slick and shiny in the streetlights. A lot of cars were in the lot, and Emily suspected the proprietors would be thrilled to be making so much money this time of year. She wondered if the business people in the area were the ones who came up with the whole Rainbow Valentine Festival idea to begin with.

Inside, a pretty woman stood at the counter, and smiled brightly at her when she came in. Emily took note of the posters on the wall advertising the upcoming dance, as well as the rainbow flag hanging demurely in the front window. Apparently, they were going all out to attract a specific customer base this weekend.

"I don't suppose there's a room available?" Emily asked, readily returning the smile as she took note of the nametag on the innkeeper's slender chest.

"Last one," Cindy said, accepting her credit card. "But it's a double, two queens."

"That's all right. I'll take it. It beats looking for another place this time of night."

"I don't know that you'd find it. As far as I know, everything else as far down as Berwick has been booked." Cindy chatted away as she processed the registration. "Would you like some tickets for tomorrow night's dinner and dance? I still have a few available."

Emily hesitated and, for a moment, thought about finding Lana, extricating her from the clutches of the Devereaux woman, and maybe asking her out on a real date. Deciding to be optimistic, she nodded. "Sure, I'll take two. I understand it's for a good cause."

"It is." Cindy took her twenty dollars and handed over the tickets. "Breast-cancer research. You get a free pin with the tickets."

Emily tucked the tickets in her wallet, along with her receipt and the card key. "Thanks," she said, attaching the tiny metal pink ribbon to the collar of her black leather bomber jacket.

Outside, she got back in her car and moved it down the row of units to where hers was located. Overhead, the skies opened up and rain pounded down as if it were late for dinner, and Emily let out an oath as she retrieved her bag, ducking quickly into her motel room.

She hoped the bad weather wasn't an omen.

CHAPTER ELEVEN

There doesn't seem to be anyone around," Lana said finally. They'd been sitting in her Jeep for a half hour, just to be sure no further activity was going on in the Grand-Pré National Historic Site, especially nothing new in terms of security, like a police car cruising in the vicinity or the presence of a new watchman hired after the break-in, though that would be a lot like locking the stall door after the horse had disappeared over the hill. Lana had driven in the back way, along a dirt road called Miner Lane that, although icier than she would have liked, had at least been plowed. The rain had eased into a light but steady mist, while fog rose from the layer of snow like the scattered ghosts of winter. In the mist, the church was little more than an indistinct outline through the leafless trees.

"Let's do this," Michelle said, impatient but respecting the fact that as long as Lana had the car keys and the credit cards, this was her show.

"I have a head lamp in the back," Lana said as they got out. "I'll put fresh batteries in. What else do we need? A shovel? It's going to be hard digging up frozen ground."

"We're not going to dig," Michelle told her, huddled in her new winter jacket. She shivered. How the hell did Canadians put up with this weather? It was inhuman. "But I could use a rope and something sharp. Do you have an ax?"

Lana frowned at her "I have a hatchet. Planning on chopping down a tree?"

"God, I hope not," Michelle said reverently as she accepted the items Lana handed her from the kit stored in the back of her Jeep. "We're going to leave tracks in the snow."

"Can't be helped," Lana said. "Where are we headed?"

"To the old well. It shouldn't be too far from the church they built."

Lana lifted her brows, a familiar expression of mingled interest and wariness, but proceeded to climb over the bank that lined the road, plunging into the field where the snow reached almost to her knees. It was a struggle for them to cross the small meadow to the line of trees bordering the back of the site, each step threatening to twist a joint, and if Michelle wasn't so sure of what she was going to find, she would have turned around and gone home. The rain left a layer of moisture on her face, chilling it, and a cold dampness was seeping through her jeans. Fortunately, her boots were completely waterproof and kept her feet warm and dry.

The snow was shallower beneath the trees but grew deeper once they cleared that area and began walking by the church. The top of the well, a circle of stones, was barely visible above the white, and they clambered over to it through the soggy drifts. Michelle was sweating by the time she reached it, and from the forceful way Lana was breathing, she wasn't in much better shape.

"Now what?" Lana demanded as they leaned against the cold rocks. A bitter wind blew in from the Minas Basin, which lay not far from where they stood, hidden from their view by dikes built by the Acadians and still standing firm, solid earthen mounds holding back the tidal marsh.

"This way," Michelle said and began to pace, fifty paces exactly, to the northeast. In the distance, she could see a monument, the stone cross erected by John Frederic Herbin, who had purchased the land believed to be the site of the Saint Charles-des-Mines Church in 1907 to preserve it for the Acadian community. No one could find the foundation of the original church, but they had discovered an old cemetery lay beneath the monument.

She stopped beneath the shelter of a huge sugar-maple tree, rising a hundred and sixty feet above her, the dark branches swaying in the wind. It was still here, exactly where her research had put it. Not cut down in all that time, not blown over in all the wind and ice storms that had followed in the centuries since, not killed by insects or disease. Still standing as it had in 1755, two hundred and sixty years earlier, a fully mature tree even then.

"What are you doing?" Lana demanded as she made her way over to where Michelle was standing, staring up in wonder.

"When the British came, Father Beauséjour knew he had to hide the cross from them," Michelle said in a hushed, trembling voice. "He put it in a box and gave it to Thomas, his eight-year-old altar boy, and sent him to hide it. Thomas did what he always liked to do. He climbed the tree closest to the church. This was his favorite. He hid it in a knot where the two largest branches intersected."

"Jesus," Lana said, head tilted back as she looked up, as well. "You think it's still up there?"

"It has to be," Michelle said. "There's no record of it ever being found. The only recollection of where it was hidden was a cryptic notation in Thomas's diary, handed down through the generations after his family was expelled from Acadia and sent to Louisiana. No one paid much attention to it until I found the letters from Beauséjour to Father Hebert in Port Royal."

"That's how Hector got it?"

"He's descended from Thomas Duperies. He hadn't read it either until I showed it to him."

"Oh, boy." Lana exhaled audibly, her breath a white cloud. "Now what?"

"Now I climb up there and get it."

"Are you crazy?" Lana stared at her. "Do you know how dangerous that is?"

"I didn't come all this way for nothing," Michelle said firmly, setting her jaw. "Give me a boost." The lowest branch was well out of the reach of her short stature.

"Oh, my God, I guess I'm the one who must be crazy," Lana groaned, but she went over to the base of the tree and hooked her gloved fingers together, holding them out for Michelle to step onto.

Rope slung over her shoulder in case she needed it, hatchet tucked into her belt, Michelle clambered up the trunk with Lana's help until she was able to grasp the branch and haul herself the rest of the way up. Perched unsteadily at the crook where the branch met the trunk, she looked down in the pale circle of Lana's face.

"For God's sakes, be careful," Lana said, voice tight, her concern evident.

"I will," Michelle promised untruthfully. "Signal me if anyone comes."

"Signal how?"

"Whistle. You do know how to whistle, don't you?"

"Oh, for Chrissakes," Lana snapped, clearly recognizing the movie reference. But she moved off a little to keep a lookout, arms wrapped around herself as she leaned into the fierce wind, long dark hair whipping beneath her wool toque.

A wind that made her going even more perilous. Michelle had to test every hand and foothold, careful not to slip on the slick bark. More than once, she had to use the hatchet as a climbing ax, wincing as she cut into the wood and hoping she wasn't doing any kind of lasting damage to the stately tree. It was, after all, the enduring protector of its treasure. The rope turned out to be more nuisance than help, and halfway up, she let it drop down with a hissed warning for Lana to watch out. As she resumed her ascent, her hold grew more precarious, her body more exposed to the wind and mist as the branches thinned.

Then she was there, near the top, the entire tree swaying alarmingly back and forth, making her dizzy. Or perhaps it was the exhilaration that was making her light-headed as she stared at the gnarled knot located where the branch met the trunk, just underneath, sheltered from the elements all these centuries.

Hand shaking, she reached into the small hollow, and her heart leaped as she felt the outlines of a small box beneath her fingertips. She closed her eyes and, just for a moment, savored the thrill of her discovery, the knowledge that the cross had been here all along, unseen and unknown, while all the historians and archeologists had dug and explored beneath, never really seeing what had been in their midst all along.

Carefully, she drew it out into view. It was metal, corroded but still intact, and she wanted nothing more than to open it, but she was a hundred feet up in the air during a rainstorm with a death grip on the trunk and her feet planted on an icy branch. It would have to wait, as much as she might wish otherwise. She zipped open her jacket and tucked the box inside, the metal ice-cold against her chest, but she barely noticed the discomfort as she began her descent, trying not to rush even though every molecule in her body wanted nothing more than to be on the ground.

Halfway down, reaching for a branch, she slipped. Fear replaced her exhilaration as she was suddenly out of control, gravity seizing her with ruthless force. She didn't know how many branches she hit on the way down. They served to break her descent, but they hurt, and then abruptly, she was free of them and falling the rest of the way to the ground, where she landed in the snow on her back, the air exploding out of her like a popped balloon. For a few seconds, she couldn't get her lungs to work, and her only consolation was that she had found the cross and trusted Lana enough to know she would give her full credit for the discovery, posthumously as it was.

"Holy Christ, Michelle, are you all right?" Her classic features panicked, Lana leaned over her, and Michelle was surprised she could still see her. She supposed that meant she was still alive, and then the pain rushed in, assuring her that, at least for the moment, she was.

"I don't know," she managed to croak. "I fell."

"I saw," Lana said. "You sounded like a sack of potatoes when you landed. Don't move. I'll call the EMTs."

"No, don't," Michelle said, raising her hand to forestall her. Wincing, she tested a few things. "I think I'm okay. I can feel everything. I don't think anything's broken. Help me up."

"I don't think that's a good idea," Lana said, her tone a touch annoyed now. "Michelle, seriously, you fell out of a tree."

"I know, and I'm fine," Michelle said, forcing herself up into a sitting position. "Just had the wind knocked out of me for a moment. The snow cushioned my fall."

And several branches, she added silently, feeling the multitude of painful spots now clamoring for attention. She hoped it was just from bruising and not anything more serious.

"Help me up."

Shaking her head, Lana reached down and supported her as she managed to get to her feet. Upright, Michelle reassessed her condition and decided that her initial diagnosis was correct and that she was a great deal luckier than she deserved. With Lana's arm around her, they started the arduous journey back to the Jeep, slipping and sliding in the snow as the wind and rain blasted them unmercifully.

Finally inside the shelter of the vehicle, Lana started the engine and air began blasting from the vents, at first cold but warming up quickly. Michelle's hands shook as she pulled the box from inside her coat.

"Turn on the overhead light," she croaked as she rested the box on her lap. After stripping off her gloves, her fingers trembled as she fumbled with the tiny latch. She hoped she wouldn't have to pry it open. It was a simple box, devoid of ornamentation, made of tin or perhaps silver. It was hard to tell. She managed to slip her nail beneath the hook, and with an effort, she pried it open.

There was a packet, something wrapped in oilskin, and her heart pounded, making her chest feel hollow, as she carefully uncovered what was inside. It was a folded parchment, a letter of some kind, covered in scrawled handwriting, faded and barely visible, written in French. Michelle heard a sound, unaware it was coming from her, a thin sound of shock and grief.

There was no cross here, gold or otherwise.

CHAPTER TWELVE

L ana shut the door quietly behind her, not wanting to wake Michelle. She had finally fallen asleep, and Lana hoped that the restoring properties of slumber would heal a bit of the utter devastation Michelle had experienced. She had barely said a word since that moment in the Jeep when she opened the box to discover, not the cross as she'd expected, but just another mystery. Back at the motel, Lana had convinced her to take a hot shower and change into a T-shirt before getting into bed. By the time she'd drifted off, the tears drying on her cheeks, the pale gray of dawn was filtering through the motel window.

Exhausted, but unable to sleep, Lana decided to get some fresh air and some breakfast. In the east, the sky was brightening as the dark clouds from the night before began to clear. The sun, unseen for too many days, appeared on the horizon, bright and dazzling, and for a brief moment, the golden rays made her feel a bit better. She hoped some food in her belly and, more importantly, some hot coffee, would further ease her disappointment, though she doubted anything would ever grant solace to Michelle's shattered heart.

As she crossed the parking lot, heading for the diner, the bright-red color of a Dodge Challenger parked a few doors down caught her eye. She paused to admire its sporty lines, stunned as the door to that motel unit opened and Emily Stone came out. Dressed in a lined leather brown bomber jacket, jeans and boots, her thick, blond hair hanging loose around her face and spilling down her back, she looked completely different out of uniform.

Emily spotted her, the pale-blue eyes lighting up, and she lifted her hand in a small gesture of greeting. "Lana, are you all right?"

Lana blinked and nodded, astonished. "I'm fine," she said. "Why? What are you doing here?"

"I read your note." Emily's expression became serious. "What the hell are you thinking, Lana?"

Startled, Lana laughed. "I didn't expect you to get it so soon." She paused. "Wait, how did you get it? What were you doing in my house? I haven't even been gone a day."

Emily lowered her head, looking shamed. "I'm sorry," she said. "I was worried about you. A rental car washed up in Lattie's Brook and I guess—I don't know why, but I had a suspicion it belonged to your friend." She lifted her eyes, meeting Lana's gaze. "I went to your place and it was empty, even though you said you weren't going anywhere for a few days. So I used your spare key."

"And you followed us here?"

"Well, I knew you were heading for Grand-Pré, and this was the closest motel. I got in late last night, booked the last room they had, and was going to look for you this morning. I guess I don't have to now." Her familiar features grew stern, more authoritative. "Lana, you can't break into a historic site. You're not that person."

"Uh," Lana began, squirming a bit. "That's—uh, it's sort of water under the bridge at this point. And we didn't break in, exactly. We just sort of—well, trespassed a little."

Emily stared at her, gaze darkening, but after a second, she let out her breath, almost a sigh. "Did you find what you were looking for?"

"Yes and no," Lana said, then felt her stomach rumble. "Can I tell you the rest over breakfast?"

Emily hesitated, apparently surprised, then suddenly smiled. It was an amazing smile, changing her whole face, and Lana found it suddenly hard to inhale. "Sure, on me," she said. "The diner?"

"Why not?" Lana responded, falling into step with her. "They do have a breakfast menu. No hash browns, though."

"I'll have to make do," Emily deadpanned, and Lana laughed heartily. It seemed to surprise Emily again, and the glance she shot her as they sat down at the table was a mix of uncertainty and delight. "So, what happened last night?"

The prompt arrival of the waitress interrupted Lana's reply, and they spent the next few minutes ordering: omelet and toast for her, two eggs over easy, ham, and toast for Emily. Once the waitress left, Lana filled Emily in on the events of the previous evening or, in this case, hours earlier in the darkest part of the early morning.

"So you haven't been to sleep for twenty-four hours," Emily said, once she was finished, worry evident in her light eyes. Lana was surprised but touched that was her main concern.

"No, I haven't," Lana admitted, and suddenly stifled a yawn. "Still too excited to sleep, I guess."

"Is that why you're doing this? Because it's exciting?"

Startled, Lana looked inside herself. "I suppose," she said slowly. "It's just—it's been so long since anything has felt—good, you know?"

"I do." Emily paused, a shadow ghosting over her face. "So you and this Devereaux woman, you're together now?"

"Oh, God, no," Lana responded without thinking. Then she stopped, embarrassed. "I mean, I wanted to help her out. It's an adventure. And it's got me out of the house, at least."

"That it did," Emily said, her features severe. "But lying to a police officer, trespassing on federal land, disturbing a national historical site? Not exactly what I'd recommend for an adventure."

Lana winced. "Yes, how much trouble are we in, exactly?"

Emily maintained her stern expression for a few seconds more and then relaxed, the furrow between her brow disappearing. "Well, apparently there are no witnesses to your trespass, and it wouldn't be fair to charge you on the basis of things told to me as a friend. Those are only finable offenses, anyway, not the sort that require criminal proceedings. As for Devereaux, if she reports what happened, then I doubt anything will come of losing the car. Since there were no injuries, technically, she has five days to report it before she's held accountable, and insurance will cover it. I'm more concerned by the fact that she said she was run off the road by these two men. Do you know that for a fact?"

Lana thought about it. "It's what she told me. Why would she lie? And the two men do exist. The innkeeper said she saw them. In fact, I think they were the ones who broke into the church yesterday morning."

"God, okay. I'll take her to the detachment in Wolfville. It's the closest," Emily said, sounding exasperated. "She can make a statement there." She shook her head, as if shaking off dark thoughts. "So much for my day off."

"This is your day off?" Lana asked, stricken. "And you wasted it looking for me? I'm so sorry."

Emily blinked as if taken aback and regarded her intently. "I'm not. And looking for you is never a waste of my time, Lana. Ever."

"Oh." Lana felt heat rise in her cheeks. So Michelle had been right. Emily was interested in her. How could she have missed that? "Still, it's a shame you have to deal with this."

"I have a long weekend. It's not a problem." Emily dropped her head, suddenly seeming a little bashful as her eyes skidded away from Lana's. "Besides, I didn't know about all the events going on this weekend. Otherwise, I might have asked you to go with me."

"Oh." Lana considered that comment for a second, surprised at how much it pleased her. And intrigued her. "Who knows? I might have said yes."

"Really?" Emily lifted her head, the corners of her eyes crinkling as she smiled.

"Absolutely." Lana glanced around, feeling a bit vulnerable. "You know, it's too early for the brunch the inn is hosting, but I heard there were other events going on this afternoon at Acadia

University. Seminars and various displays regarding women's cultural studies."

"Well, if I can wrap things up with Devereaux this morning, maybe we can go check some of them out," Emily said casually, then sobered. "Where is she now, anyway?"

"In our room. She finally fell asleep, poor thing. I guess she'll probably want to go home as soon as she can. I should drive her to the airport."

"There's a car-rental place in New Minas," Emily said immediately. "She can get a new vehicle there. I'll go with her and smooth over the loss of her previous vehicle. We wouldn't want her to remain in the province any longer than she has to."

Lana swallowed back her smile, realizing a little jealousy flavored Emily's comments. She found it oddly flattering.

Then, as Lana realized what she was thinking, she did smile because she knew Sarah would be laughing at her at this point. The corresponding surge of sorrow and grief that the thought of her wife always inspired wasn't nearly as overpowering this time, and Lana hoped that was a sign that she was ready to, if not move on completely from her loss, then at least to start experiencing life again.

As if going off on a treasure hunt with a complete stranger wasn't proof enough of that already, she scoffed internally. It was just too bad there hadn't been a payoff of some kind, assuming one didn't count the opportunity to get to know Emily a bit better. And wasn't this how she used to be, before Sarah's death? Someone who'd never been afraid of taking a chance? Someone who'd enjoyed life to the fullest? Rediscovering that part of her was a treasure in itself.

She leaned back as their food arrived, and for the next few minutes, they were busy buttering toast, breaking the top of the yolks for dipping and forking up the tasty mix of eggs, ham, cheese, onions, green peppers, and mushrooms. Lana was impressed at how delicious it was, or perhaps she was just able to taste it fully again after not having much of an appetite for so long.

"What will happen to the two men?" she asked, sipping her orange juice.

"Well, after Devereaux makes her statement, there'll be an arrest warrant put out for them. It's her word against theirs about the accident, of course, but if they're driving the same car, the FIS might be able to match paint and damage to the rental car, and if they did break into the church, some of the artifacts might still be on them. That would initiate a list of charges that would put them behind bars for quite a while."

"FIS?"

"Forensic Identification Services," Emily explained. "You know, like the CSI people on television, except, of course, they don't carry guns or question witnesses or chase after suspects. They just do the science."

"Right. I should have figured that out."

Emily shrugged. "It's just lingo. Hang out with me long enough and you'll pick up on it."

"Maybe I will," Lana said, and daringly touched Emily's hand that was resting on the table.

Emily glanced up and met her eyes, and for a moment, the heat in that gaze was enough to take Lana's breath away. But she didn't say anything else, and Lana realized she was the one who would have to make all the moves, that Emily wasn't about to press the issue in any way.

A whole new adventure worth pursuing.

CHAPTER THIRTEEN

Michelle's eyelids were gummy and stuck together when she woke. It was an effort to open them and her head felt hollow, as if she'd been unconscious rather than merely asleep. On the other hand, she thought as she sat up, raking her fingers through her tangled hair, maybe she had been. Maybe falling out of that tree had left her concussed. Not that anyone would care. She certainly didn't.

Dully, she looked across the room, wondering idly where Lana was. A glance at the digital clock on the nightstand let her know she'd been asleep for about four hours. Just enough to leave her feeling logy and drained of energy. Her gaze settled on the metal box sitting forlornly on the dresser, and immediately, she felt sick. She'd gambled everything on this trip, using up her meager savings and maxing out her cards for plane tickets and rental car, taking a leap that her research would pay off financially, economically, and emotionally, proving once and for all that she knew what she was doing. Instead, all she had left was a credit-card debt, unemployment, and an utter sense of failure.

Sliding out of bed, she tottered over to the dresser, where she stared at the box, trying to find some kind of solace in knowing that it dated from 1755. It might be worth something, though Acadian artifacts weren't exactly a booming business in the illegal-antiquities trade. Exhaling heavily, she opened the box and pulled out the parchment, unfolding it as carefully as she could, acutely aware she should be using protective gloves while handling it, but not really concerned about it at this point.

With it laid out flat, she could see the note better in the morning sunshine streaming through the window than she had in the dim illumination of the Jeep's interior light the night before. The lettering was still faded and almost unreadable, but one legible phrase caught her eye.

J'ai déplacé la croix dorée à Chéticamp.
I've moved the cross to Cheticamp.

All of a sudden, the empty feeling disappeared, replaced by a rising excitement. The cross had actually been there. It really did exist. It might yet exist in Cheticamp, which, if Michelle remembered correctly, was a fishing village in Cape Breton that had existed since 1660, a place where many Acadians had moved after returning to Nova Scotia once the war between the British and French had ended.

The door to the unit opened, and Michelle turned to Lana with a huge smile on her face, one that promptly went away when she saw who accompanied her.

"What the hell's she doing here?"

Lana paused, looking surprised, and over her shoulder, Emily's features arranged themselves into that impassive, professional expression that screamed cop. Michelle immediately forced a smile, regretting her initial reaction and hoping she could slide past it.

"Sorry, you surprised me," she added quickly. "I'm feeling a bit light-headed."

Lana looked immediately concerned. "You need to see a doctor. You fell out of a tree. Here, sit down."

"Yes, do sit down," Emily said coldly.

Michelle allowed herself to be maneuvered into one of the armchairs, while Lana took the other. Emily remained standing by the door, leaning back against the wall, arms crossed over her chest. Her hair was down, and although the dislike was clear in her blue eyes, Michelle could see how attractive she was. Rounded, open, and honest features, with intelligent eyes and a kind mouth, while her body was solidly athletic but nicely curved. Not much wonder Lana let her hang around.

"I've just made an amazing find," she told Lana, seizing her hands and wringing them tightly. "I may know where the cross is."

"What? Where?" Lana's face lit up, her dark eyes sparkling as she responded to Michelle's excitement. "What have you discovered?"

Michelle turned to Emily. "Do you have one of those forensic kits in your car?"

"Why would I have one of those?" Emily appeared a little taken aback. "I'm off duty."

"All right, then, do you at least have some rubber gloves? For picking up evidence or something?"

Michelle noticed that Emily's accent wasn't quite the same as Lana's. It was more lively, almost as if there was an Irish influence. Drunk Irish, maybe. The vowels were slightly off, as if she was changing her mind halfway through a word and deciding to say something else.

"I may have," Emily said guardedly.

"Go get them."

"Why do you want them?" Emily countered.

"Michelle, what is this about?" Lana demanded.

"I need to examine the letter further." Michelle turned to Lana, her expression pleading as she tightened her grip on her hands. "The cross may be in Cheticamp."

"Cheticamp?" Lana echoed. "In Cape Breton?"

"Yes, and we can find it. I just need some supplies in order to do a full analysis on the letter. Then I can compare it to the writing in the journal. If Father Beauséjour wrote the letter, as I suspect, then certain entries in his diary that didn't seem so important before take on a much greater significance."

"I don't know much about historical documents, but couldn't it take years to research all this?"

"I think it's all there in the diary. But I have to know the full contents of this letter and who wrote it. To do that, I have to find a way to bring out the ink. We're so close, Lana. We've come this far."

"Far enough, I think," Emily put in.

Lana hesitated, and then she looked at Emily. "What harm could it do?" she asked, a touch of pleading in her intonation.

Emily's expression altered, became more animated, alarm appearing in those pale eyes. "What harm? Lana, she's talking about examining a document that belongs in a museum."

"A document that I discovered and that no one else would even know about if it wasn't for me." Michelle frowned at her. "Why are you here, again?"

"I'm here because you're involved in criminal activity."

"Really, because I think you're only here for Lana," Michelle responded dryly, recognizing she'd scored a direct hit when Emily turned a lovely shade of pink. "And honestly, there's nothing to worry about. We're just pursuing a historical lead. That's how discoveries are made!"

"And what about the two men who forced you off the road?"

Startled, Michelle turned to Lana. "You told her about that?"

"She read the note I left her," Lana said, sounding somewhat defensive.

"How'd you do that?" Michelle asked, turning back to Emily, who immediately became redder and even looked a bit guilty. "Did you break into her house? She wasn't even gone forty-eight hours, which I believe is standard procedure, if my television viewing is right. Now, who's the one involved in criminal activity?"

Lana slipped her hands from Michelle's grip and held them up in a placating motion, one in Emily's direction. "All right, let's just everyone calm down. We're getting ahead of ourselves." She turned a somber look on Michelle. "Listen, you need to report the accident. Emily says you have five days since no one was injured and it's only been two, so there's no harm done. But the car's already been found, which means the police will be looking for the driver. Tell them that you're all right and that the flooding and power outages were why you didn't call it in right away. They won't mind about the car. They'll just be glad no one was hurt. Insurance will cover it."

"If I do that, it'll take forever, making statements and filling out paperwork," Michelle said.

"You don't exactly have a choice here," Emily said flatly.

Michelle took a breath. "All right, I'll report the accident, but I won't say I was forced off the road."

"Why not?" Emily demanded. "Did you lie about that?"

Michelle ignored her and offered Lana a significant look. "You know why not," she said, and flicked her eyes in the direction of the briefcase sitting on the dresser beside the box. Lana's breath escaped in a rush.

"The stolen files," she said, somberly. Michelle couldn't believe it. What was the point of being subtle if Lana was just going to blurt it out like that?

"The what?" Emily yelped.

"You know, if you're going to freak out about every little thing, you might as well just go away," Michelle told her, irritated.

"Are you telling me you possess stolen property?"

"It's not stolen if Duperies hasn't reported it, which I doubt he has," Michelle said quickly. "And if I don't report anything about Pierre and Juan running me off the road, then there's no crime there, either. You can't arrest any of us based on what's been said here in the privacy of our hotel room. You're not here in any official capacity. You haven't read us our rights. You haven't even officially identified yourself as a police officer."

Emily stared at her. "You're quite the jailhouse lawyer, aren't you?" she said with icy loathing. "And about as qualified."

"Enough," Lana said, her voice a whip, startling both Michelle and Emily. "I'm sorry, Emily, but she's right. If she won't cooperate, there's really nothing you can do here. But Michelle, she's right in saying that you have to report the accident. That did happen and the police know about it. That's nonnegotiable."

"Fine. I'll do that if you get me some supplies so I can examine the letter," Michelle said.

"What kind of supplies?"

"Lana!" Emily looked very unhappy.

"Emily, if we do it your way, she'll just claim losing her car was an accident, and the case will be closed," Lana said. "Then she'll hare off and pursue it all by herself. This way, if something more sinister happens, we can be right there for it."

Emily regarded her gravely, breathing steadily with what could only be measured force. Michelle noticed that her hands were clenched into fists, pressed into the outside of her thighs. "Is this really what you want?"

Lana hesitated and then nodded, looking a bit apologetic. "I want to know how it turns out," she admitted. "I want to be there to see it when it does. Maybe that's wrong, but it's the first time—" She stopped.

"It's the first time you've wanted anything since Sarah died," Emily finished for her. She dropped her head. "I get that, Lana."

"I'm sorry." Lana's voice was very soft.

"Don't be."

Michelle, watching this exchange with great interest, had a feeling things were finally falling on her side. "So, this is what I'll need," she said, breaking the heavy silence that had fallen between the other two women. Grabbing a pad of paper from the nearby desk, she began to scribble her list. "You can probably get everything at the nearest office-supply store."

"There's one in New Minas," Lana said, accepting the sheet of paper that Michelle ripped off the pad. She glanced at it, paused, and then seemed to firm her jaw, nodding slightly. She glanced over at Emily. "Coming?"

"I think I'll stay here and keep an eye on our friend," Emily said, leaning back against the wall as if she were never planning to move again. "Make sure she's still here by the time you get back."

Lana paused again, then shot a parting look at Michelle, who wasn't sure exactly what she was trying to convey, only that it was something to do with Emily. Then she scooped up the car keys that had been lying on the end table and left the room.

Leaving Emily and Michelle to regard each other with a wary dislike.

CHAPTER FOURTEEN

"Y ou know, you can always go home," Michelle suggested after Lana had left and she and Emily were alone in the motel room. "Lana and I can take it from here."

"I'm not leaving her alone with you," Emily said, furiously. "You've done quite enough damage."

Michelle leaned back in her chair, linking her hands behind her head, which lifted her body, pushing out her chest and allowing the hem of her oversized T-shirt to rise, exposing the fact that she wasn't wearing any underwear. Experience with suspects in all sorts of situations kept Emily from either looking away or changing expression, but she wanted to. She couldn't understand how Lana was involved with this woman in any way, though she realized a lot of it undoubtedly had to do with her grieving process over Sarah. The worst part was that in all the time she'd known her, she'd never seen Lana look so vibrant and alive and engaged with everything around her. Despite the situation, and all her instincts regarding Michelle, Emily couldn't believe that was a bad thing.

"What damage have I done?" Michelle asked, sounding miffed.

"Are you actually a professor?" Emily retorted, instead.

Michelle hesitated. "A graduate student."

"Uh-huh, and are you employed at all?"

"Not really."

"So you're after the cross for the money."

Again, Michelle looked offended. "No, I just want to make a difference and recover a treasure for my people. My God, didn't you ever want to do something with your life besides follow the rules?"

"I'm a regular member of the Royal Canadian Mounted Police, the best law-enforcement agency in the world," Emily said frostily. "I like rules. And I still don't know why I shouldn't have you arrested right now."

"Because if you lock me up, then you're probably going to have to arrest Lana, too, because she's been helping me since the moment I got here," Michelle pointed out in a reasonable tone. "And I doubt you want to do that, because a blind man can see how you feel about her."

Emily glared, fury roiling in her chest. "I can't believe she slept with you."

"She told you I slept with her?" Michelle sounded surprised.

"Wasn't it obvious when I saw you in her cabin?" Emily said bitterly. Then a hope dawned, a sort of optimism that Emily didn't want to feel because she knew it was foolish and likely to be crushed. "You mean she didn't?"

Michelle regarded her steadily. "Oh, yeah, we slept together. More than once, as a matter of fact. And it was fantastic. The woman really knows what she's doing in that department."

Emily hoped she wasn't letting on how much that comment stung, or worse, how much the image that popped into her head generated a sick feeling in the pit of her stomach. She wanted nothing more than to punch Michelle, wipe that smug expression right off her face. It was a measure of how much she was getting under her skin because Emily, as a rule, wasn't a violent person.

Michelle shrugged carelessly, apparently unaware of how close she was to being pummeled. "Of course, I really don't think it was about me, so much, as it was because she was finally ready for it. Let's face it. If you'd made your move before now, she wouldn't have looked twice at me. What's taking you so long?"

"Her wife died," Emily reminded her, appalled to be having this conversation but unable to extricate herself with any grace. "She's in mourning."

"Yeah, but you could have helped her get over it a lot quicker." Michelle offered a mocking grin. "Look at it this way, Ems. I'm merely a reminder of how sweet life can truly be. Now you can reap what I've sown."

"Don't call me that." Furious, Emily dug her nails into her palms and, with an effort, forced her hands to relax. "And don't be disrespectful to her."

"I'm not trying to be disrespectful," Michelle said with what sounded like great sincerity. She does sincere really well, Emily thought darkly. "On the contrary. She probably saved my life, you know. She went down that hill like Black Widow and grabbed me before the river could. She's the most incredible woman I've ever met."

Emily's opinion of Michelle rose a little, but only because she was in total agreement with her view of Lana.

"Listen, why don't you go get those gloves and I'll get dressed," Michelle suggested, offering a sunny smile. "Then we can start examining the letter as soon as Lana gets back."

"Actually, you're going to get dressed, and then we're going down to the Wolfville detachment so you can report your accident," Emily told her, her voice unyielding as she realized that Michelle had been trying to butter her up by singing Lana's praises. "Don't be long. I'll be out by the car."

As she leaned against the driver's door of her Challenger, she sagged slightly, thoughts whizzing around and around in her head. If only she could figure out a way to ditch Michelle and all her craziness while leaving Lana untouched. Unfortunately, without Lana's cooperation, which she suspected she wouldn't get at this point, she couldn't see a way to dissuade her from this little adventure. Emily would just have to go along with it and make sure no one got hurt. And try to keep both of them out of trouble along the way.

When Michelle finally came out, she was dressed in jeans and a sweater, a puffy winter coat thrown on but left hanging open in the mild morning air. All new, Emily noted, and wondered how much this was costing Lana since she had a pretty good idea Michelle wasn't paying for much.

"You know," she said as they got in her car. "They found your luggage in the trunk of the rental car."

"Where is it now?" Michelle asked, sounding mildly curious but nothing more.

"Probably at the Stewiacke detachment," Emily said, and added, "You can pick it up on your way to the airport."

"After we've found the cross," Michelle told her as they pulled out of the parking lot onto the highway.

"Do you really think you'll find it after all this time?" Emily said, scorn like acid in her throat. "You're probably just chasing your tail."

"I have faith. Everyone needs faith, Constable."

Emily made a sound, more a growl than anything else, and focused on her driving. They made the rest of the trip to Wolfville in silence. After she pulled up to the entrance of the detachment and parked her car, she looked over at Michelle expectantly. Michelle looked back, eyebrows rising.

"You're not coming in with me?"

"Oh, you're just going to spin a web full of lies to the members, and I don't want any part of it." Emily tightened her grip on the steering wheel. "When you finally go down, you're going down alone."

"Fine," Michelle said, opening her door. "I don't know how long I'll be."

"I'll wait," Emily said flatly.

It took longer than she expected, but not as long as she hoped it would, where the constables inside might decide to hold Michelle for reasons unrelated to the accident. Emily shook her head when she spotted Michelle tripping lightly down the stairs, a cheerful expression on her face. She had no doubt that the woman could talk her way in and out of most anything. Heaven knew she had Lana somehow convinced she was worth helping.

"I'm hungry. Can we stop somewhere and pick up some breakfast on the way back?" Michelle asked, once she was in the car.

"Fine," Emily said shortly. They stopped at a Subway drive-through, and Emily was unsurprised to find herself having to pay for the breakfast sandwich and coffee. After pulling away from the window, but before she pulled out onto the street, she stopped the car and reached for her notepad, jotting down the amount.

"What are you doing?" Michelle muttered through her mouthful of egg white, ham, and bacon.

"Making a tally," Emily said shortly. "I'll get what receipts I can from Lana regarding your clothes and the hotel room." She turned and offered a completely insincere smile. "I'm sure you'll want to pay us back as soon as possible."

"Of course," Michelle said frostily.

Emily snorted and shifted the car into drive. Back at the motel, she was pleased to see Lana's Jeep in the spot in front of the room, and she parked beside it. Inside, they discovered Lana curled up on the bed, her coat thrown over her, slumbering peacefully. Emily put her hand on Michelle's arm and squeezed firmly.

"Let her sleep," she said in a low voice. "You can do what you have to do in my room." She handed her the card key. "Unit five."

Michelle nodded and quietly gathered up the bags by the bed, as well as the letter from the dresser, putting it carefully back into the box. After she'd softly closed the door behind her, Emily found a blanket in the closet and replaced Lana's coat with it, lingering a moment as she looked down at the sleeping woman.

She's just so lovely, Emily thought, a sort of helplessness along with the tender feelings seeping through her. I'm in such trouble.

Delicately, she brushed a lock of dark hair away from Lana's brows, her long lashes casting soft shadows over the smooth cheeks, and it was all Emily could do not to lean down and kiss her. But as exhausted as Lana seemed, she might wake up at that, and besides, it was unseemly for Emily to be mooning over her like some sort of combination teenager/stalker. Making sure the blanket was securely tucked around Lana's shoulders, Emily tossed one last, yearning look at her and left the room, making sure the door was locked behind her.

In her room, she discovered plastic, Styrofoam, twist ties, and unpacked boxes scattered over the two queen-sized beds, the floor, and the armchairs by the window, along with Michelle's jacket, gloves, and cap. Michelle was seated at the table in the corner, the letter in front of her, a box of latex gloves beside her, and some kind of handheld scanner in her hands. Emily frowned when she saw the open laptop, and shaking her head, she straightened up the room. Discovering the receipt from one of the empty shopping bags, she blinked at the amount on the bottom. She cast an appalled glance at Michelle, who appeared oblivious, tucked it in her notebook on the page containing the amount from Subway, and found a seat on one of the beds, stacking the pillows against the headboard to give her support.

It didn't take long before she was completely bored watching Michelle do inexplicable things with the letter, so she flipped on the TV, skipping through the channels before finally settling on an *Orphan Black* rerun. Other than a single annoyed look cast in her direction, Michelle ignored her, which was fine as far as Emily was concerned, though she did deliberately turn up the volume a little, just to make a point as to whose hospitality was being enjoyed here.

Both of them seemed definitely relieved, however, when a soft knock on the door came a few hours later. "How far has she progressed?" Lana asked in a low voice after Emily let her in. She'd clearly showered and changed and was now dressed in a silk, wine-shaded blouse and dark pants, looking greatly restored from her nap.

"Hard to say," Emily said.

"Not far enough," Michelle responded pointedly, though she didn't look up from her work. "Why don't you two make yourselves scarce while I do this. It'll be less distracting."

Lana shot a glance at Emily and smiled faintly. "There's always that dinner and dance at the Warehouse."

Emily's heart suddenly thudded so hard she thought it might crack her sternum. Forcing air into her lungs, she had to rely on all her training not to break out into a sloppy smile. "Sure, that sounds great."

"Give me a minute to shower and change?"

CHAPTER FIFTEEN

Michelle snorted as soon as Emily had disappeared into the bathroom. "Well, you just made her day."

Lana glanced at her. "It's just something to pass the time while we wait for you to finish what you have to."

"Yeah? Better hope that's all it is for her, too," Michelle warned her.

Suddenly uncomfortable, Lana took a seat in one of the armchairs. "So what have you discovered so far?" she asked. "Who wrote the letter?"

"Father Beauséjour, and I believe he wrote it to Thomas. I think he wanted him to know why the cross was no longer in the box, that he'd taken it with him, and that it was still safe. But the Duperies family never returned to Nova Scotia. They all stayed in Louisiana, so Thomas never found the letter." Michelle tapped on the laptop keyboard. "I'm using the scanner to bring out the ink, making it more visible."

"Wouldn't—I don't know—lemon juice or something help with that?" Lana asked.

She still wasn't sure why she was so cheerfully shelling out money for this expedition other than the fact that this was who she used to be. Once she committed to something, she was in all the way, no holding back, from learning how to tie flies to mountain biking. Sarah had always loved that about her, Lana remembered wistfully. Or at least, she always claimed she did.

Michelle shuddered delicately at Lana's suggestion. "Any kind of chemical that would bring out the ink would also damage the parchment," she explained. "Scanning the sheet from different angles with different wavelengths brings out the contrast between ink and paper, making what's written more visible. Every scan adds more to the image on the computer. Eventually, I'll have a complete rendering of the note. It's not as good as what the high-end scanners in the lab could do, of course, but it should allow me to read most of what was written."

"But what about—" Lana stopped as the door to the bathroom opened.

Emily was wearing makeup, she thought dazedly. She'd never seen her in makeup. Or in a low-cut, cleavage-exposing shirt, or ass-hugging black jeans, or seen her hair curled in golden waves around her face.

"Wow, you clean up nice, Constable," Michelle noted.

Emily favored her with a dark look but smiled when she looked back at Lana. Using the brief diversion, Lana got a grip on herself. "You look great," she echoed in a soft voice, and Emily beamed. "Shall we go?"

"Have fun, kiddies," Michelle said cheerfully. "I won't wait up."

Outside, Emily offered Lana a serious look. "You know she's half cracked."

"She's just American," Lana said weakly.

"I don't think that's it."

But she smiled a little as she unlocked the passenger door for Lana, even opening it for her before going around to the driver's side. As Lana settled into the leather seat, she found herself sneaking quick glances at Emily while she started the car, absorbing everything about her, the sure and strong way her hands moved over the gearshift and the wheel, how she was a conscientious and alert driver, constantly checking the rearview mirror and side angles, how the illumination from oncoming cars flashed over her strong features. Her actions were commonplace and hardly worthy of notice, yet oddly arousing at the same time. It was as if Lana had never seen her before, or at least had never perceived her as anything more than someone just wearing a uniform. A kind, caring, funny uniform, of course, but not as someone to whom Lana might be attracted.

That had certainly changed in the space of only a few hours.

The Warehouse in Wolfville was a cavernous building that had been used to store apples a half century earlier. Now it was the college town's main hangout, with a long bar that ran along one side, tables at the front, and a respectably sized dance floor and DJ booth at the other. A couple of pool tables and some pinball machines were set up in a back room, and more tables could be found in a upper-level balcony that circled the area, providing a sort of gallery for patrons to watch the dancers. The entire bar was liberally decorated with Acadia Axemen-related memorabilia and, for this weekend, with a lot of additional rainbow flags, streamers, and balloons.

Lana was surprised when Emily, rather than pay the entrance fee, handed over two tickets she apparently already had in her possession. Making their way to the upper level, they found a table near the back, away from the better part of the music and noise. There they ordered their drinks, a beer for Emily and a white wine for Lana, and were informed their food waitress would be with them in a minute, though judging from the crowd, Lana suspected it would be significantly longer than that.

She glanced at Emily, who was surveying her surroundings with keen evaluation. "You're not going to arrest anyone, are you?"

Emily focused on her, smiling faintly. "If I haven't arrested your friend before now, then I doubt I'll go after anyone else tonight. Besides, it's not protocol for me to arrest someone while off duty. Unless someone's in immediate mortal danger, my duty is to call in any kind of criminal activity and act as an expert witness to whatever's going down. I'm not supposed to become directly involved."

"I didn't know that," Lana admitted. She paused and leaned closer, lowering her voice. "Are you carrying a gun?"

Emily laughed out loud. "No, there are no 'carry' permits in Canada, and even if there were, we're not supposed to have our weapons while off duty. I'm not saying some members don't have registration permits for their own personal use, so they can have rifles or handguns in their home, but I've never applied for one."

"It's not like TV at all, is it?"

"No, and it's especially not like American television." Emily paused. "You've never asked me anything like this, before."

"I guess—" Lana paused, trying to phrase it the right way. "I've just never been that—interested." She quickly touched Emily's hand. "Please don't take that the wrong way."

"I don't," Emily said, her eyes grave as they regarded her. "Even when I could talk you into eating with me, I could always tell you weren't really there. Your body was, but your heart and mind? They were somewhere else and all that was left was the grief."

"For a long time, now. I guess I didn't know how deep it really went. It wasn't even a matter of feeling bad all the time. Or feeling depressed. I just felt numb. I've been going through the motions for months." She took a breath. "Years."

Emily exhaled audibly, dropping her head to look at Lana from beneath her lashes. "I hate to admit it, and I really hate to admit she had anything to do with it, but it's obvious that meeting Michelle has—I don't know, brought you back, somehow."

"It has," Lana admitted. "I don't know how to explain it, either, but when I saw her car in the river, when I went down that hill to get her, it was almost like I could suddenly hear and see and feel again." She shrugged, finding it hard to put words to what she was experiencing. "And now that I'm on this quest with her, I can't wait to see what happens next."

Emily, about to speak, was interrupted by the appearance of their waitress. After they ordered, quesadilla for Lana with a chicken Caesar salad for Emily, and the waitress had moved away, she continued the conversation.

"So you see all this as some kind of quest. Like in one of your books."

"I guess I do," Lana said. "Look, I know Michelle is dancing back and forth over some pretty thin lines, both legal and moral. Hell, I've been doing some dancing right along with her, but it's just so exciting, Emily. It's about having an adventure as opposed to just reading or writing about it."

"The thing about an adventure is that it's only in the aftermath that it can be called that," Emily pointed out. "It can just as easily be called a tragedy or a farce, depending on the outcome. At the time, you're just treading water."

"But it doesn't feel like I'm treading water," Lana said earnestly. "It feels like I'm swimming toward something, something important. Not the cross, necessarily, but something."

Emily sighed. "That's the only reason I'm still here. I don't trust Michelle at all, but I do trust you. And if you tell me you have to do this, for whatever reason, then I'm right there with you."

Lana linked her fingers in Emily's, entwining them as she squeezed warmly. "I appreciate that," she said. "I guess I haven't been seeing what's been right in front of me when it comes to you."

"You weren't ready," Emily said. "I know that. I was willing to wait. I still am." She drew back her hand, dropping her eyes and looking a little uncomfortable. "I also know you and Michelle were—well, I know you're sleeping together."

Lana felt a twinge. "It's not quite like that," she said. "We did sleep together. We do have a room together." She stopped. "Hell, now I *am* treading water. I don't want to deceive you in any way, Emily. I'm working things out, and frankly, ever since you showed up, I've wanted—" She stopped again, searching for the right thing to say. "I don't know what I want," she admitted. "That's the part I'm still working out. I'm not trying to be unfair to you."

Emily managed a bit of a pained smile. "I understand."

"Do you?" Lana said, a bit sadly. "Because I'm not sure I do."

Emily recaptured Lana's hand, seizing it in a firm grip. "I know how I feel about you," she said earnestly. "I've felt it for a long time. I know I could be in love with you."

Lane felt those words strike to the bone. "But you don't know who I am, Emily," she protested, feeling her throat hurt. "For the past three years—for the past three and a half years, ever since Sarah was diagnosed, I feel as though I've been sleepwalking through life, just getting through it one day at a time instead of actually living it. That isn't really who I am. That isn't the person Sarah fell in love with, or who she married. That's definitely not who I was before Sarah. So how can you love that person, Emily? She doesn't really exist. She was just a shadow drifting through."

"She's part of who you are," Emily said mildly.

"Yes, but only one part, only the grief part. And I am sorely tired of grieving."

"Okay, that makes sense." Emily raked her fingers through her long hair, leaving it in disarray. "I guess you're right. I don't really know who you are. But I do know how I feel every time I'm with you, and that's real, whether you like it or not."

Lana bowed her head. "It's not that I don't like it," she said quietly. "It's not even that I might not return those feelings, because I really do like you, Emily. A lot. But I'm telling you this because, as much as you don't really know who I am, I'm not sure I know who I am at this point, either."

"Then maybe we can find out together," Emily said, and squeezed her hand again. "Will you let me come along with you on this journey?"

Lana smiled. "I'd like that."

"And maybe we can ditch Michelle in Canso?"

Lana laughed. "You're going to have to get along with her for the time being," she said. "She's the one with the treasure map. Or at least the paperwork with all the clues leading to the treasure."

"In Cheticamp." Emily shook her head. "It's not a place I'd put a treasure." She lifted her head as ABBA came on, the catchy tune drifting up from the dance floor. "Dance?"

"Why is it everyone makes fun of disco, but once it starts playing, everyone heads for the dance floor, even the young ones who've never heard it before?" Lana complained, though she didn't oppose being pulled from her seat.

"Because it's 'Mamma Mia,' and that never gets old," Emily said as she bounced down the stairs to the main floor.

"How can you resist it?"

CHAPTER SIXTEEN

Emily couldn't believe she was here, dancing with Lana, seeing her laugh and move and just be alive again. It was wonderful, but she was determined to back off at this point, keep it casual. She didn't want to scare Lana away. She'd already told her far too much about the depth of her feelings, already thrown the l-word around like it was nothing. It was time to take things very slowly.

And besides, Lana was right. Emily didn't really know who she was or had been before Sarah's illness. In fact, that woman might be a little more than she could handle, she thought as she watched Lana move lithely to the music, her throat catching at how incredibly beautiful and graceful she was.

ABBA gave way to some generic 90s tune, then back to the 80s with the very danceable and upbeat "Mickey" before they decided their dinner was probably on its way. On the upper level, Emily sank into her seat, the last tune still reverberating in her head and her heart still beating quickly from the physical exertion. Or perhaps it was merely from her dinner companion. Their return was timely as they could see their waitress, arms full of plates, approaching their corner.

After she left, Emily found herself toying with her salad, not really that hungry. Lana, on the other hand, consumed her quesadilla as if she hadn't eaten in days. She really was tackling life again, Emily thought wistfully, finding it hard to swallow when she saw Lana wipe a bit of sour cream from the corner of her mouth with her thumb, the casual yet oddly elegant gesture making her seem incredibly relaxed. It was all Emily could do not to lean across the table and replace Lana's thumb with her mouth.

Searching for something, anything to cool off that line of thought, she seized on Lana's professional life. "I was wondering, have you ever thought of writing a sequel to—"

She stopped as she spotted a group of women ascending the stairs, just coming into view over Lana's left shoulder. Amanda was among them, and while their breakup hadn't been that bad as those things went, Emily wasn't particularly thrilled to see her. Of course, she should've expected it, considering how small the community was in this part of the province. She sank a little in her seat, even as she knew that was ridiculous and hardly about to work.

Lana was regarding her, bemused. "Emily, are you all right? You look like you've seen a ghost."

"Not a ghost." Emily forced a smile as she saw Amanda's gaze turn her way, her expression shift as she recognized her. As she started her way, leaving her friends behind, Emily's heart sank. "Just an ex."

"Oh." Features suddenly curious, Lana turned as Emily rose from her seat to greet Amanda. Statuesque, with brown hair highlighted with light streaks and brilliant blue eyes, Amanda still provoked a certain attraction that rippled across Emily's midsection. She didn't like it, but she couldn't deny it, either.

"Ems, it's so great to see you. You never come to these things."

Emily felt the familiar arms pull her close in a friendly hug, felt the lips brush her cheek. Amanda had always been the exceedingly affectionate type. Emily didn't take it personally because Amanda was the same with all her friends. And her exes.

"Good to see you, too," she lied. "Here with the girls?"

Emily had lost all their friends in the separation, because of her work and because they'd been Amanda's friends to begin with. All except Joanna, probably because she was so settled and not really an activist. But mostly because she really didn't like Amanda all that much.

Amanda was regarding Lana inquiringly, and Emily quickly introduced them. "Amanda, this is Lana," she said. "Lana, this is Amanda, my—uh, friend."

"Ex." Amanda corrected her absently, nodding at Lana in greeting. She glanced at Emily, a sort of perplexed expression in her eyes, as if wondering how Emily could have snagged anyone so attractive. Emily felt her back teeth start to grind and forced herself to stop.

"It's very nice to meet you, Amanda," Lana said smoothly. She gestured at the chair on her left. "Join us for a drink?"

"Oh, I can't, thanks," Amanda said. "I'm here with friends."

She gestured toward the other table where the other five women waited. A few of them nodded at Emily or lifted their hands in a half wave of acknowledgment. Emily's shoulders tightened. She never knew what to do in these kinds of situations, to know what the etiquette was or how to manage the carefree sophistication that others did. She was just awkward and sad, not regretful of a heart offered and rejected exactly, but still conscious of the lingering hurt over a love that hadn't worked out.

"Did you come down for the whole weekend?" Amanda asked.

"Not really," Emily said honestly. "We just happened to be in the area."

Amanda, glancing back and forth between Emily and Lana, smiled. "Oh, okay. Well, it was great seeing you again. Nice to meet you, Lana."

As she headed back to her table, Emily was conscious of Lana's speculative gaze as she resumed her seat. "So, your ex?" she prompted archly.

"Yeah, okay," Emily said, taking a long swallow from her beer. "Nothing to see here. Move along."

Lana laughed. "No, I'm fascinated. You never once mentioned her during our lunches together. Bad breakup?"

"No, just one of those things." Emily poked at her salad with a bit more force than she intended, sending a piece of chicken over the side of the bowl and off the table. "Shit."

"Oh, now I know there's a story there," Lana said. "C'mon, give it up. You know all about me and Sarah."

"Actually, I know very little about you and Sarah, outside of what you were going through at the time," Emily reminded her. She could have kicked herself when she saw the shadow flit across Lana's eyes. Quickly, she pulled the conversation back to her, as much as she didn't like talking about it. "Amanda is really social," she explained, feeling a bit vulnerable as she opened up. "She liked to go out all the time. I didn't mind so much because I was working, and it wasn't like I expected her to stay home and wait for me or anything. It's just that I'm more of an outdoor, tomboy type, whereas she's really into things like this weekend. In fact, she probably helped organize it. She's involved in the community and very active when it comes to all the issues, fighting for our rights, here and in other countries."

"And you're not?"

"I do what I can, but as a Mountie, there are certain things I have to stay—uh, separate from, so I can do my job. And incessant meetings bore the hell out of me."

"That was a bone of contention?"

"Among other things," Emily said. "She also worried about me a lot, especially whenever she heard of a police officer being killed or harmed in the line of duty. She didn't understand that those are the rare exceptions rather than the rule when it comes to my job."

"But it only takes the one exception," Lana pointed out. "Wrong place, wrong time."

"I know, but that's true of everyone," Emily said. "After all, I'm not the one who braved flooding to rescue some American, and I'm not the one who decided to hare off on some treasure hunt with a complete stranger, who also might have a couple of thugs after her."

Lana laughed. "There is that." She glanced over her shoulder, taking a longer look in Amanda's direction. "Still, it is interesting when meeting exes. It gives an insight into the sort of woman you're attracted to. How long were you together?"

"Two and a half years," Emily said.

"Live together?"

"For two years, in my apartment." Emily toyed with her salad. "Amanda didn't like that, either. She kept trying to get us to move, but I liked being in the downtown. It's convenient to everything, especially work."

"That practical side again," Lana noted. "So you wouldn't like living out where I am."

Emily smiled. "Your cabin is lovely," she said diplomatically. "I love your view."

Lana's dark eyes danced as they peered at her over her glass as she took a long sip of her white wine. "And what finally broke you up?"

Emily inclined her head in the direction of Amanda's table. "See the woman on her left, the brunette with the short hair?"

Lana smoothly dropped her knife on the floor and picked it up, taking a discreet look under her arm as she did. "Uh-huh."

Emily was impressed. "That was nicely done."

"I try," Lana said modestly.

Beautiful and capable, Emily thought. God, I am in such trouble.

"Anyway, Beth's her oldest friend, and when I say friend, I mean she would like to be a lot more and sticks with Amanda through every girlfriend, with the intention, I suppose, of picking up the pieces when it doesn't work out, as it often doesn't."

"Uh-huh, and did she contribute to those breakups?"

"As much as she could," Emily said. "Don't get me wrong, it didn't work out because Amanda and I were too different from the very beginning, but Beth constantly hanging around didn't help. Personally, I think Amanda should just sleep with her and get it out of the equation so they can either get together or move on. But I wonder if the only reason Amanda stays friends with her is that she likes having a perfect backup plan in the event she ends up alone." She winced, wondering if that was the role she'd been playing with Lana, hoping she would finally get over Sarah and see her as more than a lunch companion. In that moment, for the very first time, she felt an unexpected sympathy for Beth, something Emily never thought she'd feel. "Sorry. I'm being a complete bitch."

"No you're not," Lana said, understanding in her tone. "Clearly, the breakup hurt, so it makes sense that you still have a little resentment over it. But if you and Amanda were so different, why'd you get together in the first place?"

Emily sighed. "Chemistry, I suppose," she admitted. "I thought she was hot. She thought I was hot. It was like an explosion when we got together. Then it eventually wore off and we realized we didn't have much in common."

"It took two and half years to figure that out?"

"Oh, probably a year and a half to wear off," Emily said. "And a year of trying to make it work before we finally gave up." She shook her head. "Taught me a lesson about moving slow before taking the big leap."

"Are we moving slow?" Lana sounded honestly curious.

"We've been meeting at the diner for three years," Emily pointed out. "That's longer than Amanda and I were together."

"Really?" Lana blinked. "You haven't been with anyone in all that time?"

Emily shrugged. "Never met anyone I wanted to be with."

"But you could've," Lana told her, sounding puzzled. "You're gorgeous."

Emily was positive she was bright red at this point and profoundly glad the lighting in the bar was low. "Uh, thank you," she managed to say.

"I mean, you must have women going after you all the time just because of the uniform," Lana added. "You look really good in it, especially with the hat and the belt."

"Now you're just making fun."

"No, I assure you, you look great." Lana put her hand on Emily's knee, squeezing lightly. As she lowered her head, her expression grew more intent. "In fact, that was the reason I accepted all those invitations to eat. Even at my lowest, I could always appreciate how you looked in uniform. And honestly, you made me feel safe at a time when my whole world was ending."

Emily inhaled slowly, trying not to shiver from the sensation of Lana's hand on her leg. "I'm glad I could offer something." She closed the distance between them a little. "But I don't want you to feel safe now."

Lana's teeth were very white as she smiled. "Oh, believe me, I don't. Not in the slightest." She lifted her head as she heard the music alter below. "Now we have to dance to this."

Emily laughed. "Lead the way."

They spent the rest of the evening on the dance floor, even for the slow ones, which was a bit excruciating for Emily, holding Lana so close, smelling her perfume and the warm, natural scent of her, her body so soft and yielding against her.

"Are you playing with me?" she asked at one point, seeking out Lana's eyes. Bringing her hand up to brush Lana's hair from her cheek, she felt her heart catch as she waited for the answer. She'd intended the question to be more lighthearted than it was and hoped her voice reflected it even if the feeling in the pit of her stomach didn't.

Lana, hands linked behind Emily's neck as they swayed together, shook her head, her face serious. "No," she said, her voice soft but very sincere. "I'm definitely not playing with you, Emily. But I'm not totally back in the game, either."

"Fair enough." Emily wanted nothing more than to kiss her right then and there, but she resisted. Instead, she pulled Lana closer, feeling incredibly tender as Lana rested her head on her shoulder, snuggled up against her as they danced. In a way this was better, more intimate than a kiss. Lana was dancing with her because she wanted to be, not because Emily happened to be there. Heaven knew, there were plenty enough other women in the

Warehouse who'd be glad to take a turn, judging from the looks directed Lana's way.

They made the drive back to the motel after the dance in a comfortable silence, Lana sitting beside her with a sort of half-smile on her face, as if remembering how rewarding the simple pleasure of a date could be. After parking the car in front of her unit, Emily started to go around the car to open her door, but Lana was ahead of her and they met at the hood.

"I had a really great time," Lana told her. She took Emily's arm, moving closer to her. "You're a wonderful dancer."

"You are, too," Emily said. She was conscious of her nearness and thankful they had several layers of winter jackets and sweaters between them, Otherwise, she suspected their hands would be all over each other. As it was, she contented herself with taking Lana's gloved fingers into her own, squeezing lightly. "We'll have to do this again, sometime."

"Soon," Lana agreed. "I like being with you, Emily. I like how it makes me feel. I like how it makes me want things again." She lowered her voice. "I like how it makes me want you."

"And it only took three years," Emily said dryly.

Lana laughed, a wonderfully husky laugh, deep in her throat, sending a jolting arc of sensation directly from Emily's heart to her center. Moistening her lips, she leaned forward, elated when Lana tilted her head slightly to the side, lips parting, inviting her in. After such a long time imagining it, she needed to know how Lana really tasted, how it would feel to finally kiss her.

A jarring and most unwelcome voice at precisely the wrong time caught Emily off guard, and she jerked back, startled, mere millimeters short of her goal.

"Hey, y'all. How was dinner?"

CHAPTER SEVENTEEN

The sound of a car door shutting just outside the motel door made Michelle lift her head from the computer screen. A quick glance at the time in the menu bar let her know it was probably Lana and Emily back from their date, though whether they were calling it that or not remained to be seen. She got up from the table and went over to the window, peering through the blinds to see Lana and Emily lingering by the hood of the red Challenger, standing close and talking as if reluctant to end the evening. They kept touching each other, despite the obvious barrier of their winter clothing, Lana's hand on Emily's arm, Emily holding Lana's gloved hand, both leaning so close into each other the white clouds from their breaths condensed in the air around them. Michelle felt a pang of envy, or perhaps it was just longing to be like them, these hearty, unfathomable women who liked to make out in frigid winter as if they were on Bourbon Street and it was 85 degrees.

Michelle went over to the door and opened it, watching as Lana laughed at something Emily said, a low, smoky laugh full of promise. Emily seemed to take that as an invitation and leaned forward, her lips mere inches from Lana's, who didn't seem inclined to pull back.

"Hey, y'all," Michelle said cheerfully and loudly. "How was dinner?"

Emily jerked back comically, and even Lana appeared a bit startled. Michelle stifled a laugh, leaning casually against the doorframe as if completely unaware what was in progress. Though for all she knew, they could have been parked somewhere else fucking their brains out before coming back to the motel. But from the expression of deep disappointment in Emily's eyes, along with a darkening anger, Michelle didn't think so.

After all, she knew full well how satisfying Lana could be. Otherwise, Emily wouldn't be nearly as frustrated as she so apparently was. No, what Michelle had interrupted had "first kiss" potential written all over it. What a shame.

"I think I've pinpointed where Father Beauséjour took the cross," Michelle said as the two women came over to her, and they all went into Emily's room, shutting out the damp air. "How long does it take to get to Cheticamp from here?"

"A few hours," Emily said shortly. "We're not going to do it tonight. We'll leave after breakfast tomorrow. We can cut through Rawdon, drop off Lana's Jeep, and get on the highway in Truro."

Michelle wasn't sure she liked Emily suddenly being in charge of their travel arrangements, but since she didn't have a vehicle, she didn't have much say. She forced a smile and moved closer to Lana.

"It sounds like a plan." Leaning against Lana's side with intimate familiarity, she slipped an arm around her waist and peered up into her face, smiling winsomely. "Ready to turn in?"

Lana looked a bit uneasy and glanced at Emily, who smiled unpleasantly at Michelle. "Actually, I think you should stay in my room, tonight, Michelle," Emily said. "That way, Lana can get some sleep."

"Oh." Michelle straightened and pulled away from Lana, dropping her arm. "So you and Lana are taking her room? Is that how it is now?"

"No. I'm staying here with you," Emily told her in that calm, even, officious tone. "We'll each take a bed."

"What? Why?"

"I just want to keep an eye on you," Emily said. "Keep you from temptation."

"What kind of temptation?" Michelle demanded, baffled.

"All kinds." Emily glanced at Lana and her face softened perceptibly. "I'll see you tomorrow?"

Lana, who'd been taking this all in with a slight smile, nodded briefly. "All right. We'll meet for breakfast?"

Michelle protested. "What about my stuff?"

"I'll bring it over," Lana told her. "It won't take long."

Feeling as if she was being outmaneuvered, which she didn't like at all, Michelle plopped down in the armchair and began to shut down the laptop. A few minutes later there was a soft knock that Emily answered, accepted the small duffle bag from Lana, said a couple of things Michelle couldn't quite hear, only that Lana found them amusing according to her soft laugh, and then shut the door.

Tossing the bag on the bed farthest from the bathroom, Emily shrugged out of her leather jacket. "Do you want the bathroom first?"

"Thank you," Michelle said coldly, retrieving her bag, where she dug out the toothbrush and the oversized T-shirt she'd been using for her nightdress. It was the same one Lana had worn their first night together, the one Michelle had worn downstairs to confound Emily, and still smelled like Lana, a slight floral scent, like lilacs, but not quite. More evocative.

As she brushed her teeth, she assessed these new circumstances. Obviously, she wasn't about to get close to Lana again, not as long as Emily was around. She felt a regretful twinge in her loins. She was here for the cross, of course, but making love to a beautiful woman while pursuing it would have been a lot more fun. Still, it was clear which way the wind was blowing as far as Emily and Lana were concerned, so it was prudent that she stay out of the middle of it.

Outside of needling Emily about it, of course. She could always find some fun, no matter what the circumstances.

They checked out the next morning right after breakfast, Lana driving her Jeep and Michelle stuffed into the passenger seat of the Challenger. Emily didn't seem particularly open to conversation, answering Michelle's varied attempts with monosyllabic responses and the occasional disdainful glance sideways until Michelle finally gave up. It proved a long, sullen trip to Lana's cabin, and Michelle was relieved when she was dispatched to the small backseat of Emily's sports coupe while Lana took her spot up front.

Michelle didn't know how appealing Nova Scotia was in the summer months, but in the winter months, with the rainy, gray weather, it was excruciatingly dull. Especially once they left the back roads outside Truro and switched to the Trans-Canada, which, from what Michelle could tell, was cut straight through the woods, separate and distinct from most of the communities they passed, noted only as names on green signs along the way.

Maybe it was pretty in the fall, she thought glumly as they crested another hill that looked down onto large swaths of forest and the double gray strip of asphalt. There weren't even that many cars, going either way.

"Isn't this place inhabited?" she asked at one point.

Lana smiled and looked back between the seats. "There's only about nine hundred thousand people in the province, and most of them are settled on the coast. This highway goes straight up the northern part of the province to Cape Breton, so there aren't as many towns along the way. And honestly, it's never going to look like anything you'd see in the States. Maybe Maine, but otherwise, it's not nearly as densely populated as any area you might know."

"You're a wealth of information," Michelle said, regarding her with interest.

"You should see me at Trivial Pursuit."

Lana offered a crooked grin and turned to look out the front window once more. Michelle saw Emily glance over at her, and her expression was such a puppy-dog mix of pride and pleasure that she rolled her eyes. There was no way around it. Emily had it bad. Michelle wondered how Lana was going to deal with it and if she would be kind about it. A day earlier, Michelle would have assumed so, but now she was realizing she didn't really know what went on behind those darkly beautiful features. Even in the very short time she'd known her, Lana seemed to be changing profoundly.

Was that what grief did to someone? Or was it just because she was letting go of that grief and this new person was who Lana really was? Michelle resolved to keep an eye on that developing situation. She shifted her gaze. Emily, on the other hand, was more of an open book: solid, upstanding, courageous, and always prepared to do the right thing. Predictable, in other words, except perhaps where Lana was concerned. Michelle resolved to keep an eye on her, as well. There might come a time when she'd have to jump a certain way, and it would be useful if she knew which way her companions would go.

"Watch out for moose," Lana noted as they passed a warning sign not long after crossing the Canso Causeway.

"I doubt we'll see one," Emily said, flashing a smile at her. "But you're right. If I had to choose, I'd rather hit a deer."

"Why?" Michelle asked, curious. "What's the difference?"

"Simple. When you hit a deer, you wreck your car, you usually kill the deer, and you might hurt yourself," Emily said, glancing at her in the rearview mirror. "When you hit a moose, you wreck your car, you usually kill yourself, and you might hurt the moose."

"Oh," Michelle said. "Yeah. Let's not do that."

They stopped at a diner just outside Cheticamp for lunch. These places didn't seem to go in for much in the way of décor, Michelle noticed, but the food was spectacular, especially the seafood. Considering that she was used to the bounty of New Orleans, she had to grudgingly admit that it was pretty damned good. She plowed her way through a variety platter containing lobster, crab, Digby scallops, fries, and a vegetable medley, Emily watching with a sort of disgusted fascination and Lana with quiet amusement.

While Emily settled the bill, Michelle found herself standing with Lana by the car. "Look," she said in a low voice, "I'm going to find a way to pay you both back for all this, no matter what happens."

"It's our choice to be here, Michelle," Lana said calmly. "Our money to spend. I can't speak for Emily, but when and if I think it's become too much, then I'll stop and go home. Either way, it's my decision. It's not on you."

"Okay," Michelle said, and got back in the car as Emily came out of the diner.

They didn't have a lot of choice regarding accommodations in Cheticamp this time of year, with most B&Bs, cottages, and motels closed for the season. They ended up at a place that rented individual cabins, two-bedroom units with a small kitchen and living area, electric heaters along the base of the walls, and a small woodstove providing warmth. The wind off the ice-choked bay was bitter as they carried their bags inside.

"All right, where do we start?" Emily asked once she had a small fire going in the stove and the chill in the room had dissipated.

"The cemetery beside St. Peter's Church," Michelle said. "I need to check out a gravestone."

"Do we have to wait until after dark?" Lana asked with interest.

"I'm just going to look at it," Michelle replied. She glanced at Emily. "Nothing illegal or questionable. I promise."

"That remains to be seen," Emily told her.

Michelle thought that was just being pessimistic and offered her an admonishing look that didn't seem to bother Emily at all.

The wind was even stronger as they got out of the car by the church, blowing in from the southeast. Michelle shivered in her winter coat, pulling the hood up over her head.

"How do you people stand this?" she muttered as they tromped across the snowy ground toward the gates guarding the cemetery. Beneath her booted feet, ice crunched, and there seemed to be a lot more snow in this area than in Grand-Pré. This was a much harsher environment, and Michelle wondered if the Acadians who had returned here ever missed the much-hotter climes of Louisiana and why they would even consider this a suitable place to settle.

Home had to be where the heart was because it certainly didn't make sense otherwise. Maybe it was just all the crazy ones that came back.

"These are *Les Suêtes* winds," Lana explained. "They're abnormally strong because of the highlands. They can regularly blow up to 230 kilometers an hour this time of year."

Michelle looked at her and saw Lana was reading from a pamphlet that she'd acquired somewhere and grinned. It was obvious the woman loved information.

"Where is this grave and why are we looking at it?" Emily asked sourly. It appeared she didn't like the weather any more than Michelle did.

"The far corner." Michelle wound her way through the ornate headstones. "It's the oldest part of the cemetery."

She stopped in front of a stone, weathered and worn, the barely legible chiseled letters indicating how old it was, but the grave itself was well tended, clear of any brambles or growth. She took off her glove and traced over the grooves in the granite, tracing out the letters, her fingers quickly growing numb.

"Father Gaston Beauséjour," she whispered. "He's here. He's right here."

Emily immediately looked alarmed. "We are *not* digging up a grave!"

CHAPTER EIGHTEEN

"I would never!" Michelle responded to Emily's comment in a completely offended tone. "What kind of person do you think I am?"

Since Lana had been thinking much the same thing, she couldn't really regard Michelle's outrage as justifiable, but she did lift her hand, making a nonverbal suggestion to Emily that perhaps she shouldn't take it any further. Emily lifted her brows at the gesture but set her jaw, her lips thinning as if she was swallowing back another comment.

"What does this signify?" Lana said patiently. "Obviously he died here, in 1803, according to the stone. Is this where he hid the cross?" She glanced over at the magnificent structure that was St. Peter's, serving a central role in the spiritual life of the small Acadian village. "He had nothing to do with the church. It was built in 1893, a century after he was gone. Even the church that came before it in Le Buttereau was built in 1868. Again, long after his time."

Emily goggled. "How do you know that?" she demanded. "I expect it from her. She's supposed to be some sort of an expert, but I didn't know you were interested in this stuff at all." Michelle was also regarding Lana, though her expression was more amused than astounded.

Lana felt a little self-conscious. "I bought a book in New Minas when I was picking up the office supplies and read a little bit before I went to sleep last night."

"And memorized it?"

"She's just a geek," Michelle said, cheerfully, as if pleased at Emily's surprise. "Like me."

"What next?" Lana interjected strongly, forestalling any further conversation about her tendencies, geek or otherwise. Conscious of Emily still regarding her with a sort of wonder, Lana pulled up the collar of her ski jacket and moved closer to the grave, trying to read more of the weathered inscription. "I don't think this stone was put on his grave when he died. I think it was put here much later."

"You're right, it was," Michelle said. "By his grandson."

"Grandson?" Emily frowned. "I'm sorry, but wasn't Beauséjour a *Catholic* priest?"

"Things aren't always that simple," Michelle said, starting to walk back toward the car.

Emily exchanged a wide-eyed look with Lana, who shrugged and started to follow, slogging through the snow until she caught up to Michelle. "It would be helpful if you told us the whole story you've learned from your research rather than deal it out in dabs and dribbles."

"It's not that I don't want to share it," Michelle explained, patting Lana on the arm. "I don't know what's accurate and what's not until I actually see the evidence, like that gravestone. I knew the cross had been hidden at Grand-Pré. I knew that after the Expulsion, Beauséjour gave up the priesthood and married a woman, Ava Chaisson, with whom he had four sons. I know he returned here in 1790 with his wife when he was in his sixties while his sons stayed behind in Louisiana. But I didn't know he stopped by Grand-Pré first and took the cross from its hiding place or that he brought it here with him until we found that note to Thomas. The note changed everything."

"Do you think the cross still exists? It could take years before anyone discovers its location." Lana glanced back over her shoulder at Emily, who was trudging a few feet after them, and lowered her voice. "There was really no need for us to come up here at all."

"No, I think I have a line on it," Michelle insisted as they reached the parking lot. "There was a Beauséjour homestead across the bay. On Cheticamp Island."

"It's highly unlikely it's still there."

"Yes, but the well might be."

"What wel—"

"Recognize that car?" Emily suddenly appeared between them, nudging Michelle with her shoulder and inclining her head to the street where a dark sedan was parked. Startled, both Lana and Michelle stopped and stared in that direction.

"Huh? Car?" Michelle frowned. "What are you talking about?"

"I thought I saw it in Grand-Pré and driving behind us every so often on the way up here," Emily said. "It's a rental. Is that the car that forced you off the road?"

"I don't know," Michelle said doubtfully, after peering at it for a minute. "It could be."

"Stay here," Emily said firmly and began to walk toward it. She hadn't gone more than a few yards before it suddenly started up and pulled away, heading south, out of Cheticamp and back toward the mainland.

"What were you going to do when you got there?" Lana asked, honestly curious, when Emily rejoined them.

"Ask for identification," Emily said, as if that should be obvious. "Check to see if there was any damage on the car. I couldn't tell from this distance." She turned to Michelle. "Was it Pierre and Juan?"

"It was too far away," Michelle said evenly.

Emily looked at her for a moment and then nodded, though Lana suspected she didn't really believe her. Lana didn't either, necessarily. "How would they even know to come here?" she asked as the three of them got into Emily's Challenger.

"They might have picked up Devereaux's trail in Grand-Pré and saw that she was with us," Emily said somberly. "We'd be easy to follow. This car doesn't exactly blend in."

"No, it doesn't," Michelle complained. "We should have taken Lana's Jeep."

"It's a bright pearl blue," Lana pointed out, trying to forestall another argument. "And there aren't a lot of Wranglers on the roads around here. They're too hard on gas." She flashed a smile at Emily. "I guess neither one of us is very practical when it comes to our vehicles."

Emily returned the smile. "Are you saying my baby isn't practical?"

"Can we forestall the flirting for later?" Michelle said, an exasperated note in her voice. "If it's them, what are we going to do?"

"Well, clearly you didn't report what they allegedly did to you, so unless you change your mind and make a formal statement, there isn't much I or the rest of the members can do," Emily retorted. "There's no law against these guys traveling to the same places you are. It's only if they approach or threaten you in some fashion that something can be done."

"Besides, it might not even be them," Lana pointed out in a reasonable tone. "Just some people on the side of the road looking at the church, and their leaving as you walked toward them was merely a coincidence."

"And in that event, we don't have anything to worry about." Emily looked over her shoulder at Michelle. "What now?"

"It's getting dark," Michelle said uncertainly. "Maybe we should go back to the cottage and regroup."

"I don't have that much time to waste on this," Emily told her. "I go back to work on Tuesday, which means I have to go home tomorrow." She offered a thin smile. "You do understand the concept of work, don't you?"

Lana felt a pang. She was enjoying this adventure, but was it because Emily was with her on it? Would she be as interested in continuing if Emily went home?

She turned in her seat, fixing a look on Michelle. "This homestead. Do you know where it is?"

"I think so." Michelle reached down for her briefcase, which had been tucked under the passenger seat. After rifling through several of the pages, she came across an old map, outlining the various properties and who owned them in the village in the late 1700s. "It's on Cheticamp Island. Off Phare Road."

"Great. Let's see what's there."

They were quiet on the way to the island, having to backtrack down the highway to the road that ran over a thin strip of land connecting the island to the rest of Cape Breton. There wasn't a lot of settlement here, the houses few and far between, and Lana wondered if they stood a chance of finding anything from two hundred years earlier.

"Is it still considered an island if it's connected to the land?" Michelle asked.

"I think this bit is manmade, like the Canso Causeway," Emily said.

"Do you know that for sure?"

"No," Emily said shortly and looked over at Lana.

Michelle did too, as if Lana had all the answers. "I don't know," Lana said mildly, when she belatedly became aware of their scrutiny. "I'm just glad it's been plowed."

"Yeah, maybe we should have taken your Jeep after all," Emily said as they turned onto an ice-covered dirt road. "Just for the four-by-four option."

Through the passenger window, Lana could see the lights of Cheticamp starting to appear across the stretch of frozen water running between the land masses. It was beautiful in a stark sort of way, and was probably even more so during the summer months. She supposed anyone living here found it easier to get to the village by boat rather than drive the length of the island and back up. Two hundred years ago, they definitely would have rowed across rather than utilize fuel-driven engines.

As they drove north, signs of civilization grew even sparser until there was nothing but trees and telephone poles on one side of the dirt road and the frozen harbor on the other. "Is there anything else here?" Lana asked.

"No more present-day houses," Emily said tersely. "The road itself ends at the lighthouse on Enragée Point."

"All right," Lana said. "What exactly are we looking for?"

"I'll tell you when to stop," Michelle said, looking at the GPS on her phone. Only a couple minutes later, she reached out and put her hand on Emily's shoulder. "Pull over here."

It was dark now, the stars overhead sharp and clear in the winter sky, the waning gibbous of the moon rising in the east. From across the water, the faint sounds of the village drifted, but here on the island, she heard nothing but the wind in the tree branches and the sound of the car's engine ticking as it cooled.

"I'm not seeing anything," Emily said dourly.

"There's a driveway there," Lana said, pointing to the rear of the car. "Still has a culvert. And what looks like a trail through the woods."

"We're going to need snowshoes," Emily said with a sigh. "And we won't find anything in the dark. I guess she was right. We should go back to the cottage and try this again tomorrow morning. We should also see who owns this particular parcel of land or if it's federal, granting us access to walk over it."

"On a weekend?" Lana said, skeptical.

"That's what the Internet's for," Emily remarked.

Michelle, who was staring forlornly into the forest, didn't seem to be listening to any of their discussion. Instead, she suddenly took off, plunging into the snow and struggling up the trail.

"Oh, I don't think that's a good idea," Lana said, startled.

"Hey, come back here!" Emily said firmly.

Michelle ignored them both, continuing to break a path through the trees, the moonlight casting muted shadows across the snow. Lana and Emily exchanged a glance. "Let me get the flashlight," Emily said, apparently resigned.

While she did that, Lana started off after Michelle, slipping and sliding as she slogged through the wet snow.

"Christ on a crutch," she heard Emily mutter after a minute or two as she brought up the rear, the beam from her flashlight stabbing through the forest.

It was a surreal experience, the struggle through the knee-high drifts, but eventually, they reached a clearing, and in the center rose a small mound that Michelle immediately headed for. Once she reached it, she began brushing away the obscuring snow to reveal a pyramid of stones.

"Did he bury the cross under there?" Emily asked, panting as she caught up to Michelle.

Lana wasn't in much better shape, the perspiration chilling her beneath her clothes. It wasn't a good idea to sweat in the winter, no matter how mild the temperatures. Dangerous even.

Michelle didn't respond as she kept pushing at the rounded stones, trying to free them from the frozen pile.

"Michelle!" Lana took her arm, gently, stopping her futile attack on the ruins. "This is stupid. It's dark and it's cold and there's no way for you to get into that without tools. Let's try again tomorrow." She shook her gently for emphasis. "At least you know it's there. There's someplace to look."

"Assuming that's even the well from the original homestead," Emily pointed out in a practical tone. "It could be just a pile of rocks."

Michelle looked at her with pure dislike before shaking off Lana's hand and stomping away. Lana let out her breath, a frosty cloud in the night air as she stared after her, too surprised to move.

"Well," Emily said after a moment. "I can't say you don't take me interesting places."

CHAPTER NINETEEN

Over a plate of snow crab, potatoes, and grilled vegetables, Emily watched Lana covertly. She was seated across from her in the booth, beside Michelle, who was sullenly eating her dinner rather than attacking it like she normally did. Emily didn't know if she liked this aspect of Michelle, but unlike all the other demeanors she'd presented, this one felt honest, at least. They were in a restaurant located at the bottom of the lane leading to the rented cabins, a charming little establishment with checkered tablecloths, candles, and a nautical décor.

"So I talked to the clerk," Emily said, forking up a generous chunk of crab and dipping it into the garlic butter. "We can rent some snowshoes. I have a crowbar in the trunk. Do you think we'll need anything else?"

"There's a stone in the well," Michelle said. "And a passage in Father Beauséjour's journal where he described carving a symbol on it, how it took him some time because the stone was made of granite and hard to work."

"And the significance of this stone?"

"I don't know," Michelle admitted, with a flash of what might be anger in those emerald eyes. "But it was the only unusual action mentioned in his journals during his time in Cheticamp. Initially, I didn't pay attention to it because I was so sure the cross was in Grand-Pré. Now we know he retrieved it and brought it here."

"And hid it in a well?" Emily was skeptical.

"It's possible," Michelle said. "He had to hide his identity, not only as an ex-priest, but also as a French prince. Bastard or otherwise, it wouldn't be good for someone living on British territory to have such strong ties to the French throne. After his death, his oldest son came all the way here from Louisiana to gather up all his papers and journals, which is why I found them at Tulane. They were passed down in his family before being donated to the university, where they moldered in their archives until I came across them."

"And just exactly how and why did you come across them, again?" Emily asked pointedly.

Michelle shot her a baleful look. "I'm going back to the cabin," she said flatly. "Don't worry. I can walk from here."

Emily was conscious of Lana's stern expression as Michelle rose from the table, threw on her coat that had been hanging nearby, and stomped out of the restaurant. Leaving them, of course, with the bill.

"You don't have to be so mean to her," Lana said quietly.

Emily spread out her hands, stung. "I'm not being mean to her. I just want to get to the bottom of things," she said. "Haven't you noticed that she talks a lot but doesn't really say anything and half of what she does say isn't always true?"

"I do think she's young for an associate professor," Lana said.

"There! Right there!" Emily interrupted her, jumping all over the remark. "She told me she was an unemployed grad student, not a professor. And even if she is a student, I'm not sure she goes to Tulane. But you're right. She is young, younger than she's been presenting herself. I think there's a whole lot more going on here than just finding some long-lost Acadian cross, Lana. That's why I'm worried."

"You don't have to worry about me," Lana said, her tone gentling.

"I'm not worried about you," Emily blurted. "I'm worried about her. I'm worried about what she's hiding."

"So you're concerned that there isn't a cross?"

"No, I think that part's true," Emily said. "She did pull that box out of the tree, after all. But this whole bit about Duperies and the two men? That's murky as hell. That's the part she's covering up. And I don't know why, if she has all this documentation, even if she did lift it from some shady character, she doesn't just go to the authorities here in Nova Scotia. They'd be thrilled to find out where the church in Grand-Pré is really located and who Father Beauséjour really was. Probably thrilled enough to give her a job while they search for it with a lot more resources than we have." She paused. "By the way, isn't there a fort named Beauséjour?"

Lana blinked and reached into her purse, pulling out the book she'd bought in New Minas. Flipping to the back, she ran her finger down the index, found the page, and went to it.

"Fort Beauséjour was built by the French during Father Le Loutre's War, which took place from 1751 to 1755," Lana read aloud.

"Great, another Catholic priest getting mixed up in politics," Emily said dryly. "A whole war named after him."

Lana shot her a quelling glance before continuing. "It was also known as the Micmac War, and it *was* a religious war started when the British tried to settle Protestants in the region and establish military control over Nova Scotia and New Brunswick. Anyway, the fort is located in Aulac, New Brunswick and was named for the ridge it was built on. The British destroyed it, and according to this, it's notable because it signaled the conclusion of hostilities between the two European superpowers of England and France and determined which empire would control Acadia and, ultimately, North America. The area was later known as Fort Cumberland and is a historic site today, but I don't think it has anything to do with our Beauséjour."

"No?" Emily poked at her potatoes. "You could be right. He may have just taken the name when he came to Canada from France. Especially if he was hiding from enemies of the French king. God knows what his real name was."

"That's possible," Lana said and suddenly smiled. "I never thought I'd be sitting in Cheticamp discussing the history of Nova Scotia with you."

"Especially since history wasn't my best subject in school," Emily admitted. "All of this is new to me. I guess I'm learning a lot, whether I want to or not."

"It has been educational." Lana took a bite of her scallops, chewing slowly before swallowing and fixing her gaze on Emily. "I'm really glad you're here."

"I am, too, even if it doesn't sound like that sometimes," Emily said. "There are worse ways to spend my weekend, and I have to admit, I might even be having a little fun."

"I'm glad." Lana peered at her from beneath her lashes. "What do you normally do for fun?"

Emily shrugged. "Nothing much. I read, of course. I like to run. I rock climb. I play tennis with my friend, Joanna. I play pickup women's hockey at the rink."

"What do you mean, you 'read, of course'?"

"Well, I've read your stuff," Emily said. "After I met you, it didn't take long before I discovered you were an author."

Lana shook her head. "I didn't realize. You never told me."

"Why would I?"

"It would have let me know you were probably playing for my team."

"And that would have made a difference?"

Lana took a second to think about it. "Maybe not," Pushing her plate aside, she put her elbows on the table and rested her chin on her hands. "So, it sounds like you're very athletic."

"I don't know how athletic I am," Emily said modestly. "I never said I do any of those things well."

"Oh, I bet you do them all very well indeed," Lana said, and it seemed her voice grew deeper.

Emily suddenly found it hard to swallow. "What about you?" she managed to say. "I know you haven't found much joy in anything lately, but what do you like to do?"

"I fly-fish," Lana said, her gaze smoky. "It's very good for working out story ideas. The tranquillity of being on the water allows a lot of time to think. I also like to hike." She paused. "And I ride."

"Horses?" Emily was embarrassed that her voice sounded squeaky.

Lana let out a throaty laugh. "Yes, horses. Not women, though I've done plenty of that, too, in my bad old days."

"I was actually thinking motorcycles, but okay," Emily said, joining in her laughter. "Honestly, I've learned more about you in the past two days than I have in the past three years."

Lana sobered a little. "And do you like what you're learning?"

"Very much." Emily tilted her head, and took a chance. "So, would you like to go for a drive?"

"Now?"

"Well, Michelle's back at the cottage, and I'd like to spend a little more time with you," Emily said honestly. "Alone."

Lana reached for her purse. "I'll get my coat."

"And I'll get the bill."

This time of night, there weren't very many places to go in Cheticamp for the sake of the view, but Emily did find a back road that led upward, stopping on a bluff overlooking the lights of the village. She left the car running for the heat and the radio, which was playing some of her favorite songs, slow and romantic.

"I can't imagine what you intend, bringing me all the way up here," Lana said dryly.

Emily took a long, slow breath. "I just wanted to kiss you, without threat of interruption." She glanced over at her. "If that's all right."

Lana lifted a brow. "And if it isn't?"

"Then I guess we'll sit here, listen to music, and admire the view," Emily said without hesitation.

"I see." Lana's crooked grin and the decided lilt in her voice made Emily's stomach clench. How could she have ever thought the pale imitation she'd known the past three years was the woman sitting beside her? "And is this your type of music? Country?"

Emily shrugged, trying to keep it light. "I like classic rock, 70s, 80s, that sort of thing," she admitted. "Current country hearkens back to that in a lot of ways. I don't like rap or hip-hop at all."

"Jazz?"

Emily tapped her fingers on the steering wheel. "I wouldn't say it's a favorite, but I'll listen to it," she said. She looked at her again. "I'm going to kiss you, now."

"Could you stop with the threats and actually do it?"

That made Emily laugh, and she had to abort her motion toward Lana.

"Oh, please," Lana said and leaned over, putting her hand on Emily's cheek and pulled her head to her.

Her lips were amazing, soft and yielding, tasting of scallops and beer, and Emily thought if she could survive the sheer heaven of it, she could survive anything. She kissed her back, lips parting to allow access to her tongue, allowing the kiss to deepen as she slipped her arms around Lana, hugging her close. The feeling of her lush body against her own nearly made her weep. It was all she could have expected and nothing at all like she'd dreamed, just so much better.

She only drew back when she felt Lana's hand worm its way beneath her jacket and fasten on her breast through her shirt. "Uh, not in a car," she said softly. "It should be someplace better. Our first time, I mean."

"Ah, a romantic," Lana murmured as she removed her hand, though she kept her lips mere millimeters away from Emily, her breath warm and flowing over her lips. "I just knew you would be. So what? We make out like a couple of kids before going back to the cabin with the female equivalent of blue balls? Go to sleep in separate beds just because Michelle is there?"

"You say that like it's a bad thing," Emily told her. "There's something to be said for anticipating the moment." She paused, sobering as she drew back even more. "I'm not in this for a quickie, Lana, or a one-night stand. You mean too much to me. And no, I don't want someone else hanging around when the time comes, especially the Devereaux woman."

Lana nodded. "All right, that's fair." She drew her fingers lightly down Emily's cheek, her thumb moving gently over her lip as she gazed at her, her eyes limpid, dark pools in the dim illumination of the dashboard lights. "You really do know how to turn a girl's head, Constable Stone."

"I just want you to know where I stand," Emily said, scared but also aware that if there was to be anything between them, she had to be honest from the beginning. The sensation of Lana's thumb tracing a delicate pattern over her bottom lip made her close her eyes, trembling from the sheer power of her touch.

Lana leaned closer and replaced her thumb with her mouth, kissing Emily and nibbling at her lip before kissing her again. "Okay, for you, I'll try to remember what it's like to make out."

She sighed. "With my clothes on."

CHAPTER TWENTY

Lana shifted uncomfortably in her seat as they drove back to the cabins, feeling the moisture at the juncture of her legs and knowing her panties were soaked through. It was insane how turned on she was, not just from kissing Emily, but by the restraint she was expected to display. It occurred to Lana that perhaps Emily wasn't as much pursuing her as she was skillfully playing her like a trout on a line, letting her think she was swimming free even as she was well and truly hooked, all the while being pulled ever closer to the ensnaring net.

She rested her fingers against her lips, her heart thudding pleasantly, though when she glanced over at Emily and saw that small smile playing about her lips, she wanted to smack her. Or tear her clothes off and have her right there in the driver's seat. She imagined what Emily would be like in bed, what her body would look like, how she would taste and respond to her touch.

That only made things worse, of course, and she squirmed a bit as the desire raked through her lower belly like a dagger. Her nipples were painfully sensitive against the cups of her bra, and she felt as if she might orgasm just from the motion of the car pulling into the parking lot.

When they were parked and the engine was turned off, before Emily could unfasten her seat belt, Lana seized her head, holding it in place as she kissed her until they were both breathless. She was damned if she was the only one going to bed tonight unsatisfied.

She was the first one out of the car and Emily followed her, walking somewhat unsteadily as they went into the cabin. It was dark, the only light coming from the glass door of the stove from the flickering fire. Emily snapped on the overhead light, chasing away the romantic dimness with a flood of harsh brilliance. Lana blinked as she went to check on Michelle, worried she might have actually ditched them.

But Michelle was there and had taken the room with the double bed, leaving the other with the two single beds for them. Lana growled deep in her throat, swallowed it back, and turned back to look at Emily, forcing a pleasant expression. "Do you want the bathroom first?"

Emily smiled. "Are you sure?"

"Yes. I want to take a shower." Lana bared her teeth at her. "A cold one."

Looking far too smug for her own good, Emily retrieved her toothbrush and T-shirt from the bag and disappeared behind the door of the lavatory located between the two small bedrooms. Lana went over to the stove, added some wood, and stoked it for the night. She remained there, watching the flames rippling over the wood and wondering how she could feel so aroused, amused, and annoyed all at the same time.

"Hey." Emily poked her head out of the small hallway leading to the bedrooms. "It's all yours." She offered a slightly lascivious smile. "Good night, Lana."

"Good night, Emily," Lana said with clenched jaw.

After retrieving her own toothbrush and nightclothes from her duffle bag, Lana went in the bathroom, shutting the door firmly behind her and locking it for good measure. She undressed and turned on the shower, making it hot rather than cold. As the water cascaded over her, she used the motel soap to lather herself, hands roaming over her body, imagining it was Emily's touch on her rather than her own.

"Damn her," she muttered quietly, rubbing her fingertips over her nipples, squeezing them harder than a lover might, and then she reached between her legs. There was no way she would be able to lie in that single bed a few feet away from Emily feeling like this. She needed a release of some kind, even if it might not be as satisfying as it would have had she some company in the shower with her.

It briefly occurred to her that Michelle would readily welcome her into the double bed, but that would be such a terrible idea all around, Lana entertained it only for the sake of the fantasy. The thought of two beautiful women sharing the cabin with her, neither of which she could touch the way she wanted, gave Lana's self-stimulation a piquant edge that masturbation usually couldn't provide.

As she caressed her breasts roughly with her left hand, she imagined Michelle standing in front of her, touching and kissing her. As her fingers dipped and fondled and rubbed against her clit, she imagined that Emily was standing behind her, soft curves pressed against her back, her strong arm wrapped around her, her firm hand granting such skilled delight.

Lana cried out when she came, a sort of helpless groan that ripped from her throat and one she dearly hoped that the sound of the shower and the thickness of the walls obscured. Her knees buckled, and without the steadfast support of the tub surround, she'd have fallen down.

As self-driven orgasms went, it wasn't too bad.

Feeling far more relaxed and in charge of herself, she washed her hair, finished her shower, and brushed her teeth. In the second bedroom, she could hear Emily's steady breathing and wondered if she was asleep or just lying there. She didn't turn on the light to find out, navigating her way from touch, the memory of how the room was laid out, and the dim illumination of a street light coming in through the window blinds. As she crawled into bed, settling on the narrow mattress, she pulled the covers up to her neck and allowed the lassitude provided by her shower and orgasm to take her away, drifting easily into sleep that lasted until the morning, when the weak winter sunshine falling across her eyelids finally woke her up.

A quick glance sideways revealed that Emily was already up, the bed neatly made, her belongings removed from the bedroom. Stretching, Lana could still feel a pleasant warmth in her lower belly and, suddenly energetic, flipped back the covers. She brushed her hair, using the mirror over the dresser, and then got dressed in thermals, both pants and shirt under a pair of jeans and a sweatshirt. She pulled on a pair of thick, wool socks and padded out to the kitchen, where Michelle was working on the laptop.

"Where's Emily?"

"Renting the snowshoes," Michelle said. "Then she's stopping by the hardware store to pick up a few things. She also said she'd bring back breakfast."

"Wonderful," Lana said as she took a seat at the table, regarding Michelle steadily. "You look better."

Michelle lifted her reddish eyebrows. "Was I sick?"

"Sullen. Ever since we went over to the island. What's up with that?"

Michelle made a face, indicating what, Lana wasn't sure. "I had a bad moment there when I saw what was left of the well," she admitted. "I suppose I was expecting something that looked like the one in Grand-Pré."

"That one was restored," Lana said. "And honestly, I don't even know if it was the actual well or just something they built to look like it, like they did the church."

"Well, it's in the right location," Michelle said. "That's how I found the tree."

"Then that shows you're on the right track," Lana said, encouragingly. "You can trust in your research. Don't give up on yourself."

"You really are the nicest person. I wish—" Michelle stopped and looked away.

Lana was intrigued. "You wish what?"

Michelle lifted her head, offering a smile that Lana recognized as forced. "Nothing," she said, and changed the subject. "Do you think the constable will be any longer?"

"I have no idea when she left," Lana pointed out. She was about to say more when she heard the sound of a car outside. "That's probably her now."

Emily entered a few minutes later, bearing a cardboard tray with three cups and a big white paper bag, devoid of any logo but smelling wonderfully greasy.

"There are no fast-food places around here," she announced as she deposited her burden on the table. "I had to go to the restaurant. Luckily, they were open and have a breakfast menu."

"That'll work," Michelle said, tearing into the bag.

"Well, I see someone got their appetite back," Emily said to Lana as they sat down at the table. The three of them shared the ham-and-egg breakfast sandwiches on English muffins, with the hash-brown patties on the side.

"Everything looks better in the morning," Lana responded. "Did you get the snowshoes?"

"They're in the car, along with rope and shovels and anything else we might need." Emily directed a pointed look at Michelle. "This is it, you know. If we don't find anything at the well, we're packing it in and going home."

"Then you can leave me here, because I'm not giving up," Michelle responded.

Lana cleared her throat. "Uh, me, either."

Emily's expression altered as she turned to Lana, surprise and disillusionment in her light eyes. "Really?"

Lana shrugged, feeling a little abashed. "I've come this far," she explained weakly.

"Besides, we're going to find something at the well," Michelle said firmly. "Either the cross itself or a clue about where we have to go next."

"Fine," Emily said, but she didn't sound happy.

"I know you have to get back to work," Lana said, putting her hand on Emily's and squeezing her fingers. "Listen, if we don't find anything, we'll all go back to Kennetcook. Michelle and I can regroup at my place, come up with a more logical plan." She glanced at Michelle. "All right?"

"That would be fine." Michelle regarded Emily, slyly. "A few days alone with you at home will give me a chance to go over everything we've learned so far."

At that, Emily looked even unhappier and pulled her hand away from Lana's grip.

She didn't speak much on the drive to Cheticamp Island, leaving it to Michelle and Lana to provide the conversation. Lana knew she'd disappointed her, but on the other hand, it wasn't as if they were really involved. At the beginning of something, maybe, but not at a point where Emily could tell Lana what to do in any way. It was Lana's life, and she was the one who chose how to live it.

Once they arrived at their destination, they spent a hilarious half hour watching Michelle try to navigate with snowshoes. Lana was quite comfortable with them, since she and Sarah had enjoyed hiking in the woods, regardless of season, while Emily also displayed a passing familiarity with wearing them. But they might as well have strapped two couch cushions to Michelle's feet for all the ability she possessed. Lana was relieved to see the tension leaving Emily's shoulders, with her even managing a laugh as they pulled Michelle out of yet another snowbank.

"Why can't I just walk there?" Michelle demanded as Lana brushed the snow off her. "I did it last night."

"We may have to go deeper into the woods," Lana said, "depending on what we find. Believe me, snowshoes are better. C'mon, keep trying. You'll get the hang of it."

Finally, they made it to the clearing, and Michelle wasted little time in taking the crowbar to the stones. Lana helped her while Emily made a circuit of the area, trying to determine what else, if anything, was around. It looked quite different in the daytime, the sun making sharp shadows on the snow, a whisper of breeze through the trees.

"I don't believe this is the well," Lana said after an hour of moving stones to discover only bare ground. They broke for lunch—tuna sandwiches, potato chips, and apples with bottles of juice, pulled out of Emily's backpack. "I think Emily was right. This is just a pile of rocks."

"Who would bother stacking all those here? What's the point?" Michelle demanded, voice tight with disappointment. She'd barely touched the impromptu picnic. "It doesn't make any sense."

"It does if you're planting a garden," Lana explained with a wry grin. "Nova Scotia was formed by retreating glaciers from the last ice age. As the ice melted, it dropped everything it had picked up on the way down from the north. So anyone who gardens has to pick out a ton of rocks just to plant. And then do it all over again the next spring when other stones migrate to the surface with the frost. I have a similar pile in my backyard, right behind the garage."

"So you think this might have been a garden at one time?" Michelle asked.

"It would explain why there's a pile of rocks here," Emily said. "And from the size of this pile, it wasn't just a garden, but a whole field."

Michelle suddenly looked excited again, prompting Emily to exchange one of her looks with Lana, who barely noticed, infected by Michelle's enthusiasm as she pulled a drawing from her jacket.

"Look," she said, showing the other two. It was an old etching of a farm, Beauséjour's, Lana realized, probably not to scale but enough to reveal a rough layout. "The fields are closest to the shore. The actual farm was farther inland."

Lana looked into the woods. "How far, do you think?"

"If we hit ocean, we've gone too far." Emily offered up a sigh, resigned as if she undoubtedly knew her companions were going to pursue this. "One thing with an island. You can't get lost for very long."

CHAPTER TWENTY-ONE

Rather proud that she was adjusting to the contraptions strapped to her feet, Michelle took the lead as they entered the woods, scrunching along the trail that Emily noted was probably an old lane of some kind, which boded well for finding the actual farm.

"Would a lane be detectable after all this time?" she heard Lana ask.

"There's no way of knowing when this particular plot of land stopped being inhabited," Emily told her. "People could have been living here for centuries. It would definitely be easier than having to clear away the woods for a new farm."

"So the well might not actually be there anymore?" Michelle stopped, looking back at them as they caught up to her.

"Or it might have been used well into the twentieth century," Lana reminded her reassuringly. "The driveway is still around. So we know some kind of housing was here up until the time the Department of Highways started maintaining the roads in the 40s. They're responsible for putting in the culverts." She glanced at Emily. "Are you sure this is federal land now?"

"I couldn't find any deed of ownership," Emily said. "Someone might have died without heirs, and the government would have had to claim it after a certain amount of time. And it's not as if this is all prime real estate. Not a lot of people want to live here." She looked around at the trees and the snow. "It makes you wonder why the Acadians settled here in the first place."

"Fishing," Lana said, promptly. "Up until a few decades ago, it primarily drove the province's economy. And Cheticamp has a great harbor, protected by this very island. One of their biggest tourist attractions is whale-watching expeditions in the summer."

"Let's just hope we come across something recognizable," Emily said.

Michelle was tired of her unrelenting practicality, but she couldn't think of a way to get rid of her. Especially now. It was clear something had happened last night between her and Lana. Maybe they finally had that first kiss, she thought grumpily, and promptly tripped over her snowshoes.

"Are you all right?" Lana asked as she and Emily helped her to her feet.

"Yes," she said tersely. She stopped, staring at the forest around them and, more importantly, at the way the land was contoured. "I think this is it."

"Really?" Emily looked at all the trees. "What makes you think so?"

Michelle waddled over to a mound in the snow. "Because this is a wall. It's too straight for nature." She brushed away the snow and discovered large stones stacked on each other, held together with mortar. "I think this was the house or maybe a barn."

"Huh," Emily said. "Of course, it doesn't mean it was the same one from 1790."

"No, but I think you were right. It was easier to build on top of a ready-made cellar than dig a new one. See how the ground's depressed? There was once a foundation here." Michelle looked at her drawing and pointed to the north. "If so, the well should be over in that direction."

Emily and Lana exchanged one of those looks that were becoming increasingly annoying to Michelle, but followed as she left the trail and began to cut through the forest. Now that she knew what she was looking at, she could see how the trees had grown up and over what had once been buildings and cleared land.

It took a bit longer than she expected, but when she spotted the hump in the snow, she knew exactly what it was. A swell of excitement rippled through her chest, and as she made her way toward the small rise, she waved the others on. Nearby stood a large tree almost twenty meters high, a majestic English oak, rare in Canada, and probably deliberately planted there at least two hundred years earlier, if its size was any indication.

"Here," she said, unfastening her snowshoes. "This is it!"

"If you say so," Emily said doubtfully.

"Give me the crowbar!" Michelle demanded.

"You mean, 'Please, give me the crowbar'?" But Emily slipped out of the backpack she was wearing and pulled out the iron bar, handing it to Michelle, who wasted no time prying away at the frozen mound of stone.

"Is this part legal?" Michelle heard Lana ask in a low voice from somewhere behind her.

"I have no idea," Emily admitted. She walked around until she was in view of Michelle, resting her hand on the large trunk of the oak tree. "I'm fuzzy as hell on laws dealing with antiquities and historic sites and people looking for stuff like this. Outside the possible trespassing aspect, which isn't really applicable here on federal land, so long as she's not cutting down trees or damaging the environment, I don't think there's any rule against digging up a pile of rocks." She exhaled gustily, a white cloud drifting away. "I'll find out soon enough if I'm wrong and we're all arrested."

"I'm right here, you know," Michelle said, stabbing at a particularly stubborn bit of stonework. "Are you going to help me or just watch?"

With their assistance, Michelle soon had the collapsed top removed, revealing a dark hole that descended a few hundred feet. Emily used her flashlight, a heavy black truncheon type with a large lens, to look down into it, the bright LED beam flashing over the squared-off rock sides, through a tangle of roots, and glinting off the bottom far below.

"Still has water," she said thoughtfully. "Must be spring-fed." She looked at Michelle. "Now what?"

Michelle, peering down into the depths, was beyond excitement at this point. "There," she said, her voice almost squeaky. "Shine the light there."

Emily lifted her brows but did as requested, centering the beam on a section of stone some ten feet below them. "Huh," she said.

Michelle lifted her eyes to meet Lana's, smiling widely. "It's a cross," she said breathlessly. "Carved into the stone."

"Way down there," Lana said calmly, but she smiled as well. "How do we get to it?"

"I'll climb down," Michelle said immediately.

"Or we could just contact the authorities and have this done properly," Emily remarked.

"That would take forever," Michelle said, anger replacing her excitement. "Look, I'm going down. You can help me or not."

Lana put her hand on Emily's elbow. "We might as well help her," she said gently. "Even if we could drag Michelle away from here, she'd just find a way to come back on her own and do it without us. That could be dangerous."

"Could be? It *is* dangerous," Emily argued. "From my experience climbing, I can tell you, the sides of that well don't look stable at all. See how the roots from the tree have grown through them? A touch could collapse the entire shaft and take her down with it."

"So we'll do it carefully," Michelle responded. "Y'all can bear my weight. Each of you take an arm. I won't touch the sides at all."

"That's ten feet down," Emily pointed out scornfully. "Even if we laid down and extended our arms, you're still way too short."

"But you did bring rope, didn't you?" Lana said quietly. "I saw it in your backpack."

Exasperated, Emily frowned at her. "Yes."

Michelle's jaw dropped. "How did you know we'd need it?"

"I didn't. I just happened to have it in my trunk," Emily said darkly. "Besides, I like to be prepared when I go into the woods, especially since I was pretty sure you'd want to do something stupid, and sure enough, I was right."

Michelle was already next to the hole, peering down into its depths, almost quivering from her excitement and the need to get down there. Emily hesitated another moment and then began to dig the climbing gear from her backpack—a harness, two coils of rope, and a helmet with attached headlamp.

"I didn't know you climbed," Michelle said conversationally as Emily helped her into the harness and showed her how to fasten it properly.

"There's a lot you don't know about me," Emily said flatly as she stuck an Alpina ice ax in one of the harness loops and tightened the helmet on Michelle's head, switching on the lamp. "Let's keep it that way."

Michelle laughed. "Just don't drop me, all right?" She leaned closer and lowered her voice so that only Emily would hear. "After all, Lana wouldn't like it."

Emily's eyes narrowed. "We're lucky," she growled. "There's a branch growing right over the well that looks strong enough to bear your weight." She put a finger in Michelle's face. "I can't emphasize this enough. Don't touch the sides as you descend, or it'll probably collapse and you'll end up dead."

"I get it," Michelle said, sobering at Emily's warning. "I'll be careful. I won't die today."

"Good, because Lana wouldn't like that, either."

Emily turned away and picked up the coil of rope from the ground, tossing one end of it over the branch. After belaying it around the tree trunk, she brought the other end over to Michelle's vest, winding it through the buckles until it was securely tied. Then she found the second, smaller rope, and after wrapping it around the trunk of a poplar tree, she carried the other end to Michelle and fastened it to the small of her back.

"All right, I'm going to hoist you up," she explained. "Once you're high enough, Lana will let you swing forward until you're directly over the well. When you're in position, Lana will give me the necessary amount of slack and I'll lower you down." Emily tugged a final time on Michelle's harness to make sure it was secure. "Don't you do anything at all. Let us do the work."

"I understand," Michelle said in her most serious tone. "I'm ready."

With Lana's guide rope holding her back, Michelle felt herself lift off the ground as Emily pulled hard on the rope slung across the branch. Michelle's arms and legs dangled forward at an angle until Emily was satisfied she was high enough.

"Okay, Lana, ease her into position," Emily instructed her. "Take your time."

Michelle couldn't see Lana behind her, but she felt herself slowly swing forward until she was suspended directly over the dark pit below. She felt the tug behind her disappear and knew Lana was loosening her hold, providing the necessary slack.

"Ready?" Emily asked one final time.

Michelle's heart thudded against her breastbone, both from excitement and a little fear, which only proved she did possess some common sense after all. "Let's do this."

Carefully, Emily lowered her into the hole, her concerned expression the last thing Michelle saw as the rocky walls of the well came up around her. She bent her head, the beam from her headlamp flashing over the dank surroundings, searching for the etched stone until she had it in her sights again. She kept her gaze on that section of wall until the carving was directly in front of her. "Okay, stop!" she yelled.

Immediately, her descent paused and she hung there, swaying slightly, staring at the worn engraving. Taking a deep breath, she pulled off her glove and reached out with her bare hand, delicately tracing the outline of it.

"Shit!" she exclaimed suddenly as she lost hold of her glove, and she watched it spiral down to land on the tangled roots several feet below.

"What?" came Lana's alarmed cry from above.

Michelle reassured her quickly. "Nothing! Sorry! Dropped my glove. I'm fine."

"Tell her to hurry up." Emily's voice sounded somewhat strained. "We don't have all day."

"I heard her," Michelle called up, forestalling Lana. "I'm starting."

She took the ax from her waist, making sure she had a firm grip on it, not wanting to drop it too, and used the tip to chip away gently at the mortar around the stone, working at it until she'd created a deep groove outlining it, freeing it from the surrounding rock. She tucked the ax back into her waist, suspecting Emily would be more than annoyed if she dropped that too and, with both hands, dug her fingers into the grooves outlining the stone, trying to work it free. Her pulse beat at her temples as she finally loosened it, pulling it from the wall to reveal the dark hollow it had been concealing.

Inside, she could barely make out the shape of a box—metal, black with corrosion, but undeniably there. She let out a small laugh, the only way she could express the incredible joy that filled her chest. With the stone tucked under her left arm, she reached in and took hold of the box with her right. It was heavier than she expected, and when she pulled it from its hiding place, the stone with the carved cross slipped from beneath her elbow.

She made an unwise attempt to grab it, not wanting to lose what was essentially an Acadian artifact carved by Beauséjour himself. She missed, the stone rebounding off the walls as it tumbled downward, and her reflexive motion started her swinging. As she clung tightly to the metal box, she collided with the side of the well and immediately heard a grinding sound, the unmistakable scrape of rock moving on rock.

With what seemed like impossible speed, the walls around her began to collapse.

CHAPTER TWENTY-TWO

O h, my God!" Lana felt the earth shift under her feet, and she stumbled back from the edge of the well. "Michelle!"

"Help me pull!" Emily screamed, hanging tight to the rope, her heels digging into the snowy ground as she was dragged forward.

Rushing over to her, Lana grabbed hold of the rope and began to haul frantically on it, heart in her throat as she yanked. Everything slowed down and she felt as if she were moving in molasses, the rope slippery in her grasp like a living thing. Then, they were moving backward, the weight on the other end slowly rising, though with great resistance.

"It's okay." Emily's voice penetrated as if from far away. "We've got her."

Feeling detached from her body, Lana seemed to be an observer rather than a participant while they pulled Michelle out of the collapsing pit. As Michelle dangled in the air, Lana saw that she was clutching something, hugging it tight against her chest, and realized that their efforts had borne fruit of a sort, though what kind of fruit remained to be seen.

It took a few minutes to get Michelle back onto the ground. As Emily helped her out of the harness, Lana could see how filthy she was, covered in dirt and mud, realizing that for a few seconds, the well had actually claimed Michelle before they managed to pull her free. But Michelle showed no fear, no hint that she was even thinking of her narrow escape. There was just an expression of wondrous joy, the same one that had been on Michelle's face in Grand-Pré, when she'd initially thought she had the prize in her grasp. Eyeing the metal box, Lana wondered if Michelle was right or if she'd be equally disappointed, with the box's contents yielding no more than another mystery or, worse, nothing at all.

"Are you all right?" she demanded, fear making her tone sharp.

Michelle beamed. "I'm great! We've got it, Lana. We've finally found it!"

"You sure?" Emily said as she packed the climbing gear into the backpack. "Did you look inside?"

"I didn't dare." Michelle put the box down on the ground and crouched over it. Lana noticed she didn't have any gloves anymore, her hands smeared with mud and what might even be blood from scratches and cuts.

"We can wait until we get back to the car," Lana suggested weakly. "You need some Band-Aids."

"No, we can't," Michelle said with utter conviction. She fumbled briefly at the latch and then opened the lid, revealing an oilskin packet.

Lana thought she'd throw up if it turned out to be more letters. Carefully, fingers trembling visibly, Michelle unwrapped the contents, spreading the oilskin out on the ground to reveal the contents.

It could never live up to their expectations, of course, but it glinted dully in the weak winter sun, the gold catching the light as it had always done throughout history, sparking the age-old allure and avarice. Lana's breath caught, and she clenched her hands into fists, happiness welling up into her throat and bringing tears to her eyes, not for herself, but for Michelle, for whom this clearly meant everything.

"Huh," Emily said shortly. "Nice."

Lana smiled, shaking her head a little. Apparently, it took a lot to impress Emily. Or maybe she was right to be unimpressed.

On its own, it wasn't that significant. It was just a cross—made of gold, yes, but not particularly ornate or decorated with rubies or sapphires. Approximately six inches long and three-and-a-half inches wide, a tiny engraving was displayed in the cross piece, and peering closer, Lana could see it was a coat of arms.

"Louis the XV." Michelle touched it lightly with her fingertip, her voice a mere whisper in the cool air. "The only acknowledgement he would make that Gaston Beauséjour was his son."

"We'd better get back to the car," Emily said, her tone gentle, as if afraid to disturb the moment that followed Michelle's pronouncement. "It'll be dark soon."

It took a few minutes for them to put on their snowshoes and begin their long trek out of the woods to the road, following the trail of their tracks leading in. Michelle seemed to have a lot less problem maneuvering this time, or maybe it was just because she wasn't thinking about it. She waddled steadily through the snow behind Lana and Emily, hugging the metal box close to her as if it were a cherished child, an expression of beatific peace on her face.

Lana looked over at Emily, who returned the glance with a smile. "Now what?"

"There's actually a Minister of Acadian Affairs," Emily said. "Can't remember who it is right now, but he or she is the one we should call and try to explain all this." She exhaled, almost a sigh. "It can wait until tomorrow. We have a long drive ahead of us this evening."

"I know you have to work tomorrow," Lana said, and added wistfully, "I don't suppose you could call in sick?"

Emily looked at her sharply, though her expression grew pleased when she saw Lana's entreating expression. "Wish I could," she said and took Lana's hand, squeezing it through the glove. "I do have some time off next week. Would you like to do something?"

Lana felt a ripple of desire. "Oh, yes. I would very much like to do something with you," she murmured, and the tone of her voice was suggestive enough to make Emily's cheeks grow pink.

The shadows were growing a bit long as they approached the road, the days short this time of year, the sun generally setting by half past five. They were anxious to get to the car and didn't immediately see the dark-blue sedan parked behind the red Challenger as they emerged from the woods. At least, Lana didn't, and by the time Emily had spotted it and stopped, it was too late to duck back into the cover of the trees.

The two men who got out of their car when they saw them were quite large, one with dark hair and eyes, somewhat handsome in a swarthy fashion, while the other was completely bald, a decorative tattoo running down the side of his square features and onto his thick neck. This was undoubtedly Juan and Pierre, Lana thought, fear lancing sharp and fierce through her chest.

"What do we do?" she squeaked.

Emily, watching them warily as they approached, slipped off the backpack so that she could be unencumbered by its bulk and dropped it on the ground beside her. "Stay calm," she instructed them softly.

Behind them, Michelle belatedly became aware of the changing situation. "Oh, Jesus Christ, you've got to be kidding me!" She sounded a lot more annoyed than afraid.

Emily held up her hand. "Stop right there," she said in an authoritative tone that made Lana quiver and the two men actually pause in their approach. "I am RCMP Constable Emily Stone. Please identify yourself and state your purpose for being here."

"Damn," one of them muttered. Juan, Lana guessed. He looked more Hispanic than French, though his accent wasn't dissimilar to Michelle's, that Southern flavor so out of place in the frosty climes of a Cape Breton winter. As was his clothing. Both he and Pierre were dressed in jeans, western boots, and hoodies beneath black leather jackets that Lana doubted were at all suitable for this kind of weather.

Pierre's beady eyes narrowed, and he reached into his coat pocket, pulling out a nasty bit of black metal. "Too bad for you," he said coldly as he pointed it at her.

"No." Lana didn't think. She just took a step between him and Emily.

"Lana, step away," Emily said firmly.

"Let's all just calm the fuck down, shall we?" Michelle said sharply. She shuffled around Lana and Emily, waving her finger at Pierre as she shuffled toward him. "Are you nuts? She's a cop!"

"So I heard," he said. He frowned at Emily. "I won't use this unless I have to," he added, as if that somehow made a difference.

"You're not going to use it at all," Emily responded in that calm, reasonable tone. "We're just going to talk about how we can resolve this peacefully. You've already violated several laws just by possessing an unregistered weapon."

Michelle turned and made a motion, a sharp wave indicating that Emily should be quiet. Emily's face darkened. Lana was conscious of a certain dismay blunting the edge of her fear as Michelle spoke. "Constable, let me handle this."

"Nothing to handle, Michelle," Juan said, spreading out his hands. They were scarred and very big, Lana noticed. "Hector wants to see you. He's very disappointed."

"Well, we all hate disappointing Hector, don't we?" Michelle said. Lana swallowed hard, aware that Michelle's tone wasn't fearful, just sarcastic, as if people waved guns at her all the time. Or if she actually knew Pierre and Juan as more than just a couple of bad guys chasing her.

Pierre motioned with his gun, making Emily tense and Lana feel a bit weak. "Enough," he said. "I'm hungry and cold and fuckin' tired of this. I'm ready to go home. You two, give me your phones and car keys."

Lana glanced at Emily, hesitated, and, at her brief nod, reached into her pocket for her cell even as Emily did the same, handing over the keys to the Challenger.

"Okay, you three get in the backseat," Pierre said, motioning to the sedan. "Michelle, you get in last."

"May we remove our snowshoes, first?" Emily asked with steely politeness.

"Hurry up." Juan came over and took Michelle by the arm, appearing to notice the box in her arms for the first time. "Is that it? Did you actually find it?"

Michelle, expression furious, her chin stuck out pugnaciously like a young child, grudgingly nodded. "It is," she said shortly.

Juan smiled unpleasantly. "Maybe Hector won't be so disappointed, after all."

After tossing the snowshoes into the ditch, Pierre forced the women into the back of the rental car. Lana found it difficult to move, so afraid that she could barely breathe. It was only Emily's calm, if intense demeanor that enabled her to keep functioning, to keep obeying their instructions, when all she really wanted was to drop down in the snow and curl up in a ball.

"What do you plan to do with us?" Emily demanded.

"Shut up," Pierre snapped.

He kept the gun pointed at them, half turned in the passenger seat as he watched them, while Juan settled his bulk behind the wheel. To Lana's surprise and, evidently, Emily's from the way her brows lifted, they made a U-turn on the narrow dirt road and headed north, toward Enragée Point. On the other side of Emily, Michelle was conspicuously quiet, her expression more furious than frightened. Her eyes kept darting back and forth between the men in the front, and her jaw kept flexing slightly, either because she was grinding her teeth or because she wanted to say something and was continually swallowing it back. She still held the metal box close to her, protectively, and the fierceness in her eyes indicated that she was willing to die before giving it up.

Lana, on the other hand, couldn't be more willing to trade the box for their lives. If she thought for a second any such deal would be accepted, or more importantly, if she could somehow manage to get the words out with a tongue that was glued to the back of her throat, she'd offer it up in a heartbeat.

Lana felt Emily's fingers close over hers, squeezing tight, as they drove along the dirt road, conveying what little comfort she could. Through her side window, Lana could see Cheticamp on the other shore, so near and yet so far away. There was nobody on this side of the channel, no other vehicles on the road, no more houses to pass. She was terrified that they were about to die, that they were being taken to the most remote part of the island where they'd be shot and their bodies dumped in the icy Gulf of St. Lawrence. She'd just found the sweetness in life again and bitterly regretted the past years, not because mourning Sarah had been wrong, but because she'd allowed so much time to pass without appreciating what she had. Glancing over at Emily's strong profile, she was sickened by the thought that they would never have an opportunity to find out what could have been.

Enragée Point was flat and exposed to the ocean beyond, with a single automated lighthouse and a low, squat building beside it, probably a maintenance shed, both painted white with red trim, surrounded by a chain-link fence intended to keep out the public. As Pierre forced her and Emily to get out of the car, Lana prayed that someone in Cheticamp would happen to be looking their way, though she doubted it would make a difference even if it were true. The area was too isolated, too remote. There weren't even any boats on the water.

"Take care of it," Pierre said, handing the gun to Juan. "I'll stay with Michelle."

The fence had been cut and pulled back, creating a significant opening. Juan herded Emily and Lana through it and across the meadow toward the shed. Tears welled in Lana's eyes, stinging them, and she knew her face was twisted as she struggled not to cry. She wanted to be dignified like Emily, competent and brave, showing little expression as they stumbled through the snow. When they reached the door of the shed, which had clearly been forced open, Juan motioned them inside.

Emily didn't obey, instead looking at him and then at the cement step that had been cleared of snow. A heavy chain and shiny new padlock lay on the gray concrete. Probably purchased at the same hardware store in Cheticamp where Emily had bought their supplies. "You set this up ahead of time," she said flatly.

"Yeah, we knew we had to get Michelle off by herself, because she wasn't going to come with us peacefully," Juan said shortly. "She'd make a scene and complicate things. But y'all coming out to the middle of nowhere was perfect. All we had to do then was find a place to stash you."

"I warn you, if Miss Devereaux is harmed in any way, either by you, your friend, or your boss, you'll all be charged equally, not only by American law enforcement but by Canadian, as well," Emily said as she and Lana were pushed inside the cold, dark interior of the shed.

"You don't have to worry," Juan said. His expression softened, making him look more human and less a thug. "As soon as we're back in the States, we'll let someone know you're here. As for Michelle, no one's going to hurt her, especially Hector.

"He's her dad."

CHAPTER TWENTY-THREE

Michelle glared at Pierre, who reached over and turned up the heat. He was obviously suffering from the cold weather.

"Are you crazy?" she demanded. "Kidnapping a police officer?"

"Don't worry about it," he said shortly. "And we're not kidnapping them. Juan's just going to lock them in the shed. By the time anyone finds them, we'll be long gone." He looked back over his shoulder at her. "So you found it? Really?"

Defensively, Michelle hugged the box to her chest. This wasn't going at all the way she'd planned. Instead of taking the cross back to New Orleans in triumph to receive the academic accolades she so richly deserved, she was going to be hauled back home like some wayward child, and Hector would add the cross to the private collection he kept in the basement of his mansion, visited only by himself and a few of his cronies. Not only would the world never know the cross had been found, but also no one would ever know she'd been the one to discover it.

"So what happens now?" she asked sullenly.

"Now we go the hell home," he said. The car rocked slightly as the wind from the bay shook it, and he shivered convulsively. "Man, I don't know how anyone lives around here. It's the fuckin' tundra."

"It's not even as cold as Minnesota," she said scornfully.

"I wouldn't want to live there, either."

"Can't you just tell Hector that as soon as I wrap things up here, I'm on my way home," she said in her most persuasive tone. "There's no need for any of this."

"It's too late, now," he said, a dark expression in his eyes. "You complicated it. You involved other people. You shouldn't have done that."

"You two ran me into a river," Michelle said angrily. "I could've drowned. Hector isn't going to like that."

"You're the one who drove off the road when we passed you," he said, unimpressed. "All we wanted was for you to stop and talk to us. And we would've gone back and pulled you out if that woman hadn't come along."

Michelle bit her lip, feeling guilty at the reminder. Lana would be really scared right now, not understanding what was happening. Michelle truly regretted that fact and was even a little sorry that she'd involved her in the first place, even though without Lana's help and support, it was unlikely Michelle would have been able to track down the clues leading to Cheticamp. She would have probably given up after the disappointment in Grand-Pré. Or, more likely, been forced to give up by these two idiots who didn't see anything beyond the tips of their fat noses.

She saw Juan ducking through the chain-link fence. After he got back in the car, he handed the gun back to Pierre before shifting into gear and pulling away from the snowbank.

"Are they all right?" she asked.

"They're okay." He glanced at her in the rearview mirror. She could see his eyes, dark beneath his thick brows in the narrow rectangle of reflective glass. "I locked them in. They might get a little cold, but they'll be fine."

Michelle shook her head. "This is such a mess."

"Thanks to you." Juan glanced at her again, eyes narrowing. "You're getting the backseat all dirty."

Michelle rolled her eyes, but his comment made her suddenly conscious of the state she was in, scratched and bruised and completely filthy after nearly being swallowed by the collapsing well. "I need a shower," she said. "Take me back to the cabin and let me change."

Pierre shook his head. "And give you a chance to do something stupid? I don't think so."

"I can't travel all the way home like this!" she said, annoyed. "I'm dripping mud."

"She's right. We can't go anywhere with her looking like that," Juan advised his partner. "We need to clean her up."

"Fine. We'll take her back to that cabin she was staying in." Pierre turned and fixed Michelle with a baleful glare. "But only long enough for you to clean up, and I swear, if you try anything—"

"Yeah, yeah, you'll do bad things," she said in a bored tone. "Except we both know Hector wouldn't like it, and if he doesn't like it, then you morons don't get paid. You might even," she added spitefully, "be fired."

As they passed the red Challenger, she glanced over at it, wincing at what her friends must now think of her. Not that Emily's opinion of Michelle had ever been all that high, but to know she'd be able to point to this and tell Lana she'd been right about Michelle's low character all along was positively galling. Michelle looked down at the battered metal box in her arms, wondering if it had been worth it. Then she thought of the cross inside and knew it had been.

Back at the cabin, Pierre tossed the women's phones and Emily's set of car keys on the table, while Juan went over to the kitchenette and found the packets of coffee provided by the motel. As he pulled out the coffeemaker and filled it with water, Michelle started for the bedroom to gather some clothes.

"Wait," Pierre said.

She paused with a frown, one that grew deeper when he motioned at the box. "What?"

"Leave that here," he said. "As long as we have it, I know you won't be going anywhere without us." At her hesitation, he reached out and grabbed it, pulling it forcibly from her grip. She glared at him and he offered a thin smile. "Go get cleaned up."

Furious, she found some clothes and went into the bathroom, stripping off her grimy garments, which she tossed in the sink. She tried to clean the winter jacket Lana had bought her with a washcloth, dampening it and brushing off the worst of the mud. Then she took a shower, the water running brown around her feet for quite some time before it finally cleared up.

Feeling much better, and a little more in control of things, she dressed in a pair of clean underwear, jeans, and a long-sleeved black shirt with a big logo on the front, an Acadian red, blue, and white flag, a gold star emblazoned in the corner. A souvenir she'd bought in one of the restaurant gift shops. She treated the cuts on her hands with some antibacterial cream and Band-Aids she found in the medicine cabinet above the sink. When she returned to the outer living area, carrying her jacket, she felt a qualm as she saw Pierre had removed the cross from the box and was examining it curiously.

"Is this really pure gold?" he asked, a sort of greedy wonder in his voice.

"Yes," she said slowly, a bad feeling beginning to pulse at her temples.

"Nice," he said, and looked at Juan. "I wonder how much we could get for it."

She grabbed it out of his hand before he could stop her, though he half rose out of his chair to come after her. At Juan's calming motion, he sank back down but continued to regard her with an ugly expression on his tattooed features.

Suddenly uncomfortable, she wrapped the precious cross back up in the oilskin and replaced it in the box. She wished she had some kind of lock she could add, but the most she could do was find a plastic grocery bag left over from breakfast and wrap the box inside, concealing it from view as she tied the handles together.

"It's priceless," she told him, eyeing Pierre darkly. "That's why Hector wants it so badly. But it's because of its intrinsic historical value. What it means to our people. Not because it's made out of gold."

"Still," he said, sneering a bit. "It might be worth its weight."

"Hector wouldn't like it," she said, forcing herself to glare at him.

"Hector don't like a lot of things. Like having you for a daughter."

Despite how little she thought of him and his opinion, the comment stung and she opened her mouth to retort. Juan drained the last of his coffee and slammed the mug down on the wooden table with a bit more force than necessary, making the sound rattle through the small cabin and interrupting the argument.

"Let's go," he said when he had both Pierre and Michelle's attention. "I want to get there tonight."

Michelle tried to find a way to stall, though she didn't know for what exactly. It would be impossible for her to retrieve one of the phones discarded on the table. Besides, who would she call? The police? They'd take the cross and possibly arrest her, along with Juan and Pierre.

"I'm hungry," she said.

"Big surprise," Juan said, lifting an eyebrow. "We'll stop on the way and pick up something to eat. There's gotta be a McDonald's somewhere around here."

She wanted to ask on the way to where but didn't want to show any sign of weakness, any hint that she wasn't in control, regardless of the circumstances. She sensed that could be dangerous, especially around Pierre. And Juan wasn't necessarily much better. He just seemed a little more easygoing, but she knew both of them did not-so-nice things for Hector when it came to his business.

As they stepped out of the cabin, she was surprised to see it had begun to snow, small, tiny flakes floating down from the darkening sky, a thin strip of clear air on the horizon showing the final rays of the sun. The lowering clouds made for a spectacular sunset, but as she got into the backseat of the sedan, she could see a thin layer of snow beginning to gather on the surface of the car, wafting away capriciously as Juan started the engine and backed up.

As they pulled out of the motel and out onto the highway, Pierre turned around and reached into the backseat. "Give it to me," he ordered her.

"No, I'll hold it," she said, gripping the bag tightly. A brief tug of war ensued, neither willing to let go, and Pierre snarled at her like a junkyard dog.

"Give it to him," Juan said suddenly. He looked annoyed, whether at her or at his partner wasn't entirely clear. "We'll take care of it until we get back to the States. I don't trust you with it. It makes you do stupid things."

As she reluctantly released her grip, it occurred to her that the gold in the cross might make them do stupid things, too. Like ditch her somewhere and take the cross for themselves.

"Hector will be really glad to add the cross to his collection," she said pointedly as they drove on through the swiftly gathering darkness. The falling snow added to the gloom, the wind whipping it across the highway as if winter sprites were playfully chasing each other along the pavement.

"Probably." Juan offered a crooked smile. "I'm just glad he offered a bonus if we brought the cross back along with you."

"Not as much as we could get for it from Eddy," Pierre muttered.

"What?" Juan looked at him. "What's Eddy got to do with this?"

"I'm just saying," Pierre said, waving his meaty hand for emphasis. "He could find a buyer for it, one that might pay more than Hector would. And even if he couldn't, we could melt this thing down and take the gold. That'd be worth a fortune."

"You can't melt it down," Michelle said, horrified. "It's almost three hundred years old. It's a religious relic of great historical value. Melting it down would be—would be—" She faltered, trying to find something suitable that would penetrate Pierre's greed and spark Juan's more sensible nature. "It would be blasphemy."

Juan looked uncomfortable as he was forced to slow down, the snow falling faster and beginning to collect on the pavement. Perhaps it was because of the driving conditions, but she hoped it was because of her comment. She knew he was Catholic, and it might be enough to sway him to her side. And her side was now to get the cross back to her father, where at least he would protect it.

Regardless of how much she might have already disappointed him.

CHAPTER TWENTY-FOUR

Emily saw Juan's comment register with Lana, saw her expression change, the devastation and betrayal that swept over her. Emily's own fists were clenched at her sides as fury rose, bright and strong, almost choking her as she stood there, on a knife's edge, while Juan closed the door. She listened to the clink of chain being wound around the handle and the snick of the padlock snapping shut with a muffled click, locking them in.

She forced herself to breathe steadily, tracking him as his footsteps retreated across the snow, and then the car door of the sedan slammed, the engine revved slightly, and the car's wheels began to crunch through the ice and snow, until finally it all faded away to leave nothing but the wind whistling around the eaves and the waves crashing on to the nearby shore. Through the two small windows, the fading light turned gray, then dark, the interior of the shed illuminated only when the flash of the lighthouse turned their way, making it hard to see anything as their vision was alternately dazzled and darkened.

Lana made a soft sound, a combination of grief and despair as she slumped down on a wooden workbench. Concerned, Emily went over and sat beside her, wrapping her arm around her shoulders in silent support, holding her as best she could through the ski jacket.

"I'm so sorry, Emily," Lana whispered. "I got you into this."

"This isn't your fault," Emily said strongly. "None of it."

"You're wrong. If I hadn't gone along with Michelle, if I hadn't *believed* every damn thing she said—" Her voice caught on a half sob. "Everything she told me was a lie!"

"Don't you dare apologize," Emily said, squeezing and shaking Lana a little for emphasis. "You believe the best in people, you give them your trust. If they choose to betray that, it's not on you. It's on them." She let out her breath in a huff. "Michelle fooled me, too, and I'm supposed to be the professional here."

Lana protested. "You never trusted her!"

"No, but I went along with what she was doing," Emily admitted. "I honestly believed her when she said she was seeking out this cross for the good of the Acadians." Her jaw was set so hard it ached. "Rather than for herself and her father."

Lana put her hand up to her face, covering her mouth. "What'll we do?" Her voice was muffled through her fingers.

"We find a way out of here," Emily said, reluctantly releasing her and standing up. She looked around, assessing her surroundings.

The maintenance shed was unheated, but it wasn't empty. Metal shelves held wooden crates and oil-stained cardboard boxes, while three dislodged tarps revealed, respectively, a pile of pressure-treated lumber, a couple of lawn mowers, and a collection of beach junk consisting of broken lobster traps, torn fishing nets, and some damaged buoys. The two small windows had been reinforced with metal mesh, undoubtedly to keep people out and prevent vandalism and theft, but serving equally as well to keep them inside.

"We need some light. Something better than what we have." Moving over to the door, she squinted at the area around it and was pleased when she saw the light switch. After she flipped it up, the fluorescent lights overhead flickered to life, illuminating the shed with a pallid hue.

"This is good," Emily said, making her tone strong and determined, knowing Lana needed the reassurance of her confidence, regardless of how Emily might really be feeling. "This is an unmanned facility. Someone may notice the lights being on here when they're not supposed to be."

She looked at the far end of the rectangular building and spotted another entrance, larger, with a double set of wooden doors, but when she tried them, she discovered that in addition to the interior deadbolt, they were also secured from the outside. As she examined her surroundings, Lana remained where she was, huddled in her coat, watching Emily with bleak eyes.

"I'm glad I'm not alone," she said suddenly.

Emily flashed her a smile. "I am, too."

She made another circuit of the shed, looking for anything useful. She spotted another tarp-covered mound that looked untouched, as if whoever had dislodged the first three couldn't be bothered to check this one, assuming it to be more of the same. She'd reached out to flip up the edge when Lana spoke again, only this time, her voice was very small.

"I was afraid they were going to kill us."

Immediately, Emily stopped what she was doing and went over to her, pulling her up into a strong embrace, holding her as tight as she could. "Honestly, the thought crossed my mind a few times, too," she admitted softly into Lana's ear. "And all I could think was that it wasn't fair. I'd finally dredged up the courage to ask you out."

Despite the circumstances, Lana managed a small laugh, and her bravery warmed Emily. After all, she was trained to think on her feet, regardless of circumstances, but Lana was a civilian. "I'm feeling a lot warmer, now."

Emily chuckled and nuzzled into Lana's thick dark hair. "Yeah," she said. "I am, too."

They held each other for a few minutes longer, and Emily hoped Lana was drawing as much strength from their embrace as she was. As she stepped back, she looked into Lana's soulful eyes and took the opportunity to kiss her, tenderly, offering both assurance and the promise that she'd do everything she could to make things right.

"We'll be okay," she whispered, once they finally parted.

"I know," Lana said, her voice stronger now. "What can I do?"

Reluctantly, Emily took a step back, dropping her arms. "Let's try to find a lever of some kind."

"Give me a lever and I'll move the world," Lana said, dryly.

"Or at least the door," Emily remarked, making Lana laugh out loud.

They separated and began to examine the interior of the shed in greater detail, poking through the boxes and rusted tool chests. Anything that seemed useful, they gathered up and took over to the workbench until they had a small pile of screwdrivers, hammers, and wrenches, none of which were particularly big. Emily regarded the pitiful collection and sighed.

"None of that is going to break us out," she said ruefully.

"Could we bash a hole?" Lana suggested. "Using the hammers?"

"The doors are too strong. And the windows, even if we could pry off the mesh and break the glass, are too small to squeeze through."

"What about the walls?"

Startled, Emily stared at her, then looked at the nearest wall, the wooden planks bare, the four-by-six studs visible. There was no insulation and, if she remembered correctly, no other siding, just weather-worn, water-resistant paint. "You know, that might work. Let's see if we can find any weak or rotted spots."

They each took a hammer and began to examine the walls, tapping occasionally to gauge the soundness, looking for any areas that might prove vulnerable. Finally, near the back corner, Emily saw a stain on the boards near the bottom of the wall, just beside the framing of the double doors, indicating water damage of some kind. When she used the hammer on it, the round head sank into the wood rather than rebounding as it had in other parts of the shed.

"Lana," she called out. "I think we can break out here."

Lana came over, and just as Emily was about to start smashing at the stained section, she asked in a practical tone, "What will we do once we're out?"

Pausing mid-swing, Emily thought about it. "Christ, you're right," she said, and let the hammer dangle weakly from her hand as she considered the options. "It's night and the temperature's already dropped to below zero. With the breeze coming off the water, it could be minus fifteen or twenty with the wind chill. There's nothing between us and the car, which is a good twenty klicks away. That would take about four hours to walk, and we're not dressed warm enough. The possibility of exposure is too dangerous." She exhaled and straightened. "Damn it, they really took us out of the equation. By the time we get out of here, they'll be long gone."

Lana put her hand on Emily's shoulder. "Hey, we're alive," she said. "We're together. As far as I'm concerned, that's all good."

"You're right," Emily said, even as a part of her kicked and howled inside, furious at being outsmarted by the likes of that Devereaux woman. Hiding her true feelings as best she could, she managed a weak smile. "Listen, when I don't show up for work tomorrow, the members of my detachment will come looking for me. A trace of my phone and cards will put me in Cheticamp. LoJacking my car will bring them to the island. They'll find us by tomorrow night at the latest. Until then, we have to be careful about hypothermia." She looked over at the nearby tarp. "We can use that for shelter."

Lana followed her gaze, her nose wrinkling a little. "It looks pretty dirty."

"Better than freezing to death."

As they pulled the tarp off what Emily had presumed was more building materials of some kind, she was astonished to discover something else. "Oh," she said, jaw dropping.

"Why would that be stored here?" Lana asked, amazed.

Emily shook her head in wonder and a rising exhilaration. "I don't know. I wonder if it runs."

The four-wheeler was pretty battered, the leather seat ripped, yellowish stuffing poking through, the red paint faded to a pale hue. Not an official vehicle of any kind, it didn't seem the sort of thing that should be stored in a government owned building, but Emily was more than willing to overlook the infraction. She immediately checked the engine, noting that the battery had been unhooked. There wasn't any gas in the tank either, but three red gas tanks on a shelf across the shed had sloshed promisingly during their earlier investigation.

"Can we use this?" Lana asked.

"I'll attach the battery," Emily said, her tone warily hopeful. "You get the gas cans and fill the tank. We'll see if there's enough charge for it to turn over."

They spent the next few moments working diligently, and when Emily finally straddled the machine and turned the key that was stuck in the ignition, she heard a definite response, a throaty cough. Reminded that the machine had probably been sitting there since autumn, she tried again and was rewarded by the engine starting up, complete with a powerful backfire that sounded like a shotgun blast, nearly deafening her.

The roar of the engine was overpowering in the confines of the shed, the fumes from the exhaust pungent. Emily knew she had to find a way out as soon as possible. Without waiting to confer with Lana, but making sure she was well out of the way, Emily revved the engine, threw it into gear, and aimed for the double doors.

"Oh, my God!" Lana screamed as Emily rammed into and through the wooden barrier, the doors flying open to smash into the outside of the shed with resounding bangs that must have echoed across the bay like dual pistol shots. Bouncing through the opening, Emily nearly lost contact with the hurtling vehicle but somehow managed to keep hold of the handlebars, knees gripping the frame between them with a willful desperation. Skidding to a stop on the snow outside, she looked back at Lana framed dramatically in the doorway, backlit by the fluorescent lights.

"Are you all right?" Lana demanded, her tone one of amused exasperation.

"Fine," Emily said, and laughed shakily. "I'm heading for the car. Stay here and keep warm. I'll be back for you in a while."

"Don't be ridiculous. I'm coming with you." Lana stepped down from the shed interior with dignified grace. Throwing her leg over the saddle behind Emily, she wrapped her arms tightly around her waist.

"This is going to be a cold trip," Emily warned her over her shoulder.

"When I have you to keep me warm?" Lana whispered hotly into Emily's ear. "I doubt it."

Laughing into the wind, Emily turned the four-wheeler toward the road and accelerated into the night.

CHAPTER TWENTY-FIVE

Face buried into the back of Emily's neck, Lana was warmed by the soft skin and stray strands of blond hair whipping around her head. She hugged her tightly, the four-wheeler jolting as they rumbled down the dirt road, the front headlight barely illuminating it. It didn't help that it had begun snowing while they'd been trapped in the shed. Almost an inch had accumulated already, forcing them to travel slower than they'd hoped. Even with the reduced speed, the wind they generated made it brutal on any exposed skin. Emily had been forced to stop after only a kilometer in order to wrap Lana's scarf around her face for protection.

They'd been traveling for about thirty-five minutes when the car appeared in the distance, still parked on the side of the road. Relief spread like a wave through Lana, who'd been terrified that Juan or Pierre had stolen the Challenger, leaving her and Emily to ride the four-wheeler all the way back to Cheticamp. Skidding to a stop behind the car, Emily shifted down and turned off the engine. Lana's ears rang with the cessation of noise as she stiffly got off the machine.

"They took your keys," she said, suddenly remembering the kidnapping. Her mind had been shying away from that fact, trying not to think about the sick fear and horror she'd experienced anymore than she had to, but now she felt stupid, worried that they'd come all this way for nothing.

"Yeah, they did," Emily said and went to the rear of the car, kneeling down to reach underneath the bumper to the chassis, where she withdrew a small magnetic box. "But I have a spare."

After retrieving her backpack and the snowshoes from the ditch, then tossing everything into the trunk, Emily quickly unlocked the doors. They piled into the car, and Lana felt safe for the first time in hours. Emily started the engine and turned up the heat to maximum before looking over at Lana, her expression very serious.

"They're about four hours ahead of us," she explained. "It's about eight hours to the Maine border by car, but it's more logical to assume they're heading for Sydney and the airport, to try to smuggle the cross out that way. The nearest RCMP detachment is over in Cheticamp, but by the time we finish explaining all this and get the warrants in motion, they'll probably be on a plane, which means extradition and a whole lot more paperwork, assuming the American authorities can track them down on their side."

"Going to the authorities would be the right thing to do," Lana said and looked out the windshield, watching the small white flakes land lightly on the glass. "But they *are* from New Orleans," she added. At Emily's bemused look, she nodded toward the snow. "How familiar do you think they are driving in this? It's been raining for the past week, and while there's been a little freezing rain, there's been no snow at all. Now, we've got reduced visibility and the snow is sticking to the road."

Emily's face relaxed. "So four hours might not really be four hours. They might not have reached Sydney yet, especially if they turned off in Margaree Harbour and went cross-country. Those are some pretty nasty hills at the best of times."

"And I'm positive they stopped for food at some point."

"With Michelle along? Count on it." Emily's teeth glinted white in the illumination of the dashboard lights. "They probably think we're out of the picture for a day or so, so they might not be pushing it."

"They do have a gun," Lana reminded Emily somberly.

"Yeah, they must have smuggled it across the border or had some contact here that could get them one illegally. That is a concern."

"I was really frightened at the time," Lana said, slowly. "But in retrospect, it seems they went out of their way not to hurt us." She exhaled. "If they were really hardened criminals, they would have killed us."

"They didn't kill us because they didn't have to," Emily responded in a logical tone. "They could achieve their goal without it. But if we try to prevent them from leaving the province, that could change. Any time a gun's involved, it's serious. I really should call it in." But her fingers tapped fretfully on the wheel, and she sounded greatly dissatisfied with that solution.

"You want to go after them yourself, don't you?"

Emily exhaled. "I really do. It'll be a lot less hassle with the suspects in cuffs than trying to get an arrest warrant in time to prevent them flying out." She looked at Lana. "I say we go to Sydney. It might be the only way to keep them from leaving the province. If we're too late or guessed wrong and they headed for the Halifax airport or New Brunswick instead, we can always file our report with the Sydney detachment."

Lana leaned over and kissed her, cupping her face in her gloved hands so she could squarely meet her gaze. "Whatever you want to do," she told her with complete sincerity. "I'm with you."

Emily returned the stare, her blue eyes warming perceptibly. "Sydney, it is," she said and reached for the gearshift.

Lana watched the four-wheeler disappear behind them in the side mirror, wondering how long it would take before it was found, or even how long it would be before anyone realized the lighthouse shed had been broken into. Then there was the fact they hadn't officially checked out of their cabin in Cheticamp or returned the snowshoes. She suspected her credit-card statement would display some pretty hefty and unusual charges in the upcoming month.

Ah, well, it's been worth every penny, she told herself as they turned back onto the pavement and accelerated for the mainland.

You only live once. Smiling, she rested her hand on Emily's thigh, enjoying the play of muscle and warmth through the dual layers of thermal and denim.

Emily, one hand on the wheel, her right resting on the gearshift, flashed a smile her way but didn't comment, apparently content to have Lana's hand stay right where it was as they drove on through the night. It wasn't snowing hard, yet, but the flurries were flying straight at them, making visibility a little tricky. Emily seemed comfortable with the conditions, however, and drove steadily, the V8 under the hood offering a throaty purr. The Cape Breton Highlands loomed large and foreboding on either side of them, making Lana feel claustrophobic, and with the lack of traffic, it felt as if they were the last people on Earth.

"What happens if we catch up to them?" she asked about thirty minutes later as they approached Buckwheat Corner, where the highway turned north to circumvent Bras d'Or Lake.

"We follow them," Emily said. "If I find an opportunity to call for help or separate Michelle from them, or them from their weapon, then I'll take it." She looked over at her, her brows lowering. "In the event that happens, please don't step between me and any gun." She let out her breath slowly. "What were you thinking?"

Lana shrugged lightly, reminded of how she'd positioned her body between Emily and Pierre when he first pulled out his weapon. "I was thinking I didn't want them to shoot you."

"Him shooting you was the better option?"

"I hadn't worked it out that far," Lana admitted.

"Well, don't do it again," Emily said, putting her hand over Lana's and squeezing her fingers. "I sure as hell don't want to lose you now that I've finally found you."

"I'll bear that in mind," Lana said dryly.

Headlights appeared in the distance, and Emily let go of Lana's fingers to put both of her hands on the wheel as the oncoming cars passed them. The road here was a little more difficult than the one through the hills. On Emily's side, a deep ditch separated the highway from the hillside that climbed straight up into the night sky. On Lana's side, only a guardrail separated the road from the sheer drop-off to the water below, a stretch of fresh water known as St. Patrick's Channel.

Lana tried not to think about it as the Challenger slid a little before Emily corrected. "How's the road?"

"Slick but manageable," Emily replied. "The wind off the water is making it freeze, but I've driven in a lot worse."

Red taillights appeared up ahead, complete with four-way flashers, indicating the vehicle was traveling a great deal slower than the speed limit. As they bore down on it, Emily pulled out to pass but then abruptly pulled back in, coming up on the slower car's rear bumper.

"Well, isn't this interesting," she said dryly.

"What?" Lana demanded.

"I recognize the license plate. You were right. They don't know how to drive in this."

"Oh, my God, it's them?"

"So much for their head start." Emily sounded quite pleased.

"Do you think they know we're here?"

"I doubt they recognize my headlights, which is all they can see," Emily said. "But if I pass them, they'll know the car quick enough."

"Won't they wonder why we've slowed down so much? I mean, this is ridiculous. They're not even going thirty. It would be faster to get out and walk."

"We'll follow them until we're away from the cliffs," Emily said, her eyes narrowed. "The road turns inland as we reach Baddeck. I might be able to force them to pull over there without endangering anyone. The problem is the gun. As long as that's in play, anything could happen, and most of it is bad."

"We could just stop at a gas station or something and call 911," Lana pointed out.

"That's a poss—" Emily immediately took her foot off the gas. "Did you see that!?"

Lana's jaw dropped. Someone had opened the back door of the sedan and jumped out as it was moving, hitting the slushy pavement and rolling for several feet. As Emily brought the Challenger to a gentle stop, the car in front was less graceful, the driver obviously slamming on his brakes, which was the worst thing to do in the conditions. The sedan immediately began to fishtail, skidding back and forth across the highway before turning a full three-hundred-and-sixty degree doughnut.

"It's Michelle!" Lana could scarcely believe what she was seeing.

"Open your door," Emily snapped. "Don't get out. Just grab her and pull her in."

As Lana did as ordered, she saw the car ahead come to a full stop, somehow still on the highway rather than in the ditch, probably because they'd been traveling so slowly in the first place. Michelle had stumbled to her feet and was now half sprinting, half sliding toward them. When she reached the Challenger, she let out a yelp of surprise as Lana grabbed her and pulled her in across her lap.

"Bend your knees," she screamed absurdly. "So I can get the door shut!"

Ahead of them, Juan had flung himself out of the car and was now down on one knee, aiming something at them. Lana didn't need to hear the gunshot, or the blood-chilling ding of a bullet ricocheting off the hood and zinging through the air not far from her head, to know he was shooting at them. As Michelle curled up in a ball, making herself as small as possible, Lana managed to slam her door.

"Hang on!" Emily shouted.

She quickly executed a U-turn and accelerated back the way they'd come. Lana, her arms full of Michelle, glanced in her rearview mirror and saw Juan jump back into his car and start off after them."They're chasing us," she said tersely.

"Well, unless their driving improves, they're not going to catch us," Emily said calmly.

Lana glanced down at Michelle, who was ashen, her freckles standing out against her pale skin. "Are you okay?"

"I think so," Michelle squeaked. "I knew you were following us, so I took a chance."

"It was a hell of a chance," Emily said. She glanced in the rearview mirror. "They're not giving up. Get in the back and buckle up."

Without argument, Michelle slithered into the backseat through the opening between the front seats. Quickly, she pulled on her seat belt as Lana grabbed the handle above her head with her right hand and the edge of the passenger seat with the other. Beside her, Emily drove with a competent skill as the high beams of the car behind them reflected brightly off the rearview and side mirrors.

Now this was a car chase, Lana thought wildly. Anyone could do it on a double highway with six lanes in California's perfect weather. Try doing it on the Cape Breton Trail with a deep ditch on one side, a sheer drop-off to Bras d'Or Lake on the other, and drifting snow to worry about. As she watched the needle on the speedometer tick ever upward, she knew it was only a matter of time. Something had to give.

Either Emily would lose control and go off the road or their pursuers would.

CHAPTER TWENTY-SIX

Michelle shivered in the backseat, heart thudding. She was soaked again, her new jeans torn from where she'd jumped out of the car and slid across the road. She still couldn't believe what she'd done. It was as if she'd been in a dream, trapped in the rear seat of the rental car, listening to Juan and Pierre bitch about the weather and how it forced them to go slow and that they couldn't wait to get home and how the lights in the rearview were irritating as hell and why didn't the bastard just pass them? She'd looked back and recognized the car behind them, or at least thought she did as she peered at the shadowy outlines of it through the back window.

Then she was unfastening her seat belt, opening her door, and flinging herself from the car as if in a movie. She was surprised she didn't break her neck, but she supposed if she had survived falling out of a tree and almost being swallowed up by a collapsing well, then jumping from a moving vehicle was no big deal.

Every muscle in her body ached, she had road rash down her left leg and elbow, and she thought she might have chipped a tooth. But for all that, she was rather jazzed at the fact that she'd escaped Juan and Pierre's clutches yet again.

And Lana had been there once more to save her. She gazed admiringly at her classic profile. Lana was hanging tight on to the handle above the window and gripping the side of her seat with the other, but she had a sort of thrilled, animated expression on her face that Michelle found very attractive. Lana was more like her than perhaps anyone wanted to give her credit for, particularly the woman in the driver's seat.

Emily, from what she could see, was serious, her keen gaze concerned, but she was also incredibly calm, driving through the snowy night as if it were a perfectly sunny day, glancing in the rearview mirror at her pursuers every so often but not seeming fazed at all. Regardless of any personal animosity, Michelle was forced to admit the woman had it together.

"Do you have the cross?" Lana asked.

Michelle shook her head. That was the only part of her actions she regretted. "Pierre had it resting on his lap," she explained. "I would have tried to grab it, but I didn't want to give them any warning about what I was about to do."

"I wish you'd given us some warning," Lana said, glancing back at her. "You nearly gave me a heart attack." She seemed to see Michelle for the first time, and her eyes narrowed. "You're bleeding."

"I'm all right," Michelle assured her. "Nothing serious." She leaned forward between the seats and tried to see Emily's face. "Will they catch us?"

"Unlikely," Emily said confidently. "The rental's a four-cylinder. This has eight. On their best day, they couldn't catch me. In this weather? They don't stand a chance. Frankly, it's harder for me to maintain a slow-enough speed to keep them interested in chasing us than it would be to lose them right now."

Michelle blinked at the revelation that Emily was deliberately luring them on and realized she'd concocted some sort of plan. She just hoped it was a good one. They were already traveling far faster than she was comfortable with, while the lights behind them never wavered.

"Why didn't you tell me about your father?" Lana demanded suddenly.

Michelle started. Lana was using that authoritative tone that was like a whip across the back, stinging and sharp. "My father? What are you talking about?"

Emily looked at Lana. "She doesn't know Juan told us Hector is her father." She glanced back at Michelle. "You'd better tell her. You're already on pretty thin ice with us."

Michelle's heart sank to her boots. She couldn't believe Juan had spilled the beans. "It's not like that," she said, trying not to sound too defensive. "I mean, Hector is my father, but I didn't grow up with him. He wasn't married to my mom or anything. They were just ships passing, you know? Neither of us knew until I was in my last year of high school when my mom finally told me. And I told him."

"Are you connected to Tulane University at all?" Lana was relentless, her questions hammering like body blows, one after another. "And don't you dare lie to me again, or I swear, you won't have to jump out of this car. I'll throw you the hell out myself."

Michelle gulped, and Emily offered Lana a sideways glance of pure admiration. "I go to school there," she admitted, conscious that a threat from Lana sounded so much more dire than any Juan or Pierre had made. "When I discovered Hector was into all this Acadian stuff, I became a history major. He was paying for my degree so when I discovered the letters while I was working on my thesis I told him about Father Beauséjour. Then Hector showed me Thomas's diary because they were in Grand-Pré together." She paused, trying to find a good spin and failing utterly. "I think I went a little crazy when I discovered the existence of the cross. I guess I wanted to show Hector what I could do on my own, without his money. If I could find the cross, I could somehow pay him back and prove I was a real historian at the same time. I swiped the materials from the university archives, took the diary from Hector's collection, and headed for the airport. Hector sent Juan and Pierre to bring me back. They do all his dirty work."

"But they didn't run you off the road."

"Not exactly," Michelle admitted. "I mean, they did, in a way, but it was an accident. They were just trying to get me to stop. I lost control when I came around the curve and went down over the bank. Then they saw you coming, and they kept on going rather than stick around. I don't think they knew I was in danger of going into the river."

"Juan just shot at us," Emily said coldly.

"He was probably trying to take out your radiator or your tire or something. He's not that great a shot."

"Christ," Emily muttered. "Americans and their guns."

"If they work for your father and were only trying to take you home, why the hell did you jump out of the car?" Lana sounded less angry now and more puzzled.

"Because I don't think that was the plan anymore," Michelle said. "They were talking about melting down the cross and how much they could get for it. I was afraid they were about to cheat Hector and leave me on the side of the road while they took the cross for themselves." She swallowed. "So when I saw you following us, I thought it was my only chance of rescue."

"Hang on," Emily said suddenly, putting the discussion on pause as they crested a ridge. "This next part's a bit tricky."

As they descended the long hill, rather than brake, Emily kept her foot steady, not accelerating but not slowing either, and she'd shifted into the lowest gear. At the bottom of the hill was a bridge, not very large but spanning a river swollen from snowmelt and choked with ice. The water hadn't reached the level of the road, the bridge far too high for that, but was still more expansive than Michelle suspected it should be, spreading from one hill to the other rather than flowing shallowly over rocks as it cut through a ravine of meadow and trees.

"Here we go," Emily said as they shot across the bridge without losing speed and started up the next hill. "Bridges always freeze first. A little black ice should do the trick."

The lights behind them abruptly wavered wildly back and forth. Michelle twisted in her seat, looking out the back window to see the rental car go sideways across the bridge and pinball between the thick, green metal supports before flying through the guardrail on the near side of the bridge. The headlights sailed gracefully through the darkness to land on a flat stretch of ice and water several meters below.

"Holy shit!" Michelle knew her mouth had dropped open, but she couldn't help it.

Emily stopped, threw the car in reverse, and backed down the hill until she was once more on the bridge. "Stay in the car," she ordered in the sort of tone that indicated they had better listen or face the consequences. She quickly went behind the car, opened the trunk, grabbed her backpack, and moved to the end of the bridge, peering over the side through the gaping hole in the guardrail.

Michelle, for all her bravado, didn't intend to disobey.

Lana did roll down her window so she could see, the icy air chilling the interior of the car and blowing snowflakes onto her face. Michelle unfastened her seat belt and wormed her way up front so she could watch over Lana's shoulder. They couldn't spot the other car from up here, but they could see Emily leaning over the bank, one hand on the bridge rail for support, her large black flashlight in the other, the bright beam flashing off the snow flurries dancing in the air.

"Get out of the car and stand on the roof," she said in a loud, authoritative tone. She waited, obviously for a response, then reached for the rope slung over her shoulder, presumably showing it to the men below. "I'm going to toss you the end and pull you up the bank. But first I want to see the weapon." She turned her head and looked back at Lana. "Get down," she hissed. "Below the window in case he fires."

"The gun's in the car," Michelle heard Juan yell. "Get us out of here."

"Show me the weapon!" Emily repeated, unmoving.

"We don't have it. It's still in the car. Throw us the fuckin' rope!" That was Pierre. Michelle hoped Emily didn't believe him.

"Show me the weapon or I'm getting back in my car and driving away from here," Emily said, her tone resolute. "By the time I contact the authorities and return here, you'll either have drowned or frozen to death. Take your pick."

During a pause, both Lana and Michelle shrank down in the car as they saw Emily ease back behind the bridge railing, using it as cover. "Throw the weapon away from you as far as you can."

They heard a cracking sound. Not gunfire as Michelle first thought but, rather, the grinding of ice moving against metal. "Jesus, get us out of here!" Juan screamed.

"Throw away the gun!" Emily repeated. "This is your last warning!"

"Okay, okay, I'm tossing it," Pierre shouted. "See! There it goes."

Emily stood up, rising from the protection of the bridge railing. Taking that as their cue, Lana and Michelle also straightened, craning their necks to see, though they couldn't discern much from their vantage point. Michelle was almost beside herself in frustration and made a move for the driver's door, though Lana grabbed her arm.

"No," she said firmly, her eyes dark. "Let Emily handle this. She knows what she's doing."

Emily stood up, and after placing the flashlight in the crosspiece of the bridge rail so that it angled downward to light the way, she secured her end of the rope to one of the splintered guardrail posts and tossed the other end down over the bank. "All right, Juan, tie the rope around your waist and climb up first. You or your friend make a wrong move and I pull this slipknot, releasing the rope. You can take your chances after that."

Peering through the windshield, Michelle watched as Emily stood on the bank, balanced on the balls of her feet, the rope twitching violently as someone used it to climb up the rocky slope. Juan's dark head appeared over the edge, and that's when Emily moved, grabbing him by the scruff of the neck and hauling him the rest of the way. The way she held on kept him off balance, forcing him facedown onto the wet pavement. Kneeling over him, knee dug firmly into the small of his back, she secured his hands behind him with some long white, plastic zip ties, then did the same to his ankles.

After that, she went through his pockets, retrieving his phone, as well as Michelle's, ignoring the shouts from Pierre, who continued to demand she toss the rope to him. Instead, she calmly pressed three numbers on the phone, undoubtedly 911, and spent the next few minutes speaking intently, all the while keeping Juan immobilized beneath her.

After she hung up, she dragged Juan over to the rail of the bridge and secured him to it with more zip ties. Only then did she undo the rope from around Juan's waist and move back to the bank. Michelle couldn't help it. She got out of the car before Lana could stop her, slipping a little in the slush as she raced over to Juan.

"I told you to stay in the car!" Emily said angrily.

Michelle ignored her, searching through Juan's pockets. "Do you have it?"

"It's still in the car." He tried to shake her off, limited by the way his hands were secured. "Get away from me."

"Michelle, leave him alone." Lana came up behind Michelle and pulled her away.

Michelle shook her off and ran over to where Emily was looking down over the bank. Now she could see how the rental car had landed on the flooded meadow below, the bumper caught up on some jagged rocks poking up through the ice but still rocking precariously beneath Pierre. Both men were fortunate it had landed right side up. Had it landed upside-down, they would probably be dead at this point. Pierre staggered at little as he stood on the roof, his craggy features a mask of fear.

"Hurry up!"

"Where's the cross?!" Michelle screamed.

"In the car on the front seat!" He looked wildly at Emily. "Throw me the rope. It's going to give way! Please!"

"Get the cross!" Michelle shouted at him. Frantically she looked around, trying to find a way down the sheer embankment to where the car was slowly shifting sideways with the current.

"It's not safe to go back in the car," Emily warned Pierre, though he gave no indication he might try. "I'm tossing down the rope. Tie it around your waist!"

As she did so, Michelle took a step over the edge of the bank. She couldn't lose it now. Not after everything she'd been through.

"Lana, grab her!" Emily cried.

Michelle felt herself yanked backward. Distantly, she was aware of tears streaming down her face, of struggling to reach the car below as Lana pulled her back and then finally pinned her against the bridge railing.

"Michelle, stop! You can't get down there."

"No, don't let it go!" she cried helplessly as Pierre stepped down on the car trunk that was rapidly being covered with water and took a huge leap for the bank, catching hold of the rocks there. He began to climb up, aided by the rope, and when he reached the top, he suffered the same treatment from Emily that Juan had, swiftly subdued with cleverly applied leverage and secured with zip ties.

Below, the car finally surrendered to the current, breaking loose from the bank as large chunks of ice slammed into the side and carried it downriver. It tilted downward as it reached a deeper part of the river, showing the rear underside and axle, and then it began to subside. Michelle reached out, barely conscious of Lana almost lying on top of her in order to keep her down, to keep her from plunging down the bank after it

The rear bumper with the car rental sticker was the last thing Michelle saw, and then it was gone, sinking beneath the ice and the rippling black surface.

CHAPTER TWENTY-SEVEN

The red and blue flashing lights cast surreal reflections over the surrounding hills as cruisers from both the Cheticamp and Baddeck detachments were on scene, along with a couple of ambulances, two fire trucks, and a tow truck sitting idle on the off chance it might be needed to haul out the sedan. The vehicles lined each side of the narrow highway from halfway up the hill to the bridge. Down below, on the edge of the flooded riverbanks, two RCMP constables, secured with harness, were retrieving the gun from where Pierre had thrown it into the rocks. Meanwhile, the EMTs were treating him and Juan for possible exposure. Emily hadn't released them from the bridge railing until other officers were on the scene and could take over. The two men had become considerably cold while waiting, and neither was dressed for this type of weather.

Emily supposed she should feel guilty about that, but it was difficult when she thought about how close that gunshot ricochet off the hood had come to Lana's head. Not to mention the unsightly dent and scratch that now marred the paint of her beloved Challenger. A little cold wouldn't hurt them, she thought, as she eyed them darkly.

At the moment, she was leaning against the front of her car, arms crossed over her chest, Lana standing next to her, as they watched Michelle being treated in the back of the other ambulance.

She looked very small huddled in the shelter of a blanket, her eyes blank and staring straight ahead, seemingly heedless of the attention being paid to the various lacerations she'd acquired during her ill-advised leap from the car. Despite her antipathy, Emily felt sorry for her.

"She looks lost," Lana said.

"It's hard to be that close to your heart's desire and lose it at the last moment," Emily said.

Lana leaned into her, nudging her with her shoulder. "Speaking from experience?"

Emily grinned at her. "I'm rather hoping I have my heart's desire. Unless I'm wrong?"

"Maybe just a little ahead of yourself," Lana said, but she smiled, too.

"Listen, they're probably going to take us back to Cheticamp while all this is sorted out. That was where the illegal confinement took place. It may take a few days before you can go home."

"I don't really have anyplace else to be," Lana said, with a bit of a sigh. "At least I'll be able to return the snowshoes and register for another night at the cabins. Which is good because I was *not* looking forward to that credit-card statement." She lifted her chin. "What about you?"

"Me?" Emily winced. "The paperwork alone is going to take forever. Then I'll have to explain everything to my supervisor. I don't think participating in a treasure hunt will play particularly well with him."

"Well, tell him you just came along to protect me."

"Oh, yes, I'm sure that'll make it so much better," Emily said, dryly, and inserted a Cagney impression in her tone. "Hey, Boss, I was chasing this dame, see, and it just got out of hand."

"Dame?" Lana laughed. "So you like old movies, too."

Emily, feeling the brush of snowflakes against her face, grinned. "Yep, and on a night like tonight, I'd much rather be curled up in front of the TV with popcorn and you than out here pulling a car out of the water."

"Do you think they'll actually find it tonight?"

"Depends on the current," Emily said. "According to Constable Collins, Middle River eventually empties out into Nyanza Bay, but the car will probably catch up on some rocks long before that. God knows, there's plenty of incentive to find it now, rather than wait for spring. The cross will be discovered." She glanced over at Michelle again. "In the meantime, she'll get credit for uncovering its existence, even if they downplay how she went about finding it."

"I think that's all she really wants. The acknowledgement of her research."

"Is it?" Emily felt a qualm ripple through her. "I hope you're right."

She lifted her head as Collins approached. He was young, clearly only months into the job, with one of those mustaches three decades out of date that rookies always seemed to favor.

"They'll be taking Miss Devereaux to Cape Breton Regional Hospital in Baddeck for observation overnight," he explained. "The EMTs think she may have sustained a concussion." He glanced briefly at Lana and then lowered his voice. "Did she really jump out of the car while it was moving?"

"It wasn't moving that fast," Emily said, dismissively. "But it's a good idea to have her checked out. She's been through a lot, recently. They might also want to do a psych eval."

"I should go with her," Lana said, and admonished Emily with a disapproving glance, undoubtedly because of her comment regarding Michelle's mental stability. "She doesn't have anyone else here." She put her hand on Emily's shoulder. "I'll see you later?"

"I'm not sure when," Emily admitted, displeased that Lana seemed to think she was somehow responsible for Michelle, yet warmed by such a clear display of her kind and compassionate nature. She leaned into Lana's touch. "As soon as I can, I'll catch up to you. I promise."

Lana squeezed lightly in farewell and then let go, leaving Emily feeling a bit empty as she watched her make her way over to the ambulance where they were putting Michelle on a gurney. Michelle, uncharacteristically, wasn't objecting. Perhaps she was hurt worse than they'd thought, or maybe the experiences of the past few days were simply catching up to her. She had fallen out of a tree, after all.

"Come on," she said, sighing slightly as she looked at her fellow member. "Let's get started on those statements."

Over the next few days, Emily thought often of Lana as she performed the necessary duties involving Pierre and Juan's arrests. They had to figure out a lot of charges and jump through more than a few hoops regarding the red tape of holding American citizens, which required a couple of calls to the consulate in Halifax and a whole lot of extra paperwork.

She also had to make a rather embarrassing call to her superior, who needed it all explained more than once before he grudgingly signed her leave to be away from Windsor while she assisted the detachments in Baddeck and Cheticamp. She traveled back and forth between the two communities so much, she had the road memorized. She could have driven it with her eyes closed.

Sleep itself was brief, a transitory experience in a local motel in Baddeck, and she caught her meals on the fly from local restaurants that, at least, had great food. Though she'd brought one of her uniforms with her, she had to borrow another pair of trousers and a couple more shirts from another female officer in Baddeck who was close to her size. They issued her a Sam Brown belt and firearm on a temporary basis while she was operating out of their detachment. It didn't fit as well as her own, but she made do.

She and Lana and Michelle kept missing each other, brought in at different times and different places for questioning. That included one meeting with the Minister of Acadian Affairs, Nicolle Crosiers, who seemed greatly excited to hear about the cross in the missing car.

It had yet to be found. By now, various government departments and locals were searching up and down the river in the hopes that the car would appear as the water receded, but it was entirely possible, in Emily's opinion, that they wouldn't be able to recover anything until the ice broke up in the spring. That was still a couple of months away.

Finally, after three excruciating days, she was free to return to Cheticamp and the cabin where Lana had been staying. She felt a sort of lightness in her heart as she got out of the Challenger, truly excited to be seeing her again. It didn't even bother her that Michelle had apparently also been staying in the cabin while the situation was sorted out. Well, not much, anyway.

After knocking briskly at the door, she caught her breath as Lana threw it open. Dressed in a dark-gray sweater that clung to every curve and a pair of jeans that hugged her hips and legs, Lana took one look at Emily and didn't say a word. She just stepped into her arms and hugged her tightly.

Which was exactly how Emily had wanted that to go.

She inhaled deeply as she buried her face into the soft, dark hair, breathing in Lana's scent and the warm sense of being with her again. Oh yeah, she thought with a sort of happy resignation, she's got me good.

"You okay?" she murmured.

"Now that you're here," Lana said. She drew back, regarded her for a happy moment, and then kissed her,

"It's about time you got here, Constable," came the unwelcome but irritatingly familiar voice from somewhere over Lana's shoulder. "Any word?"

Emily needed a second to gather her wits. "Any word on what?"

"The cross," Michelle said, as if it should be obvious, which, Emily thought in retrospect, it should have been.

"Still no sign of the car," Emily said as Lana released her embrace, allowing her to enter the cabin. Shaking out of her heavy police jacket, Emily hung it neatly on the hook by the door.

"Where's your gun?" Michelle asked. "You're still in uniform."

"Because I don't have that many clothes with me," Emily explained pointedly. "I'm living out of my trunk, and I haven't had a chance to change. As for my gun, we don't wear our Sam Brown belt off duty. That's left back at the detachment." She turned to look at Michelle, scanning her from head to toe, assessing her condition. "You look a lot better than the last time I saw you."

"I'm going stir-crazy here." Judging by Michelle's emerald eyes, she was considerably aggravated. "Why can't I go look for the car with everyone else?"

"Because they know what they're doing and you don't," Emily told her in a logical tone. "And it's out of your hands, now. The Department of Acadian Affairs is handling it from here, which is what they should have been doing in the first place."

"That's what I've been saying," Lana said, a long-suffering note in her voice that Emily was secretly very pleased to hear. Obviously, the allure Michelle had initially offered Lana had finally worn off.

Michelle protested. "I can't just sit here and do nothing. It's driving me crazy."

"Not just you." Lana went over and sat down on the sofa, an uncomfortable and cheap-looking piece of furniture. "Although I do agree that I'm tired of staying here. Are they finished with us?"

"Yes, good news there," Emily said with a smile. "That's why I dropped by. You're free to go. We both are."

"Finally," Michelle said. She looked at Lana. "Listen, I need to go back to the bridge and—"

"No, I'm sorry," Lana said firmly, holding up her hand. "I'm checking out, and Emily, if she's agreeable, is going to drive me home. Where you go from here is up to you, but I'm done."

"Just like that?" Michelle looked a little angry. "Don't you know how important this is to my people?"

"Your people?" Lana erupted. It felt to Emily as if this reaction had been building for some time. Perhaps being cooped up with Michelle in this cabin for a few days was all that was needed to clear away any lingering illusions Lana might have that the girl was her responsibility to look after. "Don't you get that the cross belongs here in Canada, and that it's never going back to the

States with you? Do you really think that you and your father are somehow better Acadians than those who returned home, whose descendants actually live here in what was Acadia?!"

She stopped and visibly calmed herself. "It's over," she added in a more reasonable tone. "I wanted to help you find the cross, and that's what we did. It was an incredible adventure, but now I'm done. Acadian Affairs knows where the cross is, and it's just a matter of time before they find it. If I were you, I'd go to Madame Crosiers and talk to her about assisting the department. She seemed very interested in your research and the documents you 'borrowed' from Tulane and your father. I'm sure if you play your cards right, you'll be able to parlay that into some kind of paying arrangement."

"But don't you want to see how it ends?"

"I did see how it ends." Lana shot a look at Emily. "The hero rescues the damsel and captures the bad guys. We all live happily ever after."

"So I'm the damsel in this story?" Michelle was clearly outraged.

"I'm the hero?" Emily said, vastly pleased with herself.

"Oh, God," Lana said, and put her face in her hands. "Please, just take me home."

CHAPTER TWENTY-EIGHT

Lana rested her head against the cool glass of the car window, feeling a bone-deep fatigue that made it hard to think. She felt irrationally guilty about leaving Michelle back in Cheticamp, but she knew she was a resourceful young woman. Michelle would just have to find her own ending to the story one way or another. And knowing her as Lana did, it would undoubtedly be complicated and dramatic, yet somewhat oddly and irrevocably disappointing.

Glancing sideways at Emily, who seemed content to let her be, listening to the classic rock music on the radio, Lana wondered what her ending would be. Or if they were both at a new beginning.

"Hey, we're coming up on the Truro exit," Emily said, almost as if aware of her glance, though she never took her eyes off the road. "Do you want to stop and get something to eat?"

"Can we wait until Kennetcook?" Lana asked. "I'm tired of restaurant food, but I could use some fish and chips from the diner." She paused. "That didn't sound right."

"No, I get it," Emily said with a smile. "The taste of home without actually having to cook. And that place is home for us, in a lot of ways."

"Exactly," Lana said, relieved that she understood. "By the way, did you find out anything about Hector? Is he a bad guy?"

"We couldn't find any criminal connections," Emily told her. "He just seems to be a businessman. Made most of his money in real estate, and while he's a known collector of Acadian artifacts, he doesn't seem to have a reputation for engaging in illegal activities. Not in any official capacity, at least."

"So she lied about that, too?" Lana let out her breath wearily.

"Not necessarily," Emily said in an even tone. "Just because he's never been caught or convicted of anything doesn't mean he's a good guy. He might just be really careful. In any event, Juan and Pierre aren't giving anything up, and the very expensive lawyer from the States is assisting the solicitor they hired here. It's going to take a long time before the case gets to trial."

"I'll have to testify, won't I?"

"Maybe." Emily flashed her a smile, obviously trying to be positive. "Or they might just go for a plea bargain of some kind. You never know." She tapped her fingers on the steering wheel. "I doubt Michelle will be charged with anything, unless something else comes up. I don't suppose she let anything slip while you two were staying together at the cabin?"

"All I discovered was just how obsessed she is with that cross, as if I didn't know that already." Lana thought about it for a moment. "She claimed it was because of her Acadian heritage, but that always felt—not fake, exactly, but unreal, as if she doesn't quite believe it herself. Or has just latched onto it as the reason for her actions. Maybe she grew up without a sense of belonging in the world and discovering that she had a Cajun father, that in fact, she was of Acadian blood, helped define her in some way. Perhaps the cross became a symbol of that identity. It was proof that she was part of something bigger."

"That's pretty good." Emily glanced over at her, admiration in her eyes. "Motivation. It would explain a lot."

"Maybe." Lana shook her head fretfully. "I'm just speculating."

"Well, I do know that if you hadn't became involved in this, she might have found the cross and stolen it out of Nova Scotia with no one being the wiser," Emily said. "So you can take pride in preserving an important part of our historical culture."

"It was just a matter of helping out. I really didn't do anything."

"You probably saved her life," Emily said with certainty. "And you kept her from killing herself or being arrested while she looked for the cross. She may not appreciate it now, but meeting you was very good for her."

Lana wasn't sure she agreed, especially since she hadn't prevented Michelle from falling out of a damned tree, but Emily's words did make her feel a bit better. She straightened in her seat as they came off the exit in Truro and turned left onto the 236 leading to Old Barns and Maitland, the last stretch before home. The back road was more scenic than the Trans-Canada, even in winter, and as Lana gazed across the flat fields and the muddy stretch of Cobequid Bay, she felt more comfortable, almost free, unlike the constant sense of claustrophobic oppression that the brooding hills of the Cape Breton Highlands had inspired.

"I report back to Windsor on Monday, but I'm off until then," Emily said conversationally. "Do you want to do something tomorrow?"

Lana smiled. "I'd like to do something tonight. Pick up some takeout at the diner and spend the evening in, maybe watching old movies?" She hesitated, suddenly uncertain. "Unless you need to get back home."

Emily lifted a brow. "I haven't seen my cat for nearly a week, but a friend has been checking on her since I left so she should be all right."

"I didn't know you had a cat. What else don't I know about you?"

"Oh, quite a lot of things, I would think." Emily flashed her a grin. "Takeout and a movie sounds great."

And perhaps there would be other things they could do, Lana thought happily as she leaned back in her seat and watched the scenery pass, suddenly eager to be home as quickly as possible.

The diner in Kennetcook felt oddly unfamiliar as she strolled in, maybe because she'd been through so much since the last time she'd been in. Had it been only a week? It was hard to believe so much had changed. How much she'd changed, not only emotionally, but obviously in some kind of physical outward manner. She could see it in the eyes of Wanda, who took her order, the raised brows of the cook, Bill, who nodded at her through the service opening in the kitchen, and the way Old Man Kent, huddled on his stool at the counter, rumbled a hello in response to her cheerful greeting.

She felt a little self-conscious standing there, wishing Emily had come in with her, but she'd decided to stay in the car and call her friend to let her know she still required a cat-sitter. As it was too late for lunch and too early for the supper rush, no one else stopped by as she waited, and Lana was oddly grateful. She was still getting used to being herself again. She didn't want to have to make the lengthy explanations required to all her neighbors and friends as to why she'd snapped out of her depression. Not quite yet.

When she came out of the diner, Emily glanced up at her through the windshield, smiled brightly, and quickly concluded her conversation on the phone. As Lana got into the car, the greasy, delicious smell of battered fish and fried potatoes filled the interior. Suddenly, she was starved.

"I believe you know the way from here," she said as she put on her seat belt.

Emily chuckled. "I believe I do."

They crossed over the bridge that had been underwater but was now clear of ice, the river having subsided somewhat though it remained higher than normal for this time of year. As they progressed up the hill, Lana felt herself start to relax, the familiar sights and sounds of home working their inevitable magic.

The cabin was cool when they entered through the back door. Electric baseboard heaters backed up the woodstove, but she had them set only high enough to prevent the pipes from freezing.

"I'll get a fire started," she said, tossing her bag and coat onto the island in the kitchen. "There's a bottle of wine in the cooler."

"White, of course, to go with the fish." Emily's voice held an amused note. "Do you want me to set the table?"

"Everything's in the cupboards," Lana said as she went over to the stove. She stirred the dead ashes, then loaded it with kindling and newspaper, building the base of her fire with long practice. "Actually, I wouldn't mind a shower. Can you put everything in a pan and keep it warm in the oven for now?"

"I'll handle it," Emily told her. "Take your time."

Lana grabbed her bag and dashed upstairs. In the bedroom, she quickly stripped the bed and remade it, just in case, then went into the ensuite, where she showered and pulled on a blouse and a pair of jeans. She glanced in the mirror, debated about adding makeup, decided that was being somewhat over the top, and headed back downstairs.

Emily was seated in one of the armchairs by the fire that was now burning briskly, a few logs added to it from the brass basket by the chimney. She lifted a glass to Lana, who accepted it gracefully. In the kitchen, the small wooden dining table was set, and Emily had turned on the stereo, digging out some CDs from Lana's collection, music she hadn't bothered with in years.

"This is very nice," she said, pleased that Emily had done so much. It felt domestic rather than invasive. "Ready to eat?"

Hoping the oven hadn't dried out the meal too much, she quickly served the food. Emily had even found some candles for the table, or perhaps they'd been left over from the power outage. Lana couldn't remember if she had put them away or not before taking off with Michelle. The tiny flames cast a glow over the kitchen, granting a coziness to the winter light filtering weakly through the window above the sink.

"So, this music," Emily said as they settled into eat. "You like this?"

"Yes, Norah Jones. It's a little jazzy." Lana searched her heart for any sorrow. This CD had been one of Sarah's favorites. But now listening to it was just familiar and pleasant, and nice to be sharing with Emily, who clearly needed her musical palette expanded a bit. "What do you think?"

"It's okay. It doesn't make me want to run screaming from the room or anything."

"I'm glad." Lana laughed, realizing how often she did that with Emily, now that she'd granted herself permission to be amused at things. She took a mouthful of fish and found it more flavorful than usual, the batter tangy with beer and red-pepper flakes. "So, are we dating now?"

"I think we are," Emily said as she sipped her wine. "We've had a few meals together as a couple. Let's see. Breakfast in Grand-Pré, the dinner and dance in Wolfville, that supper in Cheticamp. I guess we're up to about our fourth date now."

Lana protested. "We had more meals than that in Cheticamp. What about that picnic in the woods by the well?"

"I don't count any meal where Michelle was present. She was even there for the supper in Cheticamp, but you and I did get to make out in the car afterward, so yeah, this makes four."

"Fair enough." Lana smiled. "Come on, admit it. You liked her a little bit."

Emily shot her a wary look. "I liked what she was able to do for you," she said. "That was significant. But otherwise, I don't trust her as far as I can throw her. Honestly, it won't surprise me if, after they find the car and retrieve the cross, it doesn't suddenly disappear again."

Lana paused mid-bite. "You really think she would steal it?"

Emily spread out her hands. "Let's just say I wouldn't put it past her." She lowered her head, her pale eyes becoming darker, bluer somehow in the candlelight. "I have an idea. What if we don't talk about her anymore? Instead, let's keep the conversation on you and me."

Lana felt a little sliver of delight. "I can manage that." Reaching across the table, she took Emily's hand in hers. "So, our fourth date, you say? Shouldn't you have moved in by now?"

Emily smiled that wonderful smile. "Oh, no, we're definitely going to go slow. Take our time. Get it right. Practice the whole concept of dating in a variety of ways."

"A variety? I can't wait."

Lana could feel the heat generated between them, but she suspected Emily was quite firm on this subject. They would take their time. She just wasn't sure how that worked. And then Emily was leaning across the table, half rising from her chair so she could kiss her, lips tasting of wine and willingness.

And a promise for the night ahead.

CHAPTER TWENTY-NINE

Emily discovered she rather liked this music, especially when, after dinner, Lana suggested that they dance to it. The songs were perfect, slow and sensual, as both of them moved together in perfect rhythm while the afternoon daylight faded and darkness descended, but neither switched on a light, content to dance in the flickering illumination from the fire and the candles on the table.

Lana really was a lovely dancer, a perfect presence that filled her heart as well as her arms. Had she and Sarah danced like this? Emily hoped not. She wanted this to be for her and Lana alone, rather than some pale imitation of a cherished memory.

"I like this," Lana murmured then, as if somehow reading her mind. "And I love to dance. It was always such a struggle to get Sarah to—Well, it wasn't her thing."

"I like to dance." Emily rested her cheek against the soft cushion of Lana's thick hair. "Especially with you."

Lana made a pleased sound and snuggled closer. Emily spread her fingers over the small of Lana's back, feeling her warmth through the thin silk of her blouse. The tempo picked up a little and she drew back, extending her arms and twirling Lana before pulling her in again, Lana's back against her front, the soft curve of her buttocks cushioned against her pelvis. Arms wrapped around her waist, Emily swayed with her and drew her lips up the line of her neck, kissing the soft skin as Lana tilted her head to offer more.

Then another twirl and Lana was facing her once more. It was natural that Emily kiss that wonderfully full mouth, breathing into the warmth of it. Desire coiled in the pit of her stomach, radiating heat to her chest, and lower, as she clenched, feeling the rush of moisture at the juncture of her legs.

Lana kissed her back, open and wanting, tongue sweet as it moved against Emily's. "Let's go upstairs," she whispered against her lips.

Emily hesitated for an instant. Was it too soon? But she was already in motion, following Lana obediently as she took Emily's hand and pulled her toward the staircase. She could no more resist her than she could suddenly sprout wings and fly. She noticed that one of the stairs creaked as they ascended.

Emily had never been up on the second floor of Lana's home, and she took in the area with a glance. A loft containing bookcases and a couple of large, comfortable chairs, delimited by a wooden railing to match the staircase, overlooked the living room below. The master bedroom was large, with a queen-sized bed, and through another door, Emily glimpsed a full ensuite, gleaming chrome and glass. The bedroom walls were painted a soft green and covered with photos. Pictures of Sarah and her life together with Lana, the two of them in a canoe on a river, on horseback in the woods, at Christmas and New Year's, at a birthday party with a cake, and finally, on a beach somewhere warm with palm trees, both in bikinis. It wasn't a shrine, necessarily, but the room was unmistakably full of memories.

As Lana embraced her, Emily gentled her kiss, lessening the passion. "Here?" she asked softly. "Are you sure?"

Lana paused, seemed surprised, then glanced around. And suddenly she smiled as she apparently realized the cause of Emily's reserve. "She liked you, you know."

"She did?" Emily was taken aback. "I didn't know."

She'd only met Sarah once, when stopping Lana for speeding, and the thin, wasted woman in the passenger seat had been a sad shadow of the vibrant woman displayed in the photos. But even as sick as she was, Sarah had smiled pleasantly at her, the RCMP officer who patrolled their community and had stopped them for something so banal as going twenty kilometers over the limit. Of course, Emily had let them off with a warning rather than a ticket. They'd been on their way to the hospital in Truro for a chemotherapy treatment, but as it turned out, Sarah never returned to Kennetcook after that. Instead, she'd been admitted and then transferred to Halifax, where she died a few months later.

And the next time Emily had seen Lana, moving as if in a daze as she ordered a meal at the diner, probably because her body had finally demanded she eat and she couldn't manage to cook, Emily had asked her to join her. And every time after that, she'd made a point of scheduling her turnaround in Kennetcook so she could be at the diner, trying to coincide her break with Lana's trip back from the hospital.

"I told her that you would always make me eat my supper at the diner," Lana said, holding onto Emily and watching her, patient and kind. "Probably because you didn't trust me to eat it at home. And you'd be right. Those fish and chips on the way back from Halifax were the only food I was getting just then."

"You did order chicken burgers sometimes," Emily said, aware of how absurd the comment was but unable to think of anything else to say.

Lana smiled and nuzzled into her chin. "I promised Sarah I would eat," she continued gently. "But you were the one who helped me keep that promise. You were the one who gave me some kind of anchor during that time. You didn't know that's what you were doing, and neither did I, but that's what was happening. And then, after she passed, you were the only one I could bear spending any kind of time with. Not my family, not our friends, just this pretty RCMP constable who liked to have lunch at the diner and tell me stories about all the crazy, funny things she'd seen growing up in Newfoundland."

Tears stung the back of Emily's eyes. "I'm so sorry, Lana. I know how much you loved her. How much it hurt to lose her."

"It did." The muscles in Lana's neck were visible as she swallowed. "But it's time to let it go. She's gone, and I'm not. And being alive means being able to love, because that's what she would have wanted. It's what I want. And I want to love you."

She kissed Emily, pulling her close, and Emily could taste the saltiness of tears. "I want to love you, too," she whispered.

"So stop with the threats already, and just do it."

Startled, Emily laughed as the mood changed and everything was all right again. Kissing her fully now, she tugged at Lana's blouse, pulling it from her pants so she could unbutton it, revealing the dual swells of her breasts cupped in the white lace bra. Lana was doing the same with Emily's uniform shirt, pushing it off her shoulders and letting it fall to the floor. Their trousers soon followed, then the rest of their encumbering undergarments, leaving them scattered over the floor as they sank onto the soft cushion of the duvet, wrapped in each other's arms.

Emily found it difficult to breathe. The feeling of Lana's body against her own, so warm and soft and smooth after so long of wanting her, was nearly too much. Her kisses, shattering, were drawing something deep from Emily's soul she was almost afraid to surrender. She whimpered, feeling herself pressed back onto the mattress, Lana's hands on her, all over her, inciting the most delicious of sensations. She couldn't stop kissing her, couldn't stop touching her, wanting to be absorbed into her.

"What do you like?" Lana's voice was a husky whisper.

"Oh, you," Emily managed to say. "Touching me. This. All this. Good."

Emily could feel the edge of her teeth on her neck as Lana smiled. "Not so talkative now," she muttered, nibbling along her throat.

"No. Just here. Glad to be."

A throaty chuckle and then Lana's mouth was on Emily's breasts, tongue swirling around her nipple, her fingertips stroking languidly over her belly. Emily moaned and quivered, responding to her touch. Then Lana's hand, the palm flat on her stomach as it slid down, finally slipping between Emily's legs.

"Oh." Emily surrendered, the pleasure washing through her like floodwater across a plain, spreading to every corner of her being. Lana's fingers were teasing her, rubbing over her as her teeth and tongue ravished her nipples, the sound wet and sticky and wonderfully provocative. Lana's deep breathing offered a soft counterpoint to her own soft cries of delight. Emily could do little to return the caresses, helpless beneath Lana's skilled hands and mouth, claimed and taken, branded as hers forevermore on her heart.

As her peak shuddered through her, she clutched Lana's shoulders, fingers digging into her back, arching up into her, seeking the anchor of her presence lest she be cast adrift. And Lana, moving soft and slow over her now, let her sink back to herself, the pleasure continuing to throb through her in time with her heartbeat.

"Oh, gosh," she muttered.

Lana laughed. "Really?"

"Incredible." Emily was quick to assure her, finally coherent once more. She turned them over so she could offer Lana the same joy, taking her time now that her need had been dulled, though hardly quenched. She wanted her so badly. Every millimeter, she cherished, every sound she absorbed, every taste she drank greedily, wanting it all.

Trailing down Lana's body, pausing often to linger over every sensitive spot, testing each part to measure her level of response, Emily explored and conquered. Mouth full of her flavor, musky and sweet, she feasted, wanting to consume her. Lana was no longer so facile with her speech, unable to utter anything but the most basic of moans, open and welcoming to Emily. The shudders that raked her body left her limp afterward, unable to move as Emily trailed up her body with the same intent scrutiny with which she'd gone down, until she reached her mouth and kissed her, long and deep and unhurried.

"Magnificent," Lana whispered when Emily finally released her.

"Why, thank you," Emily said, teasing as she nipped at her bottom lip.

Lana slapped at her back, a pat really, too weak to put any force behind it. "Don't be smug."

"Smug? Just because I knew it would be like this with us?"

"Because it's enough to know what you do to me," Lana said. "You don't have to brag about it."

Emily laughed and eased off her, settling onto her side so she could look down into her face. Lana's eyes were closed, a curve to her full lips, a hint of a dimple at each corner. Emily propped her head on her left hand and used her right to explore Lana's belly and breasts casually, not necessarily to incite passion again, though that would come in time, but rather because she could. Because she was now allowed such access, granted such intimacy. It filled her heart, watching Lana reclined there in the lazy moments of receding pleasure.

"You're so beautiful," she said softly.

Lana's smile widened, and she opened her eyes to regard Emily. "You're not so bad yourself, Constable Stone."

"Even out of uniform?"

Lana turned her head to kiss Emily's shoulder. "Oh, love, had I known what was beneath it, I would have had it off you long before now."

"Pshaw," Emily said and made Lana laugh again. She so loved Lana's laugh. Absent for so long, it was unreserved and profound, indicative of the depths of her emotions, how deeply she could feel. How deeply Emily hoped Lana could feel for her.

It probably wasn't love yet, she realized. It was too soon, this thing between them, too new, but it could be. It would be. And if it took time to nurture and grow, that was so much the better.

Because then it would be real, the sort of love that lasted a lifetime.

CHAPTER THIRTY

"How old do you think Michelle is?"

Sheets tangled around them, Lana lay back against Emily, her breasts and belly a warm cushion beneath her, both propped up against a stack of pillows. They were basking in the easy glow of their togetherness, catching their breath after yet another energetic encounter. Faintly, Lana could hear the music wafting up from downstairs, through the open door of her bedroom.

"Really? That's what you're thinking right now?" But Emily sounded more amused than outraged.

"No, not like that," Lana said, her cheeks heating. "I mean, I—" She paused. "I just want you to know that I thought she was older when I first met her. Especially when we, uh—"

"Ohhh, I see," Emily said and chuckled. "Suddenly feeling a bit squeamish about bedding a kid?"

"Oh, God," Lana said, putting a hand to her face to hide her eyes. "She really wasn't a kid? Was she?"

Emily laughed and then apparently decided to take pity on her. "She's twenty-seven. I ran a background check. I know she said she found out about her father in high school, but I think it was later than that. She didn't register in university until she was twenty-five. Before that, she worked in a bar downtown." She paused. "Not a nice touristy bar, a strip club, which might actually be where she first met Hector and told him she was his daughter."

"How terrible," Lana said, saddened by the information. She'd suspected Michelle had a tough go of it while growing up. "She was a stripper?"

"No, she was a bartender, but I don't think she had a lot of opportunities growing up. Her mother was a waitress. There didn't seem to be a lot of money there." Emily lifted their hands so she could look at Lana's, running her fingertips over the back of it caressingly. "Then suddenly, Michelle was able to pay for a full four-year tuition at Tulane." She bent her head and kissed Lana on the temple. "Besides, wasn't she trying to present herself as a professor when you first met her? It's natural you assumed she was older."

Lana made a sound, half embarrassed and half begrudging. "She liked playing her roles. It was never fully the truth when a lie would do."

"She did like to tell stories, almost as much as you do."

"At least I keep mine on the pages of a book, not in real life." Lana exhaled and settled back in Emily's arms, feeling warm and protected. "Still, she never twisted my arm. I made my own choices when it came to her."

"Well, whatever else she was or did, she gets a pass with me for bringing you out of your misery. For now, at least."

"Fair enough."

Lana closed her eyes. She was tired enough for sleep but reluctant to surrender to her drowsiness, wanting to spend each moment with Emily awake and completely conscious of her presence. Emotions, long damped down, were filling her again. Sensations, previously ignored or rejected, now sizzled along her nerve endings, active and responsive. She could smell the warm perfume of Emily, hear the soft whisper of her breathing, the low thud of her heartbeat beneath her cheek, feel the silky smoothness of her skin. Emily was solid, with an athletic build, more muscular than Sarah, and not at all similar to the slight Michelle. Lana liked her bulk, liked how it made her feel to lie against her, how sheltered she felt in the warm embrace.

Lana honestly didn't know if she would fall in love with Emily but suspected it was only a matter of time. It was enough now to know she might. God knew, she certainly wanted and needed her enough.

Emily's lips trailed over her temple and cheek. "We should go down and put out those candles."

Ever practical, Lana thought, and the trait filled her with a fuller sense of security. There'd be no games with Emily, she knew, just an open and honest integrity. In a world of uncertainty, when everything could be taken in an instant, when life was short and unpredictable, finding someone like Emily to love was more than Lana probably deserved and all she could have ever hoped to have in her future.

For the moment, she just wanted to lie in Emily's arms and be happy. And she was happy, she realized. Something that, not so long ago, she never believed she'd feel again.

"Later," she added. "Let's just stay here for the time being."

"Okay." Emily tightened her embrace. "You'll never have to ask me twice."

"Good." Lana exhaled slowly. "So where do we go from here? Because, you know. Lesbian. Processing."

Emily laughed. "We date. For a few months. We see if we like the same things. I'll try fly-fishing. You can come rock climbing with me. Maybe we'll both try something new that neither of us has ever done before."

"Like what?"

"I'm not sure," Emily said, her tone thoughtful. "Sky diving?"

"Did it. There's a small airport on the way to Windsor. White-water rafting?"

"The Red River in Alberta." Emily hugged her. "Hang gliding?"

"I tried it in Wentworth off the ski hill. Snowboarding?"

"British Columbia one Christmas break."

Lana was beginning to feel a little outmatched. It sounded as if Emily had been to every province in Canada. "Do you ever miss being out West?"

"Not so much." Emily tensed a little and Lana didn't understand why. "Saskatchewan was really flat, in a way that makes you feel small and insignificant. The people were great, but I really missed the trees and the ocean. As for Manitoba, it was—" She faltered a bit. "Really rough."

Hearing the note in her voice, Lana half turned so she could look in Emily's face. "What is it?"

Emily made a face, sort of a self-abashed wince. "Sorry, that's a story that requires a little more preparation. But I will tell you all about it someday if you still want to hear it."

Lana held her gaze for a moment, recognizing that whatever it was had to be pretty intense but that Emily wasn't yet ready to share. "Okay." She kissed her softly on the lips. "I'll listen. Whenever you're ready."

"Thank you." Emily kissed her back, reaching up to tangle her fingers in Lana's hair, deepening the kiss. "So, ever try scuba diving?"

Lana smiled, desire sparking once more. Sleep was suddenly the last thing on her mind. Shoving aside the linens, she turned and straddled Emily, wrapping her arms around her neck.

"Yes, I've been scuba diving," Lana murmured against her lips. "How about this? Tried this before?"

"Oh, yes, I've done this before." Emily pulled her close. "But that's okay. This is something I don't mind trying as many times as necessary."

Emily's hands were tracing over her back as they kissed, trailing down her spine with a feather-light touch. She tasted wonderful, her tongue moving against Lana's, the tip tickling the roof of her mouth as passion rose, swift and heady. Lana couldn't get enough of it, discovering how much she truly enjoyed kissing Emily, how good it felt to be in her arms, feel her touch on her skin.

She allowed Emily to push her back a little, granting her access to her breasts, which she fondled with loving care, her palms rasping over her sensitive nipples, and then her fingertips, rolling over them, teasing them into greater sensation. Catching her breath, Lana threw her head back, baring her throat to Emily's mouth. She trailed down Lana's chest to replace her hands, lips closing over one hardened tip, tongue teasing gently.

"Oh, Emily," Lana said, the pleasure settling within her like a stone sinking into the depths of the ocean floor, as if planning to remain there forever. "Don't stop."

Emily responded with the most wonderful of nonverbal replies, continuing to attend to her breasts with her mouth as Lana held her head. Then Emily was reaching to Lana's intimate folds, slipping easily into her, making her rock on Emily's lap in an irresistible rhythm. Her thumb rotated over Lana's center, rubbing over it with intensifying skill. Lana gasped and moaned, squeezing tight around the fingers inside her that flexed and moved, finding that special spot that rocketed her past all reason.

"Yes," she hissed, bending her head so she could rest her chin on the top of Emily's head, hugging her tight as she tried to stave off the rising plateau, trying to prolong the pleasure for as long as possible.

Emily nuzzled into Lana's throat, dragging her tongue along the length of it as she deepened her touch, drawing out even more sensation. Lana could hold off no longer, plunging over the brink, spasming helplessly around Emily's hand.

Whimpering, she clung to Emily's body, seeking her strength in this moment of utter surrender. Emily eased her touch, still intimately connected but no longer driving her mad with delight, allowing Lana to finally relax into the warmth of her embrace, feeling so close to her, tenderness and affection welling so strongly inside that she nearly wept.

Emily lifted her head, and Lana covered her lips with her own, sinking deep into her kiss, absorbed by her presence.

"Yes," Emily muttered when they finally parted. "We definitely have to repeat that."

"Oh, love. What you do to me." Mouth dry from panting, Lana kissed Emily again and slipped from her embrace. "I need some ice water. Do you want anything while I'm downstairs?"

Emily granted her a lazy smile as she lay back against the pillows, lounging like a lioness after a kill, all golden and satisfied with her place in the world. "Water would be lovely. Thank you."

"Well, don't go anywhere," Lana said as she tossed on a robe, black silk, cut short to show off her legs and, from the way her eyes followed her, clearly a garment that Emily appreciated. "I'll be right back."

Padding downstairs on bare feet, Lana refilled the woodstove and checked on the candles. They'd burnt down to stubs, and wax had spread over the table. She smiled as she saw it and gathered up the plates they hadn't cleared away before they danced. She placed them in the sink and quickly washed them, then filled two glasses with ice from the fridge freezer and poured some filtered water from the pitcher. On her way upstairs, a thought struck and she decided to check her e-mail. Carrying the glasses, she made what she planned would be a brief detour into her study.

As she sat down at the computer, however, it wasn't the e-mail icon she clicked on. Instead, moving almost against her will, as if the hand on the mouse belonged to another, she slipped the arrow over to the word-processing icon, where she clicked twice. The screen flickered to bring up the familiar window, and she stared at the blank page on the large screen, the cursor flashing as it awaited her instruction. Slowly, she began to type the words, black and stark against the white background.

A title. Her name. And then, as if traveling directly from her subconscious, past her frontal lobe directly to her fingertips, the opening line, one that instantly turned into another, and then another.

The words came faster and faster, and before she knew it, she was on the second page, and then the third. So engrossed was she that it took her some time before she became aware of a presence behind her.

Shaking herself, as if waking from a dream, she turned in her chair, looking over her shoulder. Emily was standing in the doorway of the office, dressed in a T-shirt that barely covered her, leaning against the frame with her arms crossed over her chest. A half smile wreathed her face as she watched her, a combination of affection and happiness brimming in her eyes.

"Oh." Lana glanced at the water glasses she'd put on the small table beside her desk. She'd used coasters, but the condensation from the glasses had beaded and run down to puddle around the wooden circles, the ice cubes having shrunk considerably. "I'm sorry. I meant to bring up your water."

"God, Lana," Emily said, a little catch in her throat. "I don't care about the water." She smiled tremulously. "You're writing again."

Glancing back at the screen, Lana smiled. "I guess I am."

Emily came over and put her hands on Lana's shoulders, leaning against the back of the office chair as she read over her head. "*The Golden Cross*," she recited. "By L. E. Mills." She paused. "E?"

"Well, you were there, weren't you?" Lana said, feeling a bit odd. "Is that okay?"

"Of course it is," Emily said. "I'm flattered. But are you sure?"

"Well, we'll see how good you are when it comes time for me to bounce ideas off you," Lana said dryly. "I'm not an easy edit. I resist and argue and dismiss and then end up using your suggestions anyway."

She picked up her water and took a long swallow, having to wipe her hands free of the condensation on her robe, leaving a discernible stain against the silky black material. She wasn't sure how the next part would go over, but she had to be up-front with Emily, let her know what she was really getting into.

"And when I'm writing, when I'm fully into the book, I can forget everything else, like bringing you the water I promised or, for that matter, even letting you know I wasn't coming back right away. It's not the easiest thing to live with." She hesitated. "It took a while before Sarah got used to it, and even longer before she was all right with it."

"Don't worry, I can deal," Emily said, confidence strong in her tone as she squeezed Lana's shoulders lightly. "Do you need me to leave you alone right now?"

Lana reached up and snagged her hand, gripping it tightly. "No," she said, turning her head and leaning back into Emily's belly, her cheek pressed against the thin material of the T-shirt. A part of her grew calm, settled, as if it had been out wandering and now had finally found its way home. "I want you to take me upstairs and inspire me some more."

Emily bent down and kissed her jaw, nuzzling into her neck. "I think I can manage that."

The End

About the Author

Gina L. Dartt, born and raised in the Maritimes, is the author of *Unexpected Sparks* and *Unexpected Ties*, romantic mysteries that take place in her home town of Truro, Nova Scotia, published in 2002. She's also been known to write a Trek fanfic or two, which can be found on her Novel Expectations website when she's not at work or on the tennis court.

Gina is currently working on the fantasy novel, *Shadow Rider*, the first book in the new Elemental trilogy.

Gina can be contacted at gldartt@hotmail.com
Website: http://users.eastlink.ca/~ginadartt/

Books Available from Bold Strokes Books

Camp Rewind by Meghan O'Brien. A summer camp for grown-ups becomes the site of an unlikely romance between a shy, introverted divorcee and one of the Internet's most infamous cultural critics—who attends undercover. (978-1-62639-793-4)

Cross Purposes by Gina L. Dartt. In pursuit of a lost Acadian treasure, three women must not only work out the clues, but also the complicated tangle of emotion and attraction developing between them. (978-1-62639-713-2)

Imperfect Truth by C.A. Popovich. Can an imperfect truth stand in the way of love? (978-1-62639-787-3)

Life in Death by M. Ullrich. Sometimes the devastating end is your only chance for a new beginning. (978-1-62639-773-6)

Love on Liberty by MJ Williamz. Hearts collide when politics clash. (978-1-62639-639-5)

Serious Potential by Maggie Cummings. Pro golfer Tracy Allen plans to forget her ex during a visit to Bay West, a lesbian condo community in NYC, but when she meets Dr. Jennifer Betsy, she gets more than she bargained for. (978-1-62639-633-3)

Taste by Kris Bryant. Accomplished chef Taryn has walked away from her promising career in the city's top restaurant to devote her life to her five-year-old daughter and is content until Ki Blake comes along. (978-1-62639-718-7)

The Second Wave by Jean Copeland. Can star-crossed lovers have a second chance after decades apart, or does the love of a lifetime only happen once? (978-1-62639-830-6)

Valley of Fire by Missouri Vaun. Taken captive in a desert outpost after their small aircraft is hijacked, Ava and her captivating passenger discover things about each other and themselves that will change them both forever. (978-1-62639-496-4)

Basic Training of the Heart by Jaycie Morrison. In 1944, socialite Elizabeth Carlton joins the Women's Army Corps to escape family expectations and love's disappointments. Can Sergeant Gale Rains get her through Basic Training with their hearts intact? (978-1-62639-818-4)

Before by KE Payne. When Tally falls in love with her band's new recruit, she has a tough decision to make. What does she want more—Alex or the band? (978-1-62639-677-7)

Believing in Blue by Maggie Morton. Growing up gay in a small town has been hard, but it can't compare to the next challenge Wren—with her new, sky-blue wings—faces: saving two entire worlds. (978-1-62639-691-3)

Coils by Barbara Ann Wright. A modern young woman follows her aunt into the Greek Underworld and makes a pact with Medusa to win her freedom by killing a hero of legend. (978-1-62639-598-5)

Courting the Countess by Jenny Frame. When relationship-phobic Lady Henrietta Knight starts to care about housekeeper Annie Brannigan and her daughter, can she overcome her fears and promise Annie the forever that she demands? (978-1-62639-785-9)

Dapper by Jenny Frame. Amelia Honey meets the mysterious Byron De Brek and is faced with her darkest fantasies, but will her strict moral upbringing stop her from exploring what she truly wants? (978-1-62639-898-6E)

Delayed Gratification: The Honeymoon by Meghan O'Brien. A dream European honeymoon turns into a winter storm nightmare involving a delayed flight, a ditched rental car, and eventually, a surprisingly happy ending. (978-1-62639-766-8E)

For Money or Love by Heather Blackmore. Jessica Spaulding must choose between ignoring the truth to keep everything she has, and doing the right thing only to lose it all—including the woman she loves. (978-1-62639-756-9)

Hooked by Jaime Maddox. With the help of sexy Detective Mac Calabrese, Dr. Jessica Benson is working hard to overcome her past, but it may not be enough to stop a murderer. (978-1-62639-689-0)

Lands End by Jackie D. Public relations superstar Amy Kline is dealing with a media nightmare, and the last thing she expects is for restaurateur Lena Michaels to change everything, but she will. (978-1-62639-739-2)

Lysistrata Cove by Dena Hankins. Jack and Eve navigate the maelstrom of their darkest desires and find love by transgressing gender, dominance, submission, and the law on the crystal blue Caribbean Sea. (978-1-62639-821-4)

Twisted Screams by Sheri Lewis Wohl. Reluctant psychic Lorna Dutton doesn't want to forgive, but if she doesn't do just that an innocent woman will die. (978-1-62639-647-0)

A Class Act by Tammy Hayes. Buttoned-up college professor Dr. Margaret Parks doesn't know what she's getting herself into when she agrees to one date with her student, Rory Morgan, who is 15 years her junior. (978-1-62639-701-9)

Bitter Root by Laydin Michaels. Small town chef Adi Bergeron is hiding something, and Griffith McNaulty is going to find out what it is even if it gets her killed. (978-1-62639-656-2)

Capturing Forever by Erin Dutton. When family pulls Jacqueline and Casey back together, will the lessons learned in eight years apart be enough to mend the mistakes of the past? (978-1-62639-631-9)

Deception by VK Powell. DEA Agent Colby Vincent and Attorney Adena Weber are embroiled in a drug investigation involving homeless veterans and an attraction that could destroy them both. (978-1-62639-596-1)

Dyre: A Knight of Spirit and Shadows by Rachel E. Bailey. With the abduction of her queen, werewolf-bodyguard Des must follow the kidnappers' trail to Europe, where her queen—and a battle unlike any Des has ever waged—awaits her. (978-1-62639-664-7)

First Position by Melissa Brayden. Love and rivalry take center stage for Anastasia Mikhelson and Natalie Frederico in one of the most prestigious ballet companies in the nation. (978-1-62639-602-9)

Best Laid Plans by Jan Gayle. Nicky and Lauren are meant for each other, but Nicky's haunting past and Lauren's societal fears threaten to derail all possibilities of a relationship. (987-1-62639-658-6)

Exchange by CF Frizzell. When Shay Maguire rode into rural Montana, she never expected to meet the woman of her dreams—or to learn Mel Baker was held hostage by legal agreement to her right-wing father. (987-1-62639-679-1)

Just Enough Light by AJ Quinn. Will a serial killer's return to Colorado destroy Kellen Ryan and Dana Kingston's chance at love, or can the search-and-rescue team save themselves? (987-1-62639-685-2)

Rise of the Rain Queen by Fiona Zedde. Nyandoro is nobody's princess. She fights, curses, fornicates, and gets into as much trouble as her brothers. But the path to a throne is not always the one we expect. (987-1-62639-592-3)

Tales from Sea Glass Inn by Karis Walsh. Over the course of a year at Cannon Beach, tourists and locals alike find solace and passion at the Sea Glass Inn. (987-1-62639-643-2)

The Color of Love by Radclyffe. Black sheep Derian Winfield needs to convince literary agent Emily May to marry her to save the Winfield Agency and solve Emily's green card problem, but Derian didn't count on falling in love. (987-1-62639-716-3)

A Reluctant Enterprise by Gun Brooke. When two women grow up learning nothing but distrust, unworthiness, and abandonment, it's no wonder they are apprehensive and fearful when an overwhelming love just won't be denied. (978-1-62639-500-8)

Above the Law by Carsen Taite. Love is the last thing on Agent Dale Nelson's mind, but reporter Lindsey Ryan's investigation could change the way she sees everything—her career, her past, and her future. (978-1-62639-558-9)

Jane's World: The Case of the Mail Order Bride by Paige Braddock. Jane's PayBuddy account gets hacked and she inadvertently purchases a mail order bride from the Eastern Bloc. (978-1-62639-494-0)

Love's Redemption by Donna K. Ford. For ex-convict Rhea Daniels and ex-priest Morgan Scott, redemption lies in the thin line between right and wrong. (978-1-62639-673-9)

The Shewstone by Jane Fletcher. The prophetic Shewstone is in Eawynn's care, but unfortunately for her, Matt is coming to steal it. (978-1-62639-554-1)

boldstrokesbooks.com

Bold Strokes Books

Quality and Diversity in LGBTQ Literature

victory
EDITIONS

Drama

MATINEE BOOKS

SCI-FI

E-BOOKS

MYSTERY

HE
erotica

BSB
SOLILOQUY

BOLD
STROKES
BOOKS

EROTICA

LIBERTY
EDITION

YOUNG
ADULT

Romance

W·E·B·S·T·O·R·E
PRINT AND EBOOKS